TRINITY FALLS

Megan reached forward and grabbed the waistband of Ean's black gym pants. Ean came up short. The surprise stamped on his copper features was comical. Megan laughed as she sprinted past him.

She tapped the sycamore tree in front of her home and threw her arms above her head. "I won!"

Ean slowed to a stop beside her. "You cheated."

Megan was breathless from exertion and giddy with victory. "That wasn't cheating. It was strategy."

Ean's eyes dipped to her mouth. "It was cheating."

His voice was a low, wicked rumble. Megan sobered. Ean's head drew closer. His scent—sweat and musk—clouded her thoughts. The burgeoning heat in his eyes rendered her motionless. This moment was her young girl's fantasy, but his nearness stirred every inch of her woman's body. All she knew was his heat, his touch, his eyes. And all she wanted was his taste.

Also by Regina Hart

The Brooklyn Monarchs Trilogy

Fast Break

Smooth Play

Keeping Score

TRINITY FALLS

REGINA HART

Kensington Publishing Corp.
http://www.kensingtonbooks.com

DAFINA BOOKS are published by

Kensington Publishing Corp.
119 West 40th Street
New York, NY 10018

All Kensington Titles, Imprints, and Distributed Lines are available at special quantity discounts for bulk purchases for sales promotions, premiums, fund-raising, and educational or institutional use. Special book excerpts or customized printings can also be created to fit specific needs. For details, write or phone the office of the Kensington special sales manager: Kensington Publishing Corp., 119 West 40th Street, New York, NY 10018, attn: Special Sales Department, Phone: 1-800-221-2647.

ISBN-13: 978-0-7582-8652-9
ISBN-10: 0-7582-8652-X
First Kensington Mass Market Edition: September 2013

eISBN-13: 978-0-7582-8653-6
eISBN-10: 0-7582-8653-8
First Kensington Electronic Edition: September 2013

10 9 8 7 6 5 4 3 2

Printed in the United States of America

To my dream team:

- *My sister, Bernadette, for giving me the dream*
- *My husband, Michael, for supporting the dream*
- *My brother, Richard, for believing in the dream*
- *My brother, Gideon, for encouraging the dream*
- *My friend and critique partner, Marcia James, for sharing the dream*

And to Mom and Dad, always with love

ACKNOWLEDGMENT

Thank you to Dr. Martin Brick, Assistant Professor of English with Ohio Dominican University, for providing insight into the university faculty search process.

CHAPTER 1

"I can't do this." Ean Fever closed the client folder. He leaned forward and laid it on Hugh Bolden's imposing teakwood desk. Hugh was his boss and one of the principal partners with the New York law firm of Craven, Bolden & Arnez.

"Why not?" From the other side of the desk, Hugh's laser blue eyes took aim at Ean's face. His frown deepened the fine wrinkles between his thick gray brows. "It's like all the other corporate litigation cases you've worked."

"I can't represent this client." Ean steeled himself for his boss's reaction.

"'Can't' or 'won't'?" Hugh seemed more curious than confrontational.

"Won't."

The walls were closing in on him. Ean freed his gaze from the older man's steely regard to take in the spacious office. It smelled like power and prestige. Thick silver carpeting complemented the teakwood furnishings—conversation table with four white-cushioned chairs, executive desk, cabinetries and bookcases. The entertainment center, including the high-definition television, was black lacquer. The picture window behind Hugh framed several Manhattan skyscrapers as they pierced the hot August sky.

Commendations and civic awards decorated the walls and shelves. But the partner's office didn't give any insight into the man: his loved ones, his hobbies, his beverages of choice. And after almost seven years with the firm, Ean knew the older man little better than on the day he'd interviewed with him.

Hugh shifted in his chair. He crossed his right leg over his left and adjusted the crease in the pants of his navy Armani power suit. "What's on your mind, Ean? You haven't been yourself for months."

Six months. Since his father's death in February, after a long illness Ean had been unaware of. Why hadn't anyone told him? "I need a change, Hugh."

"To what? Employment law? Contracts? Torts?"

Ean shook his head as Hugh rattled off the divisions within the firm. "I have to go home."

Hugh's gaze flickered. His frown deepened. "Is your mother sick?"

Ean appreciated his boss's concern. "No." At least, not as far as he knew.

"Then why do you have to go home?"

"I'm doing this for myself."

Silence stretched. Hugh took his measure, much

as the seasoned litigator did during meetings with opposing counsel.

Tension ebbed from Ean's neck and shoulders as he gained confidence in his decision. He hadn't made this choice lightly. He'd spent the past five months weighing the pros and cons, what he felt against what he knew. In the end, the two were the same. He felt the need to return to Trinity Falls, Ohio, and knew he had to make the move now.

Would someone like Hugh Bolden understand that? The firm appeared to be everything the partner wanted. Ean couldn't allow that to happen to him.

Hugh sat back in the tall executive seat made of brown leather. His expression cleared. "Do you want a leave of absence?"

"No." Ean rose, gathering his writing tablet and silver Cross pen from the table. "You'll have my resignation before the end of the day."

He checked his bronze Omega wristwatch. It was almost ten o'clock on the last Friday morning in August. He'd already put in more than four hours.

Hugh stood. Concern was evident in his expression. "You're resigning? Isn't this sudden?"

"I don't think so." Ean slid his hands into the front pockets of his dark gray Hugo Boss pants. "I appreciate the opportunities you've given me, Hugh, including the partnership two years ago."

Hugh shook his head. "You earned the partnership. You're a brilliant lawyer, Ean. I've enjoyed working with you. Are you *sure* you want to resign? Maybe you just need some time."

His family or his career, those were Ean's choices. He already knew how it felt to lose a family member. "Craven, Bolden and Arnez is one of the best firms in the country. But my life needs to go in a different direction."

"Are you sure this is what your father would have wanted for you?" The question was surprisingly gentle coming from such a gruff man.

Ean tightened his grip on his writing tablet. No, he wasn't. Was that the reason everyone had kept him in the dark regarding his father's terminal cancer? Because his father was afraid Ean would risk his career to help care for him?

"I don't know."

Another long, silent scrutiny from Hugh's sharp eyes. "I understand. I'm sure this decision wasn't easy for you. But everything will work out. You'll make sure of it."

"Thank you." Every muscle in Ean's body relaxed with the other man's words. "It'll take me a few weeks to wrap up my open cases. I'll get Wendy up to speed on my new matters."

The second-year associate eyed his cases—and his office—with something close to lust. Would she be able to mask her pleasure at the announcement of Ean's resignation?

"What will you do back in Trinity Falls, Ohio?"

Ean offered a weak smile. "I don't know that, either."

"Stay in touch." Hugh extended his right hand.

"If you need anything—a recommendation, your job back, anything at all—call me."

Ean clasped the other man's hand. His face eased into a smile. "I appreciate that."

As he turned to leave, his black Bruno Magli shoes sank into the plush carpet. He had a lot to do, but his thoughts kept turning to his late father, widowed mother, childhood friends and the woman who'd broken his heart six years before.

"You're full of energy." Megan McCloud huffed a breath. She picked up her pace as she jogged with Doreen Fever through Trinity Falls's Freedom Park Saturday morning. She'd thought they'd have an easy jog on the last day of August, enjoying the turning foliage and waning summer. Her friend must have had other ideas.

Doreen pulled back her pace. "Ean called last night."

Megan's heart hopped once at the name of her teenage crush. "How is he?"

"He's quit his job. He's coming home. Permanently."

Megan tripped over nothing on the winding dirt path. She caught her balance and her breath. "When?"

"That was my reaction." Doreen's warm brown eyes twinkled with humor.

In her lemon yellow jersey and black running

pants, Ean's mother looked at least a decade younger than her sixty years.

Megan forced her numb limbs to keep up with Doreen as they continued jogging. "He's coming back to Trinity Falls?" *Seriously?* "Why?"

"Didn't say." There was maternal concern in the older woman's breathy voice. "He thinks it'll take eight weeks—give or take—to finish his cases and move."

Megan's heart reacted like that fourteen-year-old girl she'd been as she called to mind the eighteen-year-old Ean. He'd been larger than life to her adoring eyes: long, fluid muscles, broad shoulders and a sexy smile. But his almond-shaped olive eyes had never noticed her. All he'd seen was her older cousin, Ramona.

The path veered left around a group of bushes lit by one of the park's many security lamps. They followed the trail deeper, past morning walkers and a few other joggers.

Megan drew in the scent of warm air and packed dirt. "Is he all right?"

"He said he is." Doreen didn't seem convinced. "He sounded fine. Better than he has in a long time."

The last time Megan had seen Ean was during his father's funeral, more than six months ago. Did he even remember their exchange? She'd shaken his hand and expressed her condolences. But Ean's eyes had looked so lost—not even Ramona's touch reached him. Megan knew well the pain of losing a beloved family member. She'd lost two—four, if you included the parents she barely remembered.

Megan's thoughts returned to the present. "Did you have any idea he'd been thinking of coming back?" Had Ramona?

"None."

Megan couldn't wrap her mind around the news. "Ever since high school, all Ean's wanted to do was leave Trinity Falls. Why is he moving back?"

Doreen chuckled. "Paul used to say Ean had been born with a road map out of town."

Megan smiled at the mention of her friend's late husband. "Ean always had a plan, which is another reason this decision is so out of character."

"I know. My son has never been spontaneous." Doreen paused as they jogged past two women speed walking on the trail. "He chose his college when he was in elementary school. And he selected his law school before he graduated from high school."

Megan had been devastated when he'd picked New York University's law school. It had seemed so far away. "It was always his dream to become a partner with a prestigious New York City firm. Now that he's achieved that dream, he's going to throw it away to return to Trinity Falls, Ohio, population less than fifteen hundred?"

In the seven years since Ean had been working for that law firm, Megan could count on her hands the number of times he'd come home.

"I don't understand his decision, either. But I'm glad that he's coming home."

Megan's face warmed with guilt. Doreen's response put this situation in its proper perspective. She reined in her panic and focused on her friend. "I know you've missed him."

Doreen was silent for several paces. "A lot has changed since he's spent any real time here." She wasn't talking about the new buildings and wider roads.

Megan reacted to the tension in the other woman's voice. She reached out, giving her friend's shoulder a bracing squeeze. "As long as you're happy, Ean will be, too."

Doreen's expression was hopeful. "Do you really believe that?"

Megan let her hand drop. "How you choose to live your life is your decision, Doreen. Ean can either get on board with it or not."

Doreen mustered a halfhearted smile. "I hope he gets on board. It'll be nice to have him home again."

It would be nice for Doreen. And for Megan? That would depend on whether Ean and her cousin picked up where they'd left off.

CHAPTER 2

A little more than an hour later, Megan opened Books & Bakery, her combination bookstore and café, for business. As soon as the doors opened, two of her regular customers strolled in.

"Morning, ladies." Darius Knight greeted Megan and Doreen. The local newspaper reporter slipped onto his usual chair at the bakery counter.

"Good morning, Megan, Ms. Doreen." Dr. Quincy Spates followed Darius to the counter. The Trinity Falls University history professor took the seat beside his childhood friend.

Megan studied the two men on the other side of the counter. They'd been friends with Ean since birth or at least as long as she'd been alive. Tall, fit, intelligent and attractive, they were brothers in every way but by blood.

Darius's midnight eyes gleamed with excitement. "Have you heard the news?"

Doreen served both men a mug of coffee. "If you're talking about Ean coming home, of course,

I have. I'm his mother. And I've already told Megan. When did you two find out?"

Darius added cream and way too much sugar to his coffee. "Ean e-mailed us late last night." He inclined his head toward Quincy.

Quincy swallowed half his cup of coffee. "What do you make of his coming home?"

Megan frowned. Had he also e-mailed Ramona? What was her cousin's reaction to Ean's plans?

Doreen laid a china dish bearing a sizable square of Trinity Falls Fudge Walnut Brownie in front of Quincy. "I think the people of this good town should fear having the three of you together again."

"It's been fourteen years. I'd like to think we've matured." Darius reached toward Quincy's plate.

Quincy paused with his cup near his lips. "Touch my brownie and you'll pull back a stump."

"Yes, very mature." Doreen shook her head.

Darius dropped his hand. "What do you think, Megan?"

She thought fourteen years should have been enough time to get over her crush. Then why did her heart race every time she heard Ean's name?

Megan brought Darius his own Trinity Falls Fudge Walnut Brownie. "I think you three can be trusted to stay out of trouble this time around."

"It may not be the *three* of us, though. It may only be *two*." Darius took a big bite of the brownie.

"What do you mean?" Megan looked to Quincy. Her eyes grew wide. "Did you apply for the faculty position with the University of Pennsylvania?"

Quincy used his fork to cut a corner of the

brownie. "Yes, but I'm sure they'll have a huge pool of candidates for the position."

Megan grinned. "You'll make the final round."

Quincy shrugged broad shoulders covered in a lightweight black sweater. "I won't know anything until the fall. I may not even get a phone interview."

Megan reached out to squeeze Quincy's forearm. "They'd be foolish not to hire you."

Quincy ran a hand over his clean-shaven brown head. "It's a big decision, Megan. I'm not sure I'll take it."

Darius snorted. "You've been pining after teaching at your alma mater since you got your doctorate."

Quincy arched a brow. "No, I haven't."

"You make my ears bleed." Darius gestured with his brownie. "Your whole family moved to Florida years ago. What's keeping you here?"

Megan blinked at the challenge in Darius's question. Quincy visited his family in Florida several times a year. But something—someone?—always brought him home to Trinity Falls. Was Darius challenging Quincy to admit that?

"Did you like the university?" Doreen's question ended the awkward silence.

Quincy sliced another piece of his pastry. "It's a great institution. The faculty and staff are committed to the students."

"Does the position pay more?" Darius stuffed the last of the brownie into his mouth.

Quincy shot him a wry look. "Yes."

"Then take the job. What's the problem?" The reporter drained his coffee.

"Megan's right. They would be lucky to have you." Doreen refilled both men's mugs. "It's just too bad that you'll be leaving just as Ean's finally coming home."

Quincy dropped his dark gaze to the plate of his half-eaten pastry. Megan studied his still, silent posture. He hadn't said much about Ean's imminent return.

Megan turned her attention to Darius. "I read your article about the town council's plan to find a high-end real estate broker to buy the town center."

Darius smoothed the tight curls of his dark hair. "They're still working out the details, so I can't add anything that's not already in my article."

Megan poured herself some coffee. Steam from the drink blew across her face. "Did they at least tell you whether the current center businesses' rental agreements will be renewed?"

"No." Darius's response was succinct and tinged with regret. It added to Megan's tension.

"High-end stores in Trinity Falls?" Doreen collected Darius's empty plate. "Ramona knows the town's culture won't support exclusive labels and fashions. What is she thinking?"

"She wants to bring the big-city lifestyle to our little town." Megan's voice was tight with frustration. She carried her coffee to the counter and added cream and sweetener. "I should have realized this would happen as soon as the original center owners defaulted on the town's loan."

Her older cousin's reasons for not staying in New York when Ean had asked her to marry him were still a mystery. It was now compounded by the puzzle of her goal to bring a piece of Fifth Avenue to their sleepy little town.

"How were you supposed to know?" Darius drained his second mug of coffee. "I wonder how Ean's return will affect Ramona's plans to gentrify Trinity Falls."

Quincy stood abruptly. He put several bills on the counter. "Keep the change, Ms. Doreen."

Doreen looked as startled as Megan felt. "Thank you, Quincy. Enjoy the rest of your day."

"You do the same." Quincy waved over his shoulder as he strode to the door.

Doreen stared after Quincy. "What was that about?"

Megan remained silent, but something told her Ean's return wouldn't affect only *her* unrequited crush.

Ean jogged down the deserted, quiet street of his hometown early Monday morning. He'd arrived in Trinity Falls late Sunday night, with only enough time to fall into his childhood bed to sleep. He drew a deep breath of the chilly mid-October air as he approached his parents' home—now his mother's house.

The buildings and lamps winding through the neighborhood displayed banners heralding next year's Trinity Falls Sesquicentennial, the 150th birthday of his hometown. They read: 150 YEARS STRONG. He'd already caught the community's excitement. Was the sole heir of the town's founding family also excited? Last he'd heard, Jackson Sansbury had withdrawn from the town.

It had been a stressful six weeks since he'd announced his resignation at the end of August. Now with the scent of autumn washing over him, Ean's tension drained from his muscles. Coming home had been the right thing to do. He'd had some trouble sleeping last night. But that had been because of the crickets, not because of his caseload.

He smiled, listening to the birds rehearsing their harmony as they perched high on the trees along his street. He took another deep breath, enjoying the clean, crisp air as the sun slowly rose, turning the sky a pale gray.

"Welcome home, Ean." The disembodied voice drew him from his thoughts.

Ean looked up as he approached his neighbor's oversized, stately house, across the street from his family's home. He hadn't noticed the tiny old woman standing in the threshold of her front door. She was wrapped in a thick green sweater two sizes too large for her.

Ean stopped at the end of her paved walkway, looking up at her. "Good morning, Ms. Helen. Thanks for the welcome."

Helen Gaston, or "Ms. Helen," as the residents of Trinity Falls called her, had been ancient the day Ean was born. Since then, time had stood still for her.

"Come on in." She waved him up with a slim right arm. "Get out of the cold. I'll get you a glass of water."

How could he refuse?

Ean glanced at Ms. Helen's sesquicentennial banner as he climbed the five redbrick steps and crossed the spacious porch. He toed off his running shoes beside her front door so he wouldn't track mud from his run into his neighbor's home.

Ms. Helen stepped backward, pulling the front door wider as she moved. "I'm glad to see New York didn't leech out the good manners your parents instilled in you."

"No, ma'am, it didn't." Ean crossed into her foyer in his stocking feet. He watched Ms. Helen disappear into her kitchen.

A deep breath drew in the scent of apple potpourri. The room was inviting, with honey wood flooring and bright yellow walls. Ean wandered closer to what appeared to be original framed watercolor paintings of the view outside Ms. Helen's home. Very nice.

Heavy pale brocade curtains were drawn open over the row of windows to his left, allowing the gray morning light inside. A reclining chair was stationed in front of the windows, apparently to assist in neighborhood surveillance. In warmer weather, that chair would stand on her balcony. Ean's gaze dropped to the current issue of the women's magazine resting on the seat. Ms. Helen's nephew bought her a subscription to the monthly journal every Christmas. Did she still accuse the postal carrier of reading it before he delivered it to her?

His hostess returned from the kitchen with a tall glass of ice water. "You went running this morning in the dark."

A glance at the chair answered how his vigilant neighbor had known that. Ever since he was a child, Ms. Helen seemed to know everything that occurred in Trinity Falls, sometimes before it happened.

Ean swallowed a gulp of water. "It was dark when I started running, but the sun came up pretty quickly."

"Did you notice the streetlamps along the jogging path in the park?"

An image of the lamps, each waving a 150 YEARS STRONG flag, flashed across his memory. "Yes, they're new."

"Not that new." Ms. Helen nodded toward his house across the street. "Adding the streetlamps was your mother's idea. Did you know that?"

Ean's brows rose in surprise. "No, ma'am. I didn't know that."

Ms. Helen nodded for emphasis. "Yes, indeed. That was Doreen's idea, although Mayor Ramona McCloud takes the credit."

Ramona was mayor. His former high-school girlfriend had e-mailed him after she'd been elected three years ago. What had made her become political?

"It doesn't surprise me that my mother recommended the town council add lamps to the path.

She's been active in supporting improvements for Trinity Falls all my life."

"Longer than that." Ms. Helen nodded again. "You know she's jogging now."

Another bit of news he hadn't been aware of. "No, ma'am, she hasn't mentioned that."

"She started jogging with Megan McCloud when your father got ill. Said exercise helped clear her mind. I'd sit with your father in the mornings, until after your mother came home and cleaned herself up."

Ean felt sick. *He* should have been the one watching over his father, waiting until his mother returned from her run. "Thank you for helping my parents."

"I was happy to do it." Ms. Helen waved a thin, wrinkled hand dismissively. She glanced out the window toward his house again. "Young man, it's good that you're home. Trinity Falls needs the shake-up."

"I'm not here to shake things up."

Ms. Helen clucked her tongue. "That doesn't matter. It'll happen, anyway. Some people are shuffling around here like they're afraid to make a move. But you're not afraid, and you know how to make things happen, just like on the football field. People used to call you 'Fearless Fever.' I'm looking forward to the fireworks."

"There won't be any fireworks, ma'am. I'm not here to change anything."

"Then why did you come home, Ean Fever?"

Ean crossed his arms. His stomach was still queasy

over the fact he'd been hundreds of miles away when his parents had needed him. "I came home to take care of my mother."

Ms. Helen's expression softened. "You're a good son, Ean. And I'm sure your mother appreciates the sentiment."

"Thank you, Ms. Helen."

She continued as though Ean hadn't spoken. "But Doreen Fever is one woman who doesn't need anyone to take care of her."

Ean smiled as he waited for Ms. Helen to stop laughing over her own words. "I want to be here if she needs me."

"Trinity Falls hasn't changed much since you've been gone, a couple of new shops, a new restaurant, streetlamps in the park. But people change. That's a good thing. People shouldn't stay the same. It means they're not learning. Do you understand me?"

"Yes, ma'am."

She gestured toward him with her fragile hands. "Like you. When you were younger, it was always, 'Hi, Ms. Helen. Bye, Ms. Helen.' You were always on the go. And I'd call after you, 'Don't spend all your time on the field. Hit those books.'"

Ms. Helen's gaze returned to the window. Why did she keep looking at his home?

"I remember."

"But now that you're older, you know you need to slow down. That's why you're here, standing in my foyer, taking time to talk with me."

Ean was irritated with his teenage self. He'd been too wrapped up in what he wanted to spend a few minutes with a charming and interesting old lady. "You're right, Ms. Helen. And spending time with you is definitely a change for the better."

"Save those fancy words for your lady friends." Ms. Helen's thin cheeks blushed.

"You're breaking my heart, Ms. Helen." Ean handed her his empty glass before opening her front door. "I'd better get cleaned up. Enjoy your day."

"You do the same." Her gaze drifted toward her window and his home again.

Ean paused on the porch to shove his feet back into his running shoes. He crossed the street and navigated the curving walkway that led to his mother's front door. After unpinning his key from his running jersey, Ean pushed it into the door's lock. He swung the front door wide, then froze in the threshold. Shock rattled him at the sight of his mother standing in the center of the living room, wrapped in a stranger's arms.

"Mom?" Ean's voice shot across the great room like a bullet before he realized he was going to speak.

Doreen jumped free of the romantic embrace and whirled toward her son. "Ean."

Ean's attention jerked to the man beside his mother. Shock rocked him back on his heels. He caught his balance. "Coach?"

"Hello, Ean." Leonard George's calm voice didn't belong in this tumultuous scene.

CHAPTER 3

Ean locked the front door, using the menial task to steady his mind. What was his mother doing in the arms of his former high school math teacher and football coach?

He leaned against the door and faced his parent. "What's going on?"

"Ean." Doreen spoke haltingly. "Leo and I . . . are in a relationship."

His gaze flew to his former coach as the man stood beside his mother on the other side of the family room's thick, dark pink sofa. He was older. But then, it had been more than fourteen years since he'd quarterbacked Coach George's football team at Heritage High School.

Ean's gaze challenged his mother to take back her words. "You've been dating Coach George?"

Leonard answered for her. "We've been seeing each other for some time now."

"Please, Leo." Doreen touched his shoulder. "Let me handle this. There's no need for you to be here."

"I won't let you face this alone." Leonard took her hand from his shoulder and held on to it.

Ean wanted to drag the other man away from his mother. He fisted his hands to control the impulse.

His coach couldn't be more different from his father. Whereas Paul Fever had been tall, lean and an introvert, Leonard George was average height, bulky and a clown.

"How long has this been going on?" Ean worked the words through his tense jaw.

Doreen held her son's eyes. "For a couple of months now."

Months? "Dad's only been gone a couple of months."

His mother's features softened. "It's been a little longer than that, Ean."

His father had died Friday, February 8. It was now Monday, October 14, less than nine months later.

Ean swallowed hard to dislodge the lump of grief from his throat. "Why didn't you tell me you'd started dating?"

Why hadn't you told me my father was dying?

Doreen's gaze dropped to the thick rose carpet. She seemed to brace herself before looking at Ean again. "I thought it was too soon to tell you about my relationship with Leo. And, since you were in New York, I didn't think there was a rush to address it."

Was that also the reason she hadn't told him his father had cancer? Because he'd been in New York?

Ean struggled with his feelings, chief among

them resentment. "My decision to return to Trinity Falls must have sent you into a panic."

Why are you dating so soon after Dad's death? Why did you choose my former coach?

Ean's thoughts came to a skidding halt. He couldn't handle them. Maybe his mother was right about it being too soon to talk about this.

"We did want to tell you." Leonard's voice further agitated Ean.

Doreen continued. "When you told me you were coming home, I wanted to tell you, but I didn't know how."

"We weren't deliberately trying to hide anything from you," Leonard added.

Ean's temper snapped. "This is a private conversation between my mother and me. I'd appreciate it if you'd stop talking."

Leonard's eyebrows rose. "But this—"

Doreen put her hand on Leonard's shoulder again. "It's all right, Leo. I'll call you later."

Ean held Leonard's gaze, willing his former coach to leave. He couldn't stand to see or hear the other man right now.

"All right." Leonard kissed Doreen's hand before circling the sofa.

Ean flinched.

As he crossed to the front door, the high school coach inclined his head toward Ean. Ean didn't respond. He pulled the door open for the older man and waited for Leonard to walk through.

Ean locked the front door again before facing his mother. "What was he doing here so early?"

"He didn't spend the night, if that's what you're asking." Doreen went to the kitchen. "He usually stops by on his way to school."

Why didn't you look at me when you answered?

Ean followed his mother. "So if I'd stayed in New York, I still wouldn't know about you and Coach George?"

"Have you told me about every woman you've dated?"

"That's different."

"How?"

"I'm not a grieving widow."

Doreen poured a cup of coffee. "Don't judge me, Ean. I'm your mother, not some witness on the stand."

"I'm not judging you." He rubbed his eyes with a thumb and two fingers. "I'm trying to understand why you kept your relationship with Coach George a secret from me."

"I didn't want to have this conversation." She leaned back against the kitchen counter with her coffee mug in hand. "I didn't want you to make me feel guilty about my feelings. I didn't want you to see me differently."

"But you are different, Mom." Ean started to feel chilled in his damp jogging clothes. Or maybe it was from the awareness that his mother had changed. "I came home because I didn't want you to be lonely and sad with Dad gone. Obviously, I was worried for nothing."

Ean spun on his heels. He left the kitchen to shower and change, but the question kept playing in his mind. What other secrets were left for him to discover in this town?

Ean wasn't the only one awake in his mother's house at six o'clock the next morning. He followed the light from the foot of the stairway to the kitchen and discovered his mother sitting at the table. She was drinking coffee and reading the daily newspaper, *The Trinity Falls Monitor.*

Doreen's still-dark hair swung in thick waves above her shoulders. She was dressed in a lightweight pinkish sweater and dark blue jeans. When had his mother started wearing jeans?

They'd settled into a brittle truce yesterday after their argument about Leonard George. He wasn't happy his mother had a boyfriend—he wouldn't explain why—but he was hoping they could put the unpleasantness behind them and start over today.

Ean halted in the doorway. "Why are you up so early?"

Doreen's smile seemed forced. Her warm brown eyes were wary. "I have to get to work."

Ean froze. "You have a job? Since when?"

She lowered the *Monitor.* "I told you I worked in a bakery. It's been almost six months now."

Ean rested a shoulder against the doorjamb. "I thought all you did was bake."

"It's a bit more than that."

"How much more?"

She glanced at him, then looked away. "I run that section of the business."

Ean processed that information. His mother had a boyfriend and a job. What other secrets would he have to pry from her?

He rubbed the nape of his neck. "I thought you only spent a couple of hours a week there. Why didn't you tell me it was a full-time job?"

Doreen folded the newspaper. "I didn't want to make a big deal out of it. I don't need the money. But this job is fun. And it gets me out of the house."

"It's a big deal to me, Mom." Just as his father's illness had been a big deal to him. But his mother hadn't told him about that, either. Not until it was too late. Ean shut off those thoughts. "Tell me about your job. Where's the bakery? What do you do?"

Her face glowed with pride and pleasure. "Megan added a bakery and meal counter to Head in the Clouds Books. She changed the name to Books and Bakery about six months ago."

Ean frowned. "Megan? You mean little Meggie McCloud?"

Doreen sobered. "Don't call her that. She doesn't like that nickname."

"Ramona called her that all the time."

Doreen's expression didn't change. "Her name's Megan."

"OK." Ean shrugged. "How did you get the job there?"

Doreen's features brightened again. "Megan asked me to run the bakery. She said I could make a lot of money selling my cookies and brownies."

Ean patted his stomach. "She's right."

"Well, as I said, I don't need the money. But I'm having a lot of fun." She stood and carried her coffee cup to the dishwasher. "I'm socializing again. And I've been experimenting with recipes."

"I wish you'd told me the truth about your job, Mom."

Doreen crossed to him. She cupped the right side of his face with her palm and kissed his left cheek. "You know now." She stepped back. "I'll be home by four o'clock."

"That late?" Ean struggled with disappointment. "I just got home. I'd hoped we could spend at least today together."

"We can spend the evening together." Doreen walked past him and continued out of the kitchen. She stopped to collect her purple purse from the dining room's corner table. "And I take Sundays and Mondays off. We'll have more time together then."

"What should I do until you get home?" Ean trailed his mother to the coat closet. He sounded five years old.

"Finish unpacking. Get settled in. Look up your friends. You'll think of something."

Ean looked down at his gray jersey and black running pants. They still were fresh and dry since he hadn't gone jogging yet. "Can I come with you?"

Doreen paused in the act of slipping into her coat. "What about your exercise?"

He didn't care that he sounded like a child. But he was concerned the chasm forming between them after yesterday's argument would grow if they spent today apart.

"I'll run later." Ean settled his hands on his hips. "Do you serve breakfast?"

Doreen opened her mouth twice before words followed. "Yes. We serve breakfast, lunch and pastries."

"Great." Ean reached past his mother for his jacket. "I'll order breakfast and see where you work. Besides, it'll be good to see Megan again."

His mother seemed flustered. "Well, all right. If you're sure that's what you want to do."

He kissed her cheek. "Think of today as 'Bring Your Kid to Work Day.'"

CHAPTER 4

Ean took in the dark hardwood flooring and bright inviting wall displays of Books & Bakery. The store had changed a lot since he'd left Trinity Falls, but there was something very familiar about it. It was midway through October, and Halloween themes dominated. Special-interest tabletop displays and overstuffed red armchairs lured patrons deeper into the store, where they were hypnotized by the rows upon rows upon rows of bookcases.

Megan McCloud was born to run a bookstore. Literally. She and her cousin, Ramona, had inherited the store from their paternal grandparents, who'd inherited the establishment decades earlier from his father.

Doreen's excitement was tangible as she led Ean down the aisles. "With the money her grandparents left her, Megan has been able to modernize the store. It now has a Web presence so people can order books and specialty items online."

"What about the money Mr. and Ms. McCloud

left Ramona?" Ean looked around, fascinated by the new features cozying up to his childhood memories.

"Ramona used her inheritance to start her interior-design business."

"I remember her telling me that." Ean scanned the rows of bookcases made from the same dark wood that gleamed beneath his feet. Newly released titles were shelved beside perennial best sellers.

Everything was tidy and smelled of lemon wood polish. There was a rigid organization to the store that nevertheless contributed to the comfortable, inviting atmosphere.

"What types of specialty items has Meggie—Megan—stocked?"

"Mostly local artists' crafts, like framed artwork, greeting cards and jewelry." Doreen swept her arm in a semicircle that encompassed the store.

Ean paused at the end of the aisle, riveted by a painting on display. "Is that Ms. Helen's work?"

"It certainly is." Doreen beamed at the framed watercolor.

Ean scanned the glossy magazine covers as he followed Doreen past the periodicals. She led him toward the back of the bookstore, away from the comic-book stands lining the far left border between the store and the new café section. The display stirred memories. A vivid flashback of a heated debate between him, Quincy and Darius over who had the coolest superpower, Batman, Spider-Man or Superman? Twelve-year-old Megan McCloud, the self-appointed manager in training, warning him not to bend the pages of the comic book he was handling.

Ean trailed Doreen past the mystery and romance novels to the science-fiction and fantasy books. Some of the series lining those shelves had been stocked since his junior high years: *Star Wars, Star Trek, Battlestar Galactica.* He'd spent countless Saturday afternoons among those books. They never went out of style.

"This is it." Doreen seemed nervous and excited as she made the announcement. She crossed the threshold into a modest white-and-silver kitchen lined with modern, industrial equipment.

"Very impressive." He didn't know what he'd expected from his ex-girlfriend's awkward younger cousin. But it hadn't been this.

Ean circled the bright white-tiled kitchen floor. He pulled open the silver refrigerator door. It was well stocked with eggs, butter and other confectioner's needs. The cupboards were positioned within reach for his much shorter mother.

He imagined her adding ingredients to the electric mixer before transferring the bakery pans into the industrial-sized oven. He could even hear her humming to herself as she moved around the room, just as she did at home. All of the equipment looked clean and well cared for. The room was a baker's dream, one he hadn't realized his mother had.

"This all looks good. It has everything you need."

Doreen frowned. "You sound surprised."

Ean shoved his hands into the front pockets of

his jogging pants. "I never knew this is what you wanted to do."

"Neither did I." His mother's voice was a whisper.

"When you said you worked in a bakery, I never realized you ran it, that you were the baker. Whenever I called, you talked about gardening, knitting and visiting with friends. But you never mentioned this. You never even mentioned Megan."

"I didn't think—"

"You didn't think it was a big deal. I know, Mom. But it is." And it changed everything.

His mother had never before worked outside of the home. She didn't have to. As a financial executive with the investment firm headquartered in the neighboring town, his father had made enough money to take care of his family. That left his mother with plenty of time to spend on him. Ean's gaze swept the room and its many shiny appliances. It had replaced him as the focus of much, if not all, of his mother's attention.

Doreen hung up her coat and shrugged into her apron. "Just because I have a job doesn't mean I won't be able to spend time with you."

Ean frowned. Had his mother read his mind?

"Is there anything I can do to help you?" Ean watched as she worked the room, gathering cooking utensils and ingredients with quick, practiced movements.

She spared him a smile from over her shoulder. "You know I don't like people helping me in the kitchen. It throws me off my rhythm. Just sit down and keep me company."

The words drew a chuckle from Ean. His mother had been telling him the same thing since he was six. That's when he'd started offering to help with the baking, when all he'd really wanted was to lick the bowl.

He crossed to the corner of the kitchen and chose one of the two spindly honey wood chairs at the matching circular table. "That I can do."

"Good. And you can also tell me the real reason you decided to quit your job and come home."

Ean tensed. He hadn't expected that question, at least not this soon. He didn't know if he could answer. He opened his mouth to try, when they were interrupted.

"Who are you talking to?" The feminine voice was filled with laughter. It floated into the room just moments before its speaker.

Ean gingerly rose from the decorative chair and turned toward the threshold.

The woman was tall, perhaps five inches shorter than his own six-foot-three. Her warm honey skin glowed under the harsh lights of the industrial kitchen. Thick dark hair fell in waves to her shoulders. She had a runner's build, with long, slender limbs draped in a brown pantsuit. The suit's style was nice, though the color was less than flattering. A wide matching brown belt cinched her tight waist.

She carried herself with a grace and confidence that fascinated Ean. And when she turned her startled chocolate gaze toward him, everything in the room receded, except her and the drowning sensation crashing over him.

Without a word or a movement, she'd pinned him in place. His heart slammed against his chest, again and again and again. Her eyes seemed to target the farthest corners of his heart and soul, searching for his secrets. He had an irresistible urge to share them with her.

Who was this woman?

"Meggie?" The question croaked from his dry throat.

She gave him a long, slow blink. "Megan."

He studied her features, looking for the skittish girl in this confident woman. "You've grown up."

"So have you." Her voice was somber, different but familiar.

She'd always been so serious. More often than not, her face had been buried in a book recently purchased from her grandparents' shop. Now Ean couldn't take his eyes from the delicate features once hidden behind those pages.

How long had it been since he'd last seen her? "The last time I saw you, you were about fourteen. I was leaving for college."

"Actually, I'd attended your father's funeral in February. But it's understandable that you wouldn't remember."

Stunned, Ean glanced at his mother. Doreen's nearly imperceptible nod made him feel worse. "Thank you for attending."

Megan forced herself not to fidget. Making polite conversation with a childhood crush should rank as one of the top ten worst things an adult would ever have to do. Ean's olive green eyes locked with hers. The awkward fourteen-year-old who still lived inside her wanted to run and hide. The slightly-less-awkward twenty-eight-year-old she'd become stiffened her knees and held his gaze.

She took a calming breath. "I was sorry when your father died. He was one of my favorite people."

Ean's eyes never wavered from hers. "I hadn't realized you'd known him that well."

"He'd been my grandparents' financial advisor and then mine. But he was also a good neighbor. He looked out for me after my grandparents died. I miss him."

"Thank you. So do I." Ean looked away.

Had she said something wrong?

Megan turned to Doreen, who was blinking rapidly. "I'm sorry. I didn't mean to upset you."

Doreen wiped her eyes with her fingertips. "No, dear. Don't mind us. You said exactly the right thing."

"Mom's right." Ean's voice was kind. "Thank you."

"You're welcome." The approval in his gaze went a long way toward relieving Megan's concerns.

He'd certainly grown up in the almost fourteen years since he'd left town. He now carried in spades the appeal he'd had as a young man, an appeal that had tempted and tortured the young Megan. Her eyes traced the chiseled features beneath his copper skin, the wide forehead and square jaw that warned strangers of his stubborn personality. Yet his full lips always seemed on the verge of a wicked smile.

His body also had matured from the lanky student-athlete who had quarterbacked the high school football team to a man who wasn't a stranger to a weight room.

Megan switched her gaze from Ean to Doreen. "I'm sorry to interrupt. I'll leave you to finish catching up."

Doreen chuckled. "Did you think I was talking to myself?"

Megan gave her friend a crooked smile. "You would have thought the same."

Ean took a step toward her. "You've done a great job with the bookstore. Your grandparents would be proud."

Megan caught her breath. Doreen was the only other person who'd ever said those words to her. But Doreen was her friend; then again, Ramona was her cousin. However, she'd never given her such praise.

Megan swallowed the lump in her throat. "You said exactly the right thing." She turned to leave.

Ean's voice stopped her again. "I have great memories of this store and your grandparents."

Reluctantly, Megan turned back to him. "I never thanked you for the flowers you sent to their memorial service." Ramona had, and Megan had convinced herself her cousin's response was enough.

"My mother told me about the changes you've made to modernize the store. You're a smart businesswoman."

Megan thought she'd faint at Ean's feet. "I'd better get back to work. I have a lot to do before we open the store."

She trembled as she escaped to her office. The

store wouldn't open for another hour. She could have stayed to talk with Doreen. And Ean. No, she couldn't have. Megan collapsed into the blue executive chair behind her desk. Each minute in Ean's company had turned back time until she'd regressed to that fourteen-year-old girl confronted by her crush. His praise had taken her breath, and his olive eyes, focused just on her, had melted her insides.

Damn him.

Megan lowered her head into her hands. She couldn't handle many more encounters like those. But how could she avoid him in a town this small? Her friends were his friends. His mother worked for her. They were bound to see each other. Often. And if Ean and Ramona picked up where they'd left off? Knowing her cousin, Megan was sure Ramona would show him off to her as often as possible.

Family rivalry was hell.

"The prodigal son returns to Trinity Falls." Darius Knight's voice came from just behind Ean.

A smile stretched Ean's lips. He set his coffee mug on the counter and rose to greet his childhood friend. His smile broadened to a grin when he saw Quincy standing with Darius.

He shook both men's hands and patted their shoulders. "I needed a break from you jokers."

Darius snorted. "Then you came running back when you realized you couldn't function without us."

Ean stepped back to get a better look at the two men he hadn't seen in almost a year. Not since his father's funeral. He swallowed back that sad memory and focused on the pair's annual visits to New York.

He'd been thick as thieves with Darius and Quincy since their days in the Pee Wee Football League. Darius had been the team's prime-time tight end. Quincy had been its powerful running back. Now Darius was an intrepid reporter with the town's daily newspaper, though he looked like he belonged on the nightly news. Quincy still looked more like a football player than a university history professor.

"I heard it was the other way around." Ean waved a hand between the two friends. "The two of you couldn't function without me."

Darius shook his head in mock pity as he claimed a seat at the counter. "I'd check my sources if I were you, my friend."

Ean chuckled. It was good to be home. He looked over his shoulder at Quincy. "How've you been, Quincy?"

"The same since we last spoke a month ago." Quincy took a seat on the other side of Darius.

Ean's smile wavered at the other man's short tone. "I feel as though I've walked into a time warp. You both look the same."

Darius's eyes twinkled with evil intent. "You look older."

Ean broke into laughter. Darius hadn't changed. It was like being back on his front porch with his friends after school, sharing dreams and swapping insults.

Quincy shifted in his seat, staring down at the gray-and-white–marble countertop. "I'm sorry the town seems so prosaic to you. Maybe you should have stayed in New York."

Ean frowned. He opened his mouth to respond but was forestalled by his mother's appearance.

Doreen liberated two mugs from the collection behind the counter. "And how are you young men this morning?"

Darius and Quincy returned his mother's greeting with an easy familiarity as she gave them each a mug. This morning's meeting seemed a comfortable habit for the three of them. The sting of envy deepened the frown across Ean's brow. For months, his childhood friends and his ex-girlfriend's younger cousin had shared breakfast with his mother almost every morning. Meanwhile, he'd been in New York chasing an adolescent's dream.

"Do you two want the usual this morning?" His mother's question confirmed his suspicions.

Darius smiled up at Doreen as she filled his mug with coffee. "Yes, please."

Doreen quirked an eyebrow. "Darius Knight, that innocent smile didn't fool me when you were a child. And it certainly doesn't fool me now. My son's return doesn't give you a free pass to cause havoc like you three did as children."

Darius lifted the mug to his smiling lips. "Your suspicions wound me, Ms. Doreen."

Doreen tipped the coffee carafe to pour the hot,

fragrant drink into Quincy's mug. "Quincy was always the sensible one. But he had his hands full, trying to keep the two of you out of trouble."

Darius pretended to choke on his coffee. "Don't let his quiet demeanor fool you. Some of those misadventures were Quincy's idea."

Quincy lifted his mug of black coffee. "I don't remember it that way."

Ean offered his mother a smile as she topped off his drink. "Thank you."

Quincy's surly manner stood out against the friendly banter around the counter. Darius seemed oblivious of the tension surrounding their friend. Was Quincy always this grumpy in the morning? For his students' sakes, Ean hoped the professor didn't schedule any early-morning classes.

Doreen returned with a white Books & Bakery paper bag she handed to Quincy. "One Trinity Falls Fudge Walnut Brownie, fresh from the oven." She turned to the other customers at the counter. "Your orders will be right up."

As Doreen returned to the kitchen, Darius reached for the bag.

"Touch it and die." Quincy scowled at the other man. "If you want a brownie, order your own. Why are you always going after mine?"

Darius returned to his coffee. "You shouldn't eat sweets. They're not good for you."

Ean leaned forward to see Quincy on Darius's other side. "How's your family, Q?"

"Fine."

So much for that line of conversation.

Ean turned to Darius. "How are your parents?"

Darius's smile didn't reach his eyes. "Very happily driving each other insane, thank you. My dad's planning his retirement, and my mother's indulging every jealous bone in her body."

Ean sobered as he remembered the tension in Darius's childhood home. "I'm sorry, man."

His friend shrugged. "At least I don't live with them anymore. I can handle one Sunday dinner a month."

"What about Jack?" Ean looked from Quincy to Darius, asking about Jackson Sansbury, the last member of the town's founding family.

Darius shook his head. "He's still in mourning, man. He bought those old cabins at the lake and completely cut himself off from the town."

Ean sighed. "I'm sorry to hear that."

"Why did you come back?" Quincy's question sounded like a personal attack.

Ean studied Quincy's profile. What was eating at his friend? "I told you when we spoke last month. I'm through with the rat race. I wanted to come home to Trinity Falls."

Quincy snorted. "Growing up, you couldn't wait to leave."

Darius swallowed more coffee. "And now he's back. At least he's not afraid to go after what he wants."

Quincy glared at Darius.

The reporter ignored him. He set down his mug and turned to Ean. "So you've escaped the rat race. Do you intend to live a life of leisure in Trinity Falls?"

Ean frowned. Why was Quincy resentful of his

return? And what did Darius mean when he said Ean wasn't afraid to go after what he wanted? He needed answers, but the mulish expression on Quincy's blunt features told him he wouldn't get any—not yet.

He settled back in the swivel seat. "I have a couple of ideas. I'm going to take my time and consider them."

"I'm sure you can do that." Quincy drained his coffee. "You were making big bucks in New York. The cost of living in Trinity Falls must seem laughable to you."

"Shut up and eat your brownie, Q." Darius's voice was flat.

The tension was getting to Darius, and Ean had had enough. He checked his wristwatch. "I'm going to see Ramona. I'll catch up with you guys later."

Darius looked up. "Good to have you back, man."

Ean grinned. "Good to be back."

Quincy eyed him coldly. "Why are you going to see her? You broke up six years ago."

"Ramona and I are still friends. You know that."

Ean nodded at Darius and pondered the back of Quincy's head. What was Quincy's problem? And what was he afraid to go after?

CHAPTER 5

Ean entered the dim stairwell that would take him to Ramona's office on the second floor of the Trinity Falls Town Hall. However, his thoughts remained with Megan. He unzipped his gray London Fog winter jacket as he climbed the stairs. Megan had been a shy girl when he'd left town. She was a woman now. But the difference between the girl she'd been and the woman she'd become was more than the passage of time.

She'd always looked people straight in the eye. When she was younger, he'd found the habit unsettling. Now it challenged him. OK, it excited him. Her cousin and classmates had been coy young girls, but Megan had always been direct. As a teenager, he'd thought her odd. As a man, he found her intriguing. Maybe it wasn't Megan who'd changed. Maybe he had.

Ean opened the door to the second-floor exit and entered the hallway outside of the mayor's reception area. Ramona as Trinity Falls's mayor. Would he ever get used to it?

He pulled open the glass doors to the waiting room and crossed to the receptionist's desk. The young, red-haired woman behind the circular white counter had been a couple of grades behind him and Ramona at Heritage High School.

"Hi, Alice. Is Ramona free?"

Alice stood and beamed at him. "Hi, Ean. Welcome home."

"Thank you." He followed her to the hallway as he had on previous visits.

"Ramona's expecting you." She made a face over her shoulder at him. "Three years in office. Who'd have thought it? If I'd've bet which McCloud cousin would have run for office, I'd still've put my money on Megan."

Ean simply nodded. Alice said the same thing every year.

The thin gray carpeting masked their footsteps as they crossed the long hallway to Ramona's office. The gleaming silver metal sign on the dark wood door read: RAMONA A. MCCLOUD, MAYOR.

"No one else wanted the job." The young receptionist knocked twice, then waited for Ramona's response before opening the door. "Mayor McCloud, Mr. Ean Fever's here to see you."

Ramona turned away from her computer screen and placed her forearms on her desk. Her ebony eyes went straight to Ean. "That'll be all, Alice."

Ean stepped inside. Alice pulled the door closed behind her.

Ramona rose from her chair. Her bloodred blouse and pencil-thin black skirt hugged her siren's curves. Her thick near-black hair fell in heavy, glossy curls past her shoulders. Her café au lait skin looked radiant under perfectly applied makeup.

Ramona circled her desk and walked to the black leather sofa on her right. Red stilettos showed off her endless legs. "It's about time you came knocking on my door."

Ean stopped an arm's length from where she stood beside the sofa. Her Chanel No. 5 was familiar. "I only arrived home Sunday night."

Ramona's eyes gleamed at him as she sat, crossing her legs. "Have a seat."

Ean joined her. "You've redecorated."

"I did it myself. I needed a change." She raised her right arm, drawing his attention back to the black-and-silver décor and modern furnishings.

The room was attractive but cold, impersonal, reminding him of Hugh Bolden's office at the firm. Abstract metal sculptures posed on glass tabletops and shelves. Framed works of modern art hung from her office's white walls beside local newspaper and community magazine interviews with her.

Ramona continued. "I couldn't believe it when I got your e-mail telling me you were coming back."

"I felt the same way three years ago when you told me you were Trinity Falls's mayor." Ean settled his right ankle on his left knee. "I still don't understand how you became interested in politics."

He couldn't picture his high school sweetheart running their hometown. As teenagers, all they'd dreamed of was leaving Trinity Falls. Seven years ago, he'd made his escape when Craven, Bolden & Arnez hired him to work in their New York firm. He'd asked Ramona to join him. She'd seemed ecstatic at first. But less than a year later, she'd returned to Trinity Falls without giving him a reason for breaking up with him.

Ramona gave a low, husky laugh. "Someone had to save this town from itself."

"What was happening?"

"Nothing. That was the problem. The town was stagnating. We need to attract new industry and new people."

"The sesquicentennial celebration should help." Ean noted the miniature version of the 150 YEARS STRONG banner sitting on Ramona's desk. "Publicity for the event should attract some attention."

"But will it be enough to revitalize the economy?" Ramona shifted toward him. "We have to do more. We need to improve the town's infrastructure and add first-class features to stimulate growth."

Ean's eyes widened. "Who are you and what have you done with Ramona McCloud?"

It scared him to hear the woman he'd grown up with speaking like this. She sounded like the consummate politician, which meant she used a lot of words that said nothing.

Another husky laugh. "I could ask you the same thing for coming back here."

Ean tried again. "What was wrong with Trinity Falls?"

"There's never anything going on here. Sure, we're planning a yearlong celebration for the town's one hundred and fiftieth birthday, but all of the events are so small-town. That's why I can't believe you came back. You're not really staying, are you?" That sounded more like the old Ramona.

"Yes, I'm home for good."

Was it possible for them to rekindle their relationship? They'd once wanted the same things. It didn't seem that way anymore. Without that common purpose, did they have anything to build on?

"Why have you come back?" Her wide eyes and parted lips said she thought he'd lost his mind.

"It was time for me to come home. The work I was doing in New York wasn't fulfilling anymore." Ean stood, shifting his gaze to the window. "I don't think it ever was."

The view from town hall was so different from the panorama visible from every window at the firm. Instead of skyscrapers, there were trees. Instead of billboards, he saw blue sky. In the distance, he could see the Trinity Falls Town Center, home of Books & Bakery—and Megan McCloud.

"There's nothing to do here, but so much to do in New York." Ramona placed both feet on the ground. "You can do something different every day. And there's so much to see there."

"I enjoyed living in New York. But now I want something less hectic." He couldn't explain why he gave up his dreams of making it big in the Big Apple. Even if he could, Ramona wouldn't understand.

"You're not making any sense, Ean. New York is where we always wanted to be. Why would you throw that all away to come back to this?" She gestured toward the window.

Ean met her gaze. "Six years ago, *you* threw it all away and returned to this town. You never told me why you left the city—and me."

Ramona rolled her eyes and crossed her arms. Was that a blush darkening her rounded cheeks? "We can go back to New York together."

"I'm not going back, Ramona."

Her expression brightened. "Then maybe we can go somewhere else. It doesn't have to be New York. We can go to Los Angeles or Chicago. Or even Boston, although I hear it gets really cold there."

"If you want to leave Trinity Falls, you should." Ean returned to sit beside her. "But I'm not going with you."

Ramona leaned toward him, laying her hand on his right thigh. Her features eased into a seductive smile. "I bet I can get you to change your mind."

He considered her small, fair hand resting intimately on his lap. Sex between them had been good, but not good enough to make him change his mind about staying in Trinity Falls.

Ean gently removed her hand from his thigh. "No, you can't."

Ramona persisted. "Why don't we talk about it over dinner at my place tonight?"

Ean stood to leave. "That wouldn't be a good

idea, Ramona. But I would like to continue our friendship."

Ramona's leaving him six years ago had closed the door on their romantic relationship forever. But he wanted them to remain friends. In a town this size, it would be awkward to bear hostilities.

Ramona stood, sliding her hand up his torso to settle on his shoulder. "I remember how much you enjoyed it when we ate in. Are you sure you won't change your mind?"

The look in her eyes told him the double entendre was deliberate. "Positive."

Memories of the younger Ramona warned him it would be safer for them to go out than to have a private dinner in her home. She was less likely to make a scene in public if their evening didn't go her way.

Ramona pressed her curves against him. She pulled his head toward hers to kiss him good-bye. The kiss was deep and hot, slow and sexy. She slid her tongue between his lips and stroked the roof of his mouth. When she stepped back, Ean let her go.

Her voice was breathless. "Just a little something to help you change your mind about that dinner."

"I'm sorry, Ramona. Friendship is all I feel for you anymore." Ean turned to leave.

"What is Ramona thinking, trying to bring the big city to Trinity Falls? I just don't know." Ethel Knight sat at a table near the bakery's counter

Tuesday afternoon. "Trinity Falls is not New York, for heaven's sake."

Darius's mother pinched off a piece of her apple pie and nibbled it. She reminded Megan of a squirrel.

Don't react. Megan forced herself to remain in her seat at the counter and choke down her grilled chicken salad. She and Ramona had their conflicts, but criticism against her cousin still burned.

"If she wants to shop in New York, she should go to New York." Simon Knight spoke around a mouthful of Boston cream pie.

From his seat beside her, Darius offered Megan an apologetic look before responding to his parents. "It's easy to find fault with the government, but you should also give her credit for the positive work she's accomplished."

"Men." Ethel sniffed. "Of course you rush to Ramona's defense 'cause she's a beautiful woman. I just don't know."

"Mother, I'd say the same thing if she looked like the bottom of my shoe." Darius spun the full lazy Susan pastry tray. "Call it 'journalistic integrity.' Ramona has done a lot of good for Trinity Falls."

Megan reached over and pressed his forearm in gratitude for his defense of her cousin. Darius's movements were relaxed, almost negligent. But Megan felt the tension in his muscles and knew his parents' public displays of bickering and complaints made Darius uncomfortable.

Doreen refilled Megan's glass of ice water. "Darius is right. We may not always agree with Ramona, but we can't deny she's done a lot of good for Trinity Falls."

"I remember when you used to give pastries away for free, Doreen." Ethel's voice was sly.

"Those days are long gone." Doreen's flat tone shut the gate on memory lane. She exchanged the pitcher of water for a pot of coffee and refilled Darius's mug.

"Name one positive thing that Ramona has done for Trinity Falls while she's been in office." Simon issued the challenge with a raised chocolate-tipped index finger.

Darius didn't need to stop to consider his answer. "She fixed the intersection at the north corner of the town center. Do you remember that it had become a danger to drivers and pedestrians because of its disrepair?"

Simon grunted. "That one was easy. Ramona didn't have to come up with that. It was something that needed to get done."

Tune them out. Megan's hand shook as she stabbed lettuce and chicken against her plate and carried the forkful of salad to her mouth. She tried to chew and hum to herself at the same time.

"If it was so easy, why didn't the previous mayor do it?" Doreen topped off Simon's coffee. "She also installed the streetlamps in the park."

"But that was your idea, Doreen." Ethel's response was a crow of triumph.

"It doesn't matter whose idea it was." Doreen

returned to the counter. "The fact is, she got it done."

Megan had heard enough. "Darius is right. It's easy to sit and criticize, but if you don't like the job the council is doing, let them know."

"A man would have done a better job." Simon shoveled more pie into his mouth.

Megan's back stiffened. "Then why didn't a man run?"

Simon ignored her question. "Women are too emotional."

Megan's face heated with temper. She ignored Darius's growing tension beside her. "Why didn't *you* run, Mr. Knight?"

Simon spoke over her. "Ramona's more interested in bringing higher-end department stores to Trinity Falls. Men don't want to shop."

"Dad." Darius spun on his seat to face his father. "Our last two mayors have run unchallenged."

Simon drank his coffee. "I haven't voted for any of them."

Darius swung his seat toward the counter, turning his back to his father. "You know that old saying, Dad. 'If you don't vote, you can't criticize.'"

Megan shoved away what remained of her salad. "If you have such strong views on what's wrong with Trinity Falls and how to fix it, Mr. Knight, you should run for office yourself."

Simon snorted. "Only a fool would run for office. I'm nobody's fool."

Megan wasn't sure about that. How could Darius

have come from this couple? Her friend must have been adopted.

"My cousin has worked hard for more than three years to keep this town running—the schools, the emergency services, the health clinics and everything else. What have you done?" Megan stood. "If you don't like the job she's doing, either run against her or vote her out."

Doreen shook her head. "Be careful what you wish for."

Her friend was right. Megan's gaze slid to Simon Knight. She didn't agree with Ramona's latest plans for Trinity Falls, but things could be worse.

CHAPTER 6

Tuesday evening, Megan glanced at her red Timex wristwatch again. Only eight minutes had passed since her last time check during this interminable town council meeting. Megan shifted in her third-row seat, which probably was older than she was. She crossed her legs, folded her arms and swallowed an impatient sigh.

The metal folding chairs were arranged in the town hall's largest conference room to accommodate residents. In fact, the council's business served as a backdrop for what was more of a community social.

Ramona adjusted the microphone on the desk in front of her. "Before the council entertains presentations and new matters from the public, I would like to take a moment to update everyone on the status of the park lamps." Her pause added drama to a matter-of-fact statement. "Three months ago, the lamps were installed along the walking path in Freedom Park. The lamps are operating properly and have added a sense of increased security to residents."

A tepid round of applause limped around the room. Megan wanted to sink into her chair. Why did Ramona always have to draw attention to herself? She'd contracted to have the lamps installed in the park. But everyone in town knew the lamps had been Doreen Fever's idea.

CeCe Roben, the town council president, cleared her throat. Her auburn hair was a sleek bob framing her alabaster face. "Thank you, Mayor. I've noticed a big difference with the new lamps and feel much safer in the park at night now."

From his seat on Megan's left, Darius lowered his pen and leaned closer. He dropped his voice to a whisper. "How much of that is sincere, and how much of it is CeCe's attempt to score points with Ramona?"

Megan nodded. "I wondered the same thing."

Quincy sat forward in his chair on Megan's right. He kept his voice to the same hushed tone. "I thought you didn't believe Ramona had a good side."

The reporter shrugged. "I don't believe Publishers Clearing House is real, either, but I'll open my door if they knock."

Quincy chuckled. "I jog through the park most nights. I don't think I've ever seen CeCe there."

CeCe called for new matters, which were very few: Roads were still waiting for repair after heavy storms from the previous spring. The malicious prankster responsible for stealing road signs had struck again, leaving Guilford Lane unidentified. And the search for a new city treasurer was still under way before the current treasurer retired because of "family reasons" sparked by an affair with his brother's wife.

CeCe tapped the gavel to bring the meeting back to order. "At this time, we'd like to invite to the microphone those in attendance who would like to address the council."

Megan scanned the room. Apparently, no one felt a pressing need to air his or her concerns. Megan inclined her head at the other members of the Trinity Falls Town Center Business Owners Association. From her seat, she contemplated the microphone waiting at the front of the room. Public speaking was not her forte. Megan's heart pounded a steady rhythm against her chest. She drew in a deep breath and squared her shoulders before making her way to the podium. She felt Ramona's eyes on her every step of the way.

Megan gripped the edges of the podium and locked her knees. "Good evening, council members and Mayor."

A murmur of "good evenings" responded.

"I'm here as a representative of the Trinity Falls Town Center Business Owners Association." Was the wobble in her voice noticeable? "What additional information can you provide regarding plans to sell the center to a high-end broker to revitalize the property?"

Ramona pulled her microphone closer to her mouth. "Like what?"

Ramona's intimidation tactics were familiar—flat stare, bored tone—and they usually worked. Megan glanced over her shoulder. The members of her group, including Quincy and Darius, nodded encouragement.

Megan squared her shoulders and faced her cousin. "What types of businesses were you planning to attract? Where would you locate these new businesses?"

"We don't have answers to those questions yet." Ramona's dismissive tone slapped her down.

Megan wanted to end this exchange and return to her seat, but her group was depending on her. "You're trying to draw new businesses, but you don't know what type or where you'd put them? Then why do you want them?"

Ramona lowered her brows. "Why are you asking so many questions?"

"Ramo . . . Mayor McCloud, new businesses will impact Trinity Falls's existing retailers. The result will be increased competition for discretionary, as well as essential, spending. Businesses have to prepare for these changes—"

CeCe interrupted her. "I can understand your concern, Megan."

"I can't," Ramona muttered.

CeCe continued. "As soon as the council has the information that you're requesting, we'll share it with you and the rest of the town's business owners."

"Thank you, Councilwoman Roben." Megan nodded toward the council before leaving the podium. Her legs were like Jell-O. She was out of breath.

Again she felt Ramona's eyes burning into her. Why would the council announce its intent to attract new businesses to Trinity Falls if it didn't know the types of businesses it wanted to attract, or even where they would be located? What was really going on?

The sound of leaves crunching behind her pulled Megan from her solitary thoughts early Wednesday morning. The fellow jogger was gaining ground on her fast. Perhaps too fast. From the weight of the footfalls, the runner was probably male. Without breaking stride, Megan loped to the edge of Freedom Park's nearly deserted dirt path, signaling the newcomer that he was free to pass.

"It's not safe to run alone in the dark." Ean's rich baritone almost sent her into cardiac arrest.

It never occurred to her she would come into contact with him during her morning exercise. But here he was, with his olive green eyes focused on her.

Megan blinked. Her heart thumped once. Twice. "It's after six o'clock in the morning."

"It's still dark."

Megan puzzled over his statement as they jogged through the pools of light spilling from the lamps stationed every couple of feet. "This is Trinity Falls, not New York City."

"Unfortunately, women are accosted in small towns, too."

"That's one of the reasons these lamps were installed." Megan watched a drop of sweat trail down Ean's broad forehead, drip off his aquiline nose and land on the gunmetal gray T-shirt stretched across his broad chest.

She shifted her attention away and drew in the chill October air to cool her suddenly overheated body. Ean seemed to have adjusted his pace to match hers. Was his concern for her safety the reason he didn't just jog past her? Megan was trapped.

She tried to distract herself by focusing on the fall colors on the trees and bushes bordering the hard dirt path. Some of the vibrant leaves were strewn along the ground and grass.

She loved this time of day; the still silence of the early morning, when it felt as though she was the only person on the planet. The scent of fall was heavy in the air. She glanced at Ean in her peripheral vision. Did he sense the magic of the early morning, too? A ghost of a smile touched his full, sexy lips.

"What are you thinking about?" Her question startled her. Why had she asked him that?

"The past. The path hasn't changed much, except for these lamps." He gestured toward a tree root. "I twisted my ankle on that once, before I learned to hop over it."

"The town hasn't changed much." Megan returned her attention to the trail. "People come and eventually go. They rarely return."

"Is that a not-so-subtle reference to my home-coming?"

"Maybe." Megan's fingers trembled to smooth his thick, arched brow and wipe the sweat from his forehead. She fisted her hands.

"The bookstore's changed. A lot."

"It needed to be modernized and expanded to survive."

"Ramona's changed, too. Business and politics had never held much interest for her."

Megan struggled again with contradictory feelings for Ramona as mayor: pride that her cousin had accepted the responsibility when no one else would; relief that the town was better off now than it had been three years ago; frustration that Ramona was bullying the town into changes only she seemed to want.

Megan used the back of her wrist to wipe sweat from her upper lip. "And yet she's launched her interior-design company and is running the town."

Ean's long strides picked up. Megan maintained her pace. Maybe his increased speed would carry him away from her.

Ean wiped the sweat from his chin. "I remember you following your grandparents around the bookstore. It was as though you were grooming yourself to take over for them. Did you major in business?"

Megan bit back a groan as Ean again adjusted his stride to hers. "I had a double major in business and accounting from the University of Illinois."

Ean's brows knitted. "Illinois is a good school. Ramona hadn't mentioned that you'd gone to college out of state. I assumed you'd gone to Trinity Falls University, just as she had."

"I got a scholarship." With a wealth of relief, Megan nodded toward an old, curved tree several yards ahead on their left. "This is where I turn back. Enjoy the rest of your run."

"I'll join you." Ean's response was swift.

"That's not necessary." Megan declined his offer just as quickly.

"It's still dark. I can't leave you to jog home alone. If anything happened to you, I'd never forgive myself."

His words weakened her resistance. She fought hard not to give in. "Don't cut your run short on my account. I'll be fine."

"I can come back to the park after I take you home." And then he flashed his wicked grin. Deep dimples creased his cheeks. Hypnotic lights danced in his olive eyes.

Megan blushed at the direction her thoughts took. "All right. Thank you."

They arrived at the tree with Megan just a half step behind Ean. In silence, they circled it, then jogged back the way they'd come.

Megan glanced at Ean's strong, chiseled profile. Sweat molded the gray T-shirt to his pectorals. Her brain cells leaked from her ears. She kicked up her speed, anxious to end this torture.

Ean's voice broke the uncomfortable silence. "What hobbies do you have besides jogging?"

"Why are you asking so many personal questions?" She tossed him a cheeky grin. "Are you going to ask my sign next? My favorite color?"

Ean laughed. "I only want to get to know you better."

Her stomach seemed to drop. "What are your hobbies?"

Ean was silent for a moment. "I don't think I have any others. In New York, all I did was work and run."

She was angry for him. That wasn't a life. "Reading. I like to read."

His chuckle strummed the muscles in her lower abdomen. "Your face was always buried in a book."

"And you, Darius and Quincy were always arguing over comic books." Her blush was becoming a permanent condition.

"We weren't arguing. We were debating." His eyes warmed as they shared the memory.

Megan exhaled in relief as her grandparents' house—now her home—came into view at the end of the block. "I'll race you."

She issued the challenge to mask her desperate need to escape him. Ean laughed as he pulled away from her. A latent competitive streak stirred to life inside Megan. She dug deeper, raising her knees and pumping her arms, straining to keep up with him, hoping to pass him.

Her gaze dropped to the fine, firm muscles of his derriere. A thread of an idea sewed into her mind. Megan reached forward and grabbed the waistband of his black gym pants. Ean came up short.

The surprise stamped on his copper features was comical. Megan laughed as she sprinted past him.

She tapped the sycamore tree in front of her home and threw her arms above her head. "I won!"

Ean slowed to a stop beside her. "You cheated."

Megan was breathless from exertion and giddy with victory. "That wasn't cheating. It was strategy."

Ean's eyes dipped to her mouth. "It was cheating."

His voice was a low, wicked rumble. Megan sobered. Ean's head drew closer. His scent—sweat and musk—clouded her thoughts. The burgeoning heat in his eyes rendered her motionless. This moment was her young girl's fantasy, but his nearness stirred every inch of her woman's body. All she knew was his heat, his touch, his eyes. And all she wanted was his taste.

CHAPTER 7

Ean leaned closer. Too close. His movement wrenched Megan from her trance.

She staggered backward—away from the sycamore tree, away from Ean. Away from temptation. "Excuse me."

She stumbled up her walkway, tripped up the five redbrick front steps and fumbled into her home. With shaking hands, she relocked her door before collapsing against it. Her legs felt like water balloons. Her heart galloped like a startled horse. What had just happened?

Gripping the doorknob, Megan leaned toward the smoked side window on her right and spied on Ean. Her breath caught in her throat. He was still beside the tree. His long, lean body stood in profile as he stared at the sidewalk. Unobserved, she could allow her gaze to touch every inch of his hard, muscled form. Loose-fitting black running pants covered long, strong legs and lovingly cupped his tight glutes. His sweat-stained gray jersey molded his flat abs and chiseled pecs. Her fist clenched the doorknob. She wanted the courage to go back down her walkway and ease the ache building inside. She needed the sense to keep this locked door between them and protect her heart. What should she do, give in to desire or hold on to common sense? Before she could decide, Ean turned and jogged back toward the park.

Damn it!

Megan leaned against her front door. What had she been thinking? Ean Fever wasn't for her. Her roots were planted deep within Trinity Falls, Ohio. Almost from birth, Ean had been searching for other soil. She was too old to be weaving fantasies about the town's most popular boy falling in love with her and living happily ever after. Fairy tales were for books.

She pushed away from the door and plodded to her upstairs bathroom. Even if Ean had returned to Trinity Falls to stay, he'd come back for Ramona. She'd been rejected in favor of her cousin before. She wouldn't allow history to repeat itself.

Ean stood in Quincy's office doorway hours later, watching the former running back review papers. His childhood friend had become a university professor. Very cool.

He knocked twice on Quincy's open door. "How does it feel to be the one giving the grades instead of getting them?"

Too late, Quincy masked his surprise. "'It is better to give than to receive.'"

"Good one." Ean grinned at the glimpse of the old Quincy. "You have a minute?"

"I have to teach a class." That quickly, the window into their shared past closed.

Ignoring Quincy's attempt at a brush-off, Ean pulled the door closed behind him and settled into one of the two cushioned chairs in front of the pale modular desk. "We have plenty of time. It's nine o'clock. Darius said you only have afternoon classes on Wednesdays."

Quincy scowled. "I have to prepare for those classes."

Ean leaned into the chair and propped his right ankle onto his left knee. "I only need ten minutes."

Quincy's air of resignation was even more puzzling. "What can I do for you, Ean?"

So formal. "You can start by telling me why you're pissed off that I've come home."

"Why would I be upset?"

"That's what I'm asking."

Quincy's eyes hardened. "I'm sorry if I'm not showing you the right amount of deference, but I don't have to play follow the leader—follow *you*—anymore. I walk my own path now."

Ean's brows launched up his forehead. "'Follow the leader'? What the hell are you talking about?"

Quincy remained silent.

Maybe this confrontation hadn't been a good idea. Ean was more confused today than he'd been Tuesday morning. He dragged both hands over his head as he rose to pace. Unfortunately, Quincy's office was comfortable but small.

The framed Professor of the Year Award hanging on the off-white wall to his left distracted him. The recognition wasn't surprising. Quincy was determined to be the best at whatever he chose to do.

A small coffeepot stood on a black metal cabinet in a corner behind Quincy's chair. Two wall-to-wall bookcases faced each other from opposite sides of the office and were stuffed with books on African and African-American history. On the shelf above his computer, writing references, a dictionary and a thesaurus shared space with framed photos of family and friends.

Ean spotted a photo of him, Quincy and Darius in their grass-and-dirt–stained high school football uniforms. He remembered mugging for that photo. Quincy's father had taken it shortly after their championship game. Ean had kept a copy of that same picture on his desk at the law firm. The school had nicknamed the friends "the Terrible Trio": quarterback, running back and tight end. An unstoppable offense.

That picture hardened Ean's resolve to repair one of the most important relationships in his life. "When I was in New York, we e-mailed or called each other a couple of times a month. Everything seemed fine. Now that I'm back, you're acting as though I've stolen from you. What's changed?"

Quincy crossed his arms over his chest. "Things can't go back to the way they were."

That was a familiar theme in Trinity Falls. "Why not?"

"We aren't the people we used to be. We've grown up. We've changed."

Ean assessed his friend like any witness on the stand. Whatever was eating at him, Quincy wouldn't give up the information easily. "What are you afraid of going after?"

"What are you talking about?" Quincy's words snapped with impatience.

"At the bookstore Tuesday, Darius said *I'm* not afraid to go after what I want. What does he think you're afraid of?" Ean caught the shift in Quincy's gaze. A moment of uncertainty that revealed Ean was on the right track.

"I'm not afraid of anything." Quincy's mouth tightened as though he didn't want to divulge more than he already may have.

"We're all afraid of something."

"What are you afraid of?"

Ean clenched his teeth. Why had he opened this door? "Right now, I'm afraid I waited too long to come home."

"Maybe New York is your home now."

Those words coming from his friend hurt. "What do you want? Maybe I can help."

Quincy's expression grew mulish. "I don't need your help."

They were at an impasse. Ean stood. "Let me know if you change your mind. Your friendship means a lot to me, Q. It's one of the reasons I came home."

Surprise relaxed Quincy's tight features. Ean turned to leave the office. But he wasn't calling the game. This was only a time-out. He'd come home to return to the people and the things that mattered most to him. But had he waited too long?

"Dracula is drunk." Megan chewed the words like rocks in her mouth.

"Stan? Are you sure?" Ramona tapped Megan's shoulder with the wand she used as part of her witch costume. "Perhaps you should check again."

"I'm. Positive." Megan could barely breathe through her anger. She imagined breaking Ramona's wand into bits.

Ramona waved the wand dismissively. "What do you want me to do about it?"

Megan's eyes stretched wide. "You hired Stan Crockett—*the town drunk*—to read Halloween-themed children's books to our customers' kids."

It was the third Saturday of October, the day Books & Bakery hosted its annual Halloween costume party and children's story time. Megan heard the virtual flushing of her afternoon event as it plunged down the figurative toilet. Ramona either couldn't hear it or didn't care.

"Nice costume party, Megan." Quincy's comment was barely audible above the angry buzzing in Megan's ears and the laughter of children enjoying the Halloween games arranged around the store.

Megan turned to find Quincy standing in a

semicircle with Darius and Ean. The Terrible Trio reunited and standing in her grandparents' bookstore. She'd stepped back in time. However, each man had donned the bare minimum to be considered in costume. Quincy had pulled on a football jersey and a pair of faded blue jeans. Darius wore a gray stitch fedora. The name tag on his teal sweater read: MEMBER OF THE PRESS.

Megan stared at Ean's blue jeans, black jersey and the white bandanna tied around his head. "What are you supposed to be? A pirate?"

Ean adjusted the bandanna. "Not *what, who.* Deion Sanders."

Did he truly believe the bandanna alone pegged him as the Hall of Fame former football player? Megan feared her eyes would burst from her head. "Is this the best the three of you could do? Seriously?"

"What are you supposed to be? An Egyptian princess?" Ean's warm gaze slid over her.

Megan laid her damp palms on the skirt of her white lamé dress. "The goddess Isis."

She reached behind her to spread the gold theatrical cape or "wings." The heavy black eyeliner had been a pain to apply, even harder than wielding the hot comb to straighten the curl from her hair.

"I like it." The intensity in Ean's olive eyes made her stomach muscles quiver.

"Thanks." Megan nervously checked the gold band wrapped around the top of her head. She felt the others staring between her and Ean, and fought the urge to fidget.

Quincy turned to Ramona. "Where's your costume?"

Ramona's eyes narrowed. "I wish this were a real wand. I'd turn you into a toad. Oh! Too late."

"Ouch." Darius chuckled.

"Afternoon, everyone."

Megan turned at the newcomer's greeting. "Sheriff, is that your costume?" She clenched her teeth to keep from snarling.

Sheriff Alonzo Lopez glanced at his tan shirt, black tie and spruce green gabardine pants. His cocoa eyes looked confused. "It's my uniform. I'm on duty."

Megan cut Darius a look for his inappropriate laughter. "I'm sorry, Sheriff."

"No need to be." His calm acceptance soothed Megan. "I took the afternoon shift so my deputies with families could take their children to your party. It's a fun event for the kids."

"That was nice of you." Ramona gave him a sweet smile.

The older man's shrug was uncomfortable. "Doreen looks very nice in her movie star outfit."

"Doreen's spoken for." Darius' smile teased the older man.

"Can't a man appreciate a pretty woman without having any designs on her." Alonzo turned to Ean. "No disrespect intended."

"None taken." Ean's tense tone belied his words.

Alonzo nodded. "Well, I'd better get back to work."

"Thanks for stopping by, Sheriff." Megan laid her hand on his shoulder. "It's always good to see you."

Alonzo nodded before strolling away.

Ean caught Megan's attention. "Dracula was singing inappropriate bar songs to your customers."

Megan threw up her hands. "Oh, for Pete's sake."

Ean caught her arm as she started past him. "My mother brought him into the kitchen. She's giving him coffee."

The warmth of his touch through the sleeve of her costume made her shiver. Megan exhaled before addressing Ramona. "What were you thinking to hire Stan Crockett to read to a bunch of kids in our store?"

Quincy gaped at Ramona. "*You* hired him?"

Ramona's ebony eyes were innocent. "He needed money."

"To buy alcohol." Megan wanted to throw back her head and scream. Why wouldn't Ramona understand?

"It'll be OK, Megan." Ean released his hold on Megan's arm.

She bit her lip to keep from protesting his withdrawal.

"Ean's right, Meggie."

"Don't call me that." Her cousin added insult to injury with that obnoxious nickname.

Ramona continued, unfazed. "Doreen's giving him coffee. He'll sober right up."

"Have you seen him?" Megan's throat ached under the strain of keeping her voice level.

Darius snorted. "There isn't enough coffee in the store to sober up old Stan."

Ramona frowned. "He promised me he wouldn't drink before the reading."

"He lied." Quincy stated the obvious.

Ramona's dark eyes snapped at him. "He said he needed work to rebuild his self-esteem and get off the alcohol."

Megan took a deep breath. She counted to ten, then exhaled. "How are you going to fix this, Ramona?"

"Me?" Ramona pressed her index finger against her chest. "Why do *I* have to fix it?"

"Because . . ." Megan pressed her lips together, hating herself for not being able to stand up to her older cousin.

Quincy crossed his arms. "You hired him. You should be the one to fire him, Mona."

"Don't call me that." Ramona gave the group a stubborn look. "Let's wait and see. Once Stan's sober, he'll read to the children. It'll boost his self-esteem, and your party'll be a howling success, just as it always is."

Megan's skull started to ache. She was sympathetic to Stan. She really was. But Ramona had taken empathy to the edge of reason.

"The parents who brought their children here are on a schedule. So is the store." Megan checked her red Timex. "The reading is supposed to start in seven minutes."

"You and your schedules." Ramona rolled her

eyes. "What'll happen if story time starts late? Will the kids turn into pumpkins?"

Darius bent over, laughing.

Megan thought her head would explode. "How long will it take for Stan to get sober?"

Quincy scratched his chin. "I don't think I've ever seen him sober."

Darius shrugged. "There was that one time we saw him walking into the bar off Vine Street."

"Oh, yeah." Quincy nodded.

Megan closed her eyes briefly. "Fine. I'll take care of it."

Just as she'd dealt with other messes Ramona had made of her plans. She turned to stomp away, but a firm grasp held her in place.

Her cousin's sigh was suffering yet irritated. "I'll handle Stan." Ramona released her. She adjusted her pointed hat and smoothed her dress.

It really was a great costume. She'd gotten into the spirit of the event, as she always did. The long-sleeved black dress had a neckline that was just short of daring, a figure-hugging bodice and a pencil-thin, ankle-length skirt. The pointed black hat balanced at a cocky angle on her head. Spiders danced at the end of her dangling silver earrings. Skeleton-shaped charms hung from her necklace.

Megan wasn't the only one who watched her cousin. Quincy's mesmerized gaze followed Ramona's every move.

Megan allowed herself to hope. "You'll take Stan home?"

"Later." Ramona shook her head. "Keep him in

the kitchen, drinking coffee. I'll take him home after I read to the kids."

"*You'll* read to them?" Quincy's voice rose with surprise.

Ramona's dark gaze should have turned the university professor to ashes. "Contrary to your opinion, I can read."

Megan's headache disappeared. Her facial muscles relaxed into a smile. "Thanks, Ramona. Let's get started."

Before Ramona could have second thoughts, Megan grabbed her cousin's arm and dragged her to the front of the store. She delivered Ramona to the Halloween reading area, which she, Doreen and their student helpers had created.

After announcing story time, Megan gingerly made her way through the sea of children sprawled on the floor around Ramona. They listened, enraptured, as she started the first Halloween story. Megan had seated her cousin in an ornate red velvet throne that doubled as Santa's chair during the Christmas season. Today, two large human skulls were staked to the seat's high back, and two smaller ones were driven onto the chair's arms—all fake, of course.

"What a relief." Megan sighed as she joined Ean, Darius and Quincy at the perimeter of the entertainment.

"I told you it would work out." Ean tossed her a smile.

"I wasn't sure." Megan felt his eyes on her. His

attention made her self-conscious. She also felt powerful, sexy and aroused.

The children jumped after Ramona's dramatic pause in the story. It was a talent her cousin had perfected by tormenting a much younger Megan. Ramona adopted different voices for each character in the creepy tale.

"The witch saved Halloween." Quincy's voice was thoughtful.

"Now there's a headline." Darius unwrapped the piece of chocolate he'd taken from a candy bowl. The crystal bowl was in the shape of a fake, decaying hand. Megan's staff had placed several of them around the store.

Ean came to Ramona's defense. "Sometimes Ramona can surprise you with a generous act. She's not as aloof as she sometimes seems."

Ean spoke with affection. The bubble of feminine power in which Megan had been basking popped. She fought the urge to withdraw into herself.

How could she have entertained even for one second the smallest kernel of hope that Ean Fever could ever give her a second look—especially with Ramona around?

CHAPTER 8

"What movie do you want to see tonight?" Ean drained his glass of water Thursday morning. He'd been home for almost a month. He rose from his seat at the kitchen table to add the glass to the dishwasher.

Sharing breakfast with his mother was like old times. The difference was his father should have been at the table, too. He should be the one getting ready for work.

Ean struggled free from the weight of grief. After his mother left for work, he'd go for his morning jog. Would he see Megan in the park again? He couldn't stop thinking of their near kiss three weeks ago—and how badly he wished she hadn't run from him.

"I thought I'd make us dinner tonight." His mother's response interrupted his thoughts.

"You wouldn't rather go out? My treat." Ean returned to the table to collect his mother's empty breakfast dishes.

"I'd assumed as much." Doreen's smile was unsteady. "But I'd rather stay in for dinner. Just the two of us. And a friend."

"Who?" Ean stacked her dishes in the dishwasher, then closed its door before facing his mother.

Doreen hesitated. "Leo. I want the two of you to get reacquainted."

Ean leaned against the kitchen counter for support. "You mean you want me to accept him as your boyfriend."

Doreen inclined her head. "At my age, the term 'boyfriend' sounds odd, but you're essentially right."

It did sound odd to say his mother had a boyfriend, but Ean would embrace that word, if only to avoid the images associated with alternative terms. "I'm not going to stand in the way of your dating Coach George, but there's no reason for *me* to spend time with him."

"Yes, there is. I'm not going to divide my life into two halves just because you're uncomfortable with my relationship with Leo."

Ean recognized the determination in Doreen's warm brown eyes. She'd been giving him that look all of his life—when he protested eating his vegetables, doing his homework or cleaning his room. Now she was giving him that steely regard because he didn't want to spend time with her boyfriend. How their relationship had changed.

He crossed his arms and tried to stand his ground. "I'm not asking you to. If you want to have dinner with him tonight, I'll make other plans."

Doreen narrowed her eyes. "What if I want to have dinner with both of you?"

"We're not a family, Mom." Ean regretted the flash of pain that crossed his mother's round face at his quietly spoken words.

"I'm not trying to replace your father. I just want . . . a friend." She rubbed a hand over her face. "And I want you to accept that."

Ean let his arms drop. "How can I do that?" His throat burned at the sadness in his mother's eyes, but he wasn't ready to accept her new relationship.

"Have dinner with us tonight." Doreen spun on the heels of her white-pink-and-blue cross-training gym shoes. She strode from the kitchen.

His mother sounded impatient. What did she have to be upset about? He was the one stuck in some bizzaro version of his life. He'd thought his mother was a stay-at-home widow. Instead, she had a new man and a full-time job.

Even her appearance had changed. She'd cut her hair. Her wardrobe seemed filled with brighter colors and more modern styles. He hardly recognized her. Was Coach George the cause of all of these changes? Resentment knotted his stomach muscles.

Ean followed her. "I was worried about your being alone. With Dad gone, I thought you'd be at loose ends."

Doreen looked as confused as Ean felt. "I wasn't." She collected her purple shoulder bag from the dining room's corner table, then continued toward the coat closet in the front hallway.

"I came home to keep you company."

She gave him a startled look over her shoulder. "I never asked you to."

Ean crossed his arms over his chest. "I'm your son. You don't have to ask me."

"But it's been almost a year." She pulled her cream-colored wool coat from the closet. "Ean, you needed to come home for you, not for me. And that's fine. This is your home."

Really? It doesn't feel that way anymore. "I don't like it that you're working." He sighed. "Or dating."

Doreen shrugged into her coat. "I can tell. But I've earned the right to make my own decisions."

"Am I supposed to stand aside even if I think you're making a mistake, several of them?"

Doreen settled the strap of her bag on her shoulder. "Over the years, I haven't agreed with all of your choices, either. I didn't think you should have accepted the job with the law firm in New York, but I knew it was what you wanted."

"But I—"

"And it may surprise you to know that Ramona isn't my first choice for you or my second. Or my tenth. But I respected your right to make your own decision. Are you going to deny me the same respect?"

Ean dragged a hand over his hair. "My situation was different. Your grief over losing Dad could be affecting your decision making."

There was concern in Doreen's eyes as she searched Ean's features. "Has your grief affected your decision making?"

"No."

"Neither has mine."

"But you were his wife."

Doreen sighed. Her gaze dropped to the tiled floor. "And we were together for more than forty years. Still, I considered my options before I made my decisions. These aren't whims. They're choices. Mine."

Ean had run out of arguments. He was at a loss. "All right, Mom. I'll respect that."

Doreen stepped forward, cupped the right side of Ean's face with one hand and kissed his left cheek. "You don't have a choice. Have a nice day." With those words, she left for work.

Ean stared at the closed front door. This homecoming wasn't going at all the way he'd imagined. Had he made a mistake coming back to Trinity Falls?

Megan looked up from her grandparents' headstones Thursday afternoon. In the distance, a couple of rows away, she saw a solitary mourner standing with his head bowed before a grave site. Ean.

He was so still. Megan hesitated. She didn't want to intrude on his private time, but she sensed his thoughts were troubled. She lowered her gaze to her grandparents' headstones again and silently said good-bye.

She wanted to leave. She actually started to leave. But her steps drew her closer to Ean. "Would you rather be alone?"

He looked up, startled. "I didn't hear you."

Megan nodded over her shoulder toward the headstones that were imprinted on her heart. "Today would have been my grandparents' fiftieth wedding anniversary."

Ean returned her smile. "I'm sure they're celebrating together."

The warmth of his smile and the sincerity of his words stole her breath. Megan swallowed to dislodge the lump in her throat.

"I think so, too." She was uncomfortable with the emotion he may have heard in her voice. "Is today a special occasion for your father?"

She read again his father's headstone: *Paul Fever, 1948 to 2013, Loving Husband and Father.*

His expression grew somber. "I'm just paying my respects."

It was more than that. Megan heard it in his taut tone. He sounded lost. She fisted her hands deeper into her navy blue winter coat to keep from touching him. That was Ramona's prerogative.

"Your father was well liked and well respected in the community."

Ean returned his attention to his father's headstone. "Everything seems different with him gone."

"Everything changed for me when my grandparents died, too."

"I didn't expect my mother to change as well. I barely recognize her anymore." He caught her gaze. "You hired her to run the bakery in your bookstore."

Megan heard the accusation in his words. "Your parents had been high school sweethearts. Your father's death left your mother devastated."

"You don't have to tell me how my mother felt. I knew she was grieving." Ean's voice was rough. Was it grief, guilt, shame—all of the above?

"I'm certain Doreen put on a brave face for you. She's your mother. She wouldn't want you to worry about her. But those of us who saw her every day could tell she was hurting. She needed a distraction. I thought Books and Bakery could help."

Ean rubbed his eyes. "Why didn't someone call me? I would have come home."

"For how long? Your work schedule only allowed you a few days off at a time. Your mother needed more than that."

Ean inhaled a sharp breath. Megan's words hit him like a sucker punch. "I'm home now."

"And Doreen is very happy about that."

Ean grunted. "Really? I think I may be cramping her style. I'm sure you know she's dating."

"Coach George. You like him."

"As my coach, not as my mother's boyfriend."

"It's a good thing your mother doesn't need your approval."

Ean flashed back to the words his mother had spoken that morning.

"It may surprise you to know that Ramona wasn't my first choice for you or my second. Or my tenth. But I

respected your right to make your own decision. Are you going to deny me the same respect?"

He scowled. Megan had given his mother a job. "Did you encourage her to start dating?"

"Your mother and Coach George?" Her full lips twitched as though she battled a smile. Unnecessary amusement danced in her chocolate eyes.

Ean didn't share her humor. "How well does she even know him?"

"They've known each other since you were in high school."

He snorted. "Time doesn't determine how well you know a person."

She had the nerve to laugh. "Then it's a good thing you've come home, since you're such a stellar judge of character."

Ean didn't have a response. He wondered about the calm he found in Megan's company. Every time he tried to strike out, she found the words to defuse his pain and confusion. How was she able to do that?

He studied his father's headstone. "Did my mother tell you we argued this morning?"

"No. You just did." Her words were rich with amusement.

"She wants the three of us to have dinner together tonight." Ean shook his head. "Everything's changed. It's not the same here anymore."

"The people may have changed, but the town hasn't. Neighbors still keep an eye on each other's kids and property. The town still goes to church Sunday mornings and takes long walks Sunday afternoons. And everybody thinks they know what's best for everyone else." Megan cocked her head. "Maybe that's what's upsetting you. Doreen's dating without discussing it with you first."

"That's not true." Or was it?

"Your mother's happy, Ean. Isn't that all that matters?"

"Of course."

She eyed him shrewdly. "What would it take to make you happy?"

He wished he knew. Then he had an epiphany. "Come to dinner tonight. That would make me happy."

She stepped back. Confusion merged with the concern in her eyes. "You can't invite a guest to your mother's house for dinner without asking her first."

Ean tried a persuasive smile. "If she says yes, will you come? She likes you."

"And you'd like a shield for the evening." Megan's voice was as dry as the desert. "I'm sure there's something else I have to do tonight."

Ean cupped a hand over her left shoulder. When her slender muscles tensed, he let his hand drop. "Please, Megan. It's going to be awkward—for my mother and me. You being there will keep the tension at bay."

Megan's soft laughter challenged him. "So it's not a shield you're after. It's a referee. That sounds like fun." She turned to walk away.

Panic chilled him. Ean said good-bye to his father before falling into step beside her. He shoved his hands into the front pockets of his gray winter coat to keep from touching her again. "I only found out a week ago about them dating."

"You and Coach are both important to her. That's why she wants you to reestablish a relationship."

"I know, but I'm not ready for this." Ean scrubbed both palms over his face. "Please come to dinner. I'm not asking for myself. I'm asking for my mother."

Megan stopped in her tracks. Ean squared his shoulders and waited for her answer. A slight breeze ruffled the dark brown waves of her hair. His gaze followed the delicate line of her profile to her figure, which was masked in a thick navy coat. The memory of her dressed for Halloween as the goddess Isis superimposed itself in his mind. The soft material of her gown had hinted at her slender curves, instead of masking them.

Megan turned and stabbed a finger into his chest. "You'd better be on your best behavior."

A relieved grin split his face. "I promise."

Megan sighed again. "All right, then I'll come."

"Great. It's a date."

There was something incredibly sexy about her long, slow blink. "This isn't what you expected when you decided to come home, is it?"

Ean let his gaze slide toward a group of trees behind Megan's right shoulder. "I thought things would be the way I'd remembered them."

He and Ramona would want the same things. His mother would give him her undivided attention. Quincy wouldn't hate his guts.

"It's been fourteen years since you've lived in Trinity Falls. You can't expect people to remain the same. It's human nature to change."

Where did that leave him? "I guess you really can't go home again."

"That depends. What's your definition of 'home'?"

"What do you mean?"

"'Home' is what you make of it. You left Trinity Falls to make your home in New York. Now you're back. If you don't know what you want in a home, you'll never find one."

Ean watched Megan walk away. She was right. If he didn't know what he wanted, he'd never find it. But what did he want?

CHAPTER 9

Ean sat at the dining-room table Thursday night, staring hard at his mother's boyfriend. Most people would find it hard not to like Leonard George. Ean wasn't most people. As a high school quarterback, he'd thought his coach had been great, second only to his father. Now that the man was dating his mother, he didn't like him at all. He drained his glass of iced tea, wishing the beverage was a cold beer and the evening was over.

"Why don't we relax in the living room while we enjoy our desserts?" Doreen's smile seemed forced.

Tension returned to Ean's neck and shoulders. He'd thought the evening would end after dinner. He'd been wrong. Ean carried the serving tray of Trinity Falls Fudge Walnut Brownie, which his mother had made for dessert. He dutifully followed his mother, Leonard and Megan into the living room. A surreptitious glance at his watch showed the time to be seven-thirty. How much longer would this event last?

Doreen and Leonard sat, thigh to thigh, on the dark pink love seat to his left. He avoided looking at their linked hands. Megan had chosen the overstuffed armchair and ottoman opposite the matching sofa, on which he'd settled.

"This brownie is fabulous, Doreen." Megan speared another forkful of the dessert.

Leonard's laughter forewarned another joke. "It must have been great growing up with a mother who baked like this. But it's a good thing you played football, otherwise you would've gotten fat."

Ean lifted his gaze to find Megan's encouraging smile. He wouldn't have made it through the evening without her. "You're right."

Leonard gestured toward him with his fork. "You look like you kept up your training. Did you work out in New York?"

His former coach had been asking let's-get-reacquainted questions all evening. How had Ean enjoyed Georgetown University? What was his favorite part of attending law school at New York University? Ean would have been fine with those questions—if he wanted to get reacquainted with his coach. He didn't.

"I still run and lift weights." Ean felt Megan's eyes on him. Was she remembering their jog through Freedom Park? He'd never forget it.

Doreen glowed with pride. "He attended Georgetown on an academic scholarship."

"I remember." Leonard smiled a little too long at Doreen.

"Of course you do." Doreen touched Leonard's arm with too much familiarity.

Leonard finally seemed to remember he and Doreen weren't alone. "Ean, maybe you could come to a couple of Heritage High games."

The silence in the living room was absolute. Everyone seemed to be holding his or her breath, waiting for Ean's reaction. Tension drilled down his neck. Dinner with Leonard in the company of his mother and Megan was bad enough. Attending the coach's football games would imply he approved of Leonard's relationship with his mother. He didn't.

"Maybe." Ean stretched forward, setting his empty glass on the serving tray. Hopefully, Leonard would forget his invitation.

But the idea had been planted and Leonard was persistent. "The kids would get a kick out of it. You're a legend at the school. You conquered Trinity Falls. Then you conquered New York."

What was his former coach talking about? "I didn't conquer anything."

"Yes, you did." Leonard insisted. "It'll be fun for you and the kids. And it'll give us a chance to get reacquainted."

Ean's gaze dropped to Leonard's fingers intertwined with his mother's. The coach appeared to make Doreen happy. He wouldn't get in the way of that. But their relationship didn't mean he and Leonard had to be friends.

He spoke with finality. "Coach, I'm not making any plans right now."

"Call me Leo." Leonard's smile wavered. "I understand. You just got back to Trinity Falls. You're settling in, trying to get back into the community." He stood as he checked his watch. "It's late." Leonard helped Doreen to her feet.

She frowned at Ean before cupping the side of Leonard's face. "Thank you for coming, Leo."

Leonard's good humor was restored. "It was fun, Dorie."

Dorie?

Ean stood from the sofa, fearful that his dinner might come back up. He gathered the dessert plates and empty glasses onto the serving tray, and turned to carry the load back to the kitchen.

"I should be going, too." Megan's voice carried from across the room.

Ean looked at her over his shoulder. "Wait for me. I'll walk you home."

"It's only three blocks, Ean. I'll be fine." Megan crossed to kiss Doreen's cheek and give Leonard a hug.

Doreen took the tray from Ean and gave it to Leonard. "Leo and I will handle the cleanup. I'd feel better if you took Megan home."

"Sure." The evening had taken a turn for the better. Was it getting out of kitchen duty or the prospect of being alone with Megan, even if it was only for three blocks?

Megan accepted her purse and navy coat from

his mother. "Thanks again for dinner and dessert, Doreen. They were both delicious."

Ean stepped forward to help Megan with her coat.

"Thank you." She gave him a long, slow blink and the world slowed down.

Ean came out of his trance. "You're welcome."

In silence, he followed Megan through the front door and down the steps. The early-November night was cool with a brisk, late-fall breeze. A deep breath brought the scent of moist earth and the advent of winter. Sidewalks were lit only by their neighbors' porch lights. Halloween decorations were still on display a week later. They hung next to the sesquicentennial banners.

It was so quiet here. Ean enjoyed the silence and the comfortable presence of the woman walking beside him. No honking horns, emergency sirens, blaring television programs or driving rock music. He could hear himself think.

"Do you suppose your mother's making out with Coach Leo, now that we've left?"

Megan's question drew a mental picture Ean could do without. "I'd rather not think about it."

Her soft laughter blended into the evening. "I was just joking."

"That's not funny." Ean resisted the urge—just barely—to wrap his arm around her waist and draw her closer to him. "Thank you again for coming. Your presence really did make a difference."

"You're welcome. You did well."

He basked in her praise. "Until the end of the evening."

Megan's throaty chuckle strummed across Ean's abdominal muscles. "Leo can be a little pushy."

"That's a nice way of wording it."

"Don't worry." Megan patted Ean's arm. "Well, at least not until he shows up on your doorstep next football Friday night."

Ean felt her warmth even through his coat sleeve. He ached with the desire to press her hand to his arm.

"Let's change the subject." Ean put his hand on Megan's shoulder. He dropped it when he felt her tension through his fingertips. "I'm sorry. I forgot that you don't like to be touched."

"It depends on who's doing the touching." Her voice was wry. "How's Ramona?"

Ean smiled at her pointed question. "She's your cousin. You tell me." He looked both ways before they crossed the street.

Megan forged ahead, picking up the pace. "Don't play games, Ean. Have you two gotten back together?"

"I've only been home a couple of weeks."

"So?"

"*She* left *me* six years ago, remember?"

"Still, you probably should have invited *her* to dinner at your mother's house tonight instead of me."

Ean again recalled his mother's comment: *"It*

may surprise you to know that Ramona isn't my first choice for you or my second. Or my tenth."

"I don't think so." Ean shook off the memory. "By the way, I enjoyed watching you stand up to Ramona."

Megan's gaze flew back to his. "When did I do that?"

Ean's brows knitted in confusion. "During your store's Halloween costume party. You made her take responsibility for hiring Stan. Not one of her better ideas."

Megan gave him her slow blink. "Thank you."

"You're welcome." Why did she seem surprised by what he'd said?

She was silent, seemingly lost in her thoughts until they arrived at her home. What was on her mind?

"Thank you for walking home with me." Megan led them up the winding walkway to her front steps. She'd left her porch light on.

"It was my pleasure." And he meant it. He'd enjoyed the sound of her laughter, her gentle voice and serene silences.

Megan lifted her winged brows above her chocolate eyes. "You may not be as pleased if Ramona finds out you escorted me home."

"She'd rather I let you walk by yourself at night?" He stood only an arm's length from her. It wasn't close enough.

Megan chuckled as though he'd said the silliest

thing she'd ever heard. "You must have forgotten how possessive Ramona can be."

"She broke up with me."

"But she's not done with you."

Ean held her gaze. "What if I was done with her, Megan?"

"What do you mean?"

He knew of one way to clear up her confusion. He stepped forward and lowered his head to hers. Megan's eyes widened and her mouth parted in surprise. Ean touched the tip of his tongue to her top, then bottom lip. They were soft and sweet. He laid his mouth on hers and swept his tongue inside. Megan trembled against him. Ean wrapped his arms around her to comfort and reassure. The feel of her body in his embrace—even through the layers of clothing—drew a primitive response from him. He was man. She was woman. His body shook in reaction.

Megan pushed away from him. She mounted the bottom step before facing him. The boost in height put them at eye level. "That was a mistake."

Not to him. "Why?"

Megan started to respond, then seemed to change her mind. She turned and climbed the steps. "Good night, Ean."

He caught her wrist to stop her. Her pulse fluttered beneath his thumb. "Tell me why you think my kissing you was a mistake."

"You think Ramona stayed in Trinity Falls because she broke up with you?" Megan whispered the question.

"She did."

"You're wrong. She'd always intended to go back to you."

When Megan turned to leave this time, Ean let his hand fall free. Not because he wanted to, but because she'd caught him by surprise.

He remained on her walkway until Megan entered her house. When he heard her lock her door, he began the return trip to his home.

Ramona had intended to restart their relationship? Interesting. Maybe things would have been different six years ago. But he didn't have feelings for Ramona any longer. What would it take to convince her of that? How could he convince Megan?

CHAPTER 10

Ean wished he'd never agreed to this Saturday evening dinner with Ramona. It had started badly and was skiing downhill at Olympic speeds. She'd wanted to go into the city to dine at a fancy chain restaurant, but Ean had disagreed. He hadn't seen the point in driving for more than an hour for a meal. Besides, he wanted to try the local restaurant, Trinity Falls Cuisine. It had been under construction when he'd been home for his father's funeral in February. Ramona's terse responses as they sat in the comfortable booth conveyed her displeasure with his decision.

Ean studied the menu. "What do you recommend?"

"I wouldn't know." Her response was pitch-perfect disdain.

He raised his gaze to Ramona. Was she warm enough in that low-cut, tight black minidress? Her straight black hair hung past her shoulders, framing her impressive breasts.

Ean frowned. She hadn't even glanced at the menu. "Have you eaten here before?"

"Of course not."

Why wouldn't she have eaten at this restaurant? It was new and in the heart of their community.

"New businesses mean more employment opportunities. As mayor, don't you think you should try them at least once?"

"No."

It was going to be a long night.

Ean took in the restaurant's beige-and-gray stone walls and wood trim. The lighting was low, giving the place a romantic ambience. He still noticed the other diners looking hastily away. So it hadn't been his imagination. People were staring at them. The town's prodigal son had returned home and was out for the evening with his high-school-sweetheart-turned-town-leader. He should have anticipated the stares.

A movement toward the front of the restaurant caught his attention. Ean froze. The hostess was leading Quincy and Megan to a nearby booth.

Impulse lifted him from his seat and prodded him to call across the aisle. "Quincy."

"What are you doing?" Ramona came to life, hissing like an angry tigress. She glanced over her shoulder, then faced forward, squeezing her eyes shut.

Quincy turned toward Ean's voice. His expression stiffened when his gaze dropped to Ramona. Megan looked around, too. She seemed surprised—and dismayed?—to see him.

Ean waved them over. "Join us." *Please.*

For the second night this week, he hoped the company of friends would defuse an uncomfortable dinner.

"I don't want them here." Ramona roasted him with her glare.

Quincy and Megan consulted with each other. Megan shook her head twice in response to whatever Quincy said. Finally, the young hostess led the couple to Ean and Ramona's booth.

Quincy must have met Megan right after the bookstore closed. What were they doing here together? They couldn't be on a date. The idea threatened his appetite.

Megan carried her navy coat over her left arm. She wore a dark gray sweater dress. The color wasn't appealing, but the material traced her slim curves and ended just below her knees. Her dark, wavy hair floated around her shoulders.

Ean waited until the hostess left before speaking. "What a coincidence, running into you tonight."

"Not really."

He ignored Ramona's sarcasm and moved over to give Quincy more room.

Megan sat beside her cousin. "I thought you said you'd never eat here."

Ramona's scowl darkened. "This wasn't my idea."

Quincy opened the menu and studied its contents. "Refusing to eat at a perfectly good restaurant just because it's in your backyard is nonsensical."

Ean's eyes widened. He didn't think anyone had ever spoken so dismissively to Ramona before. A ghost of a smile softened Megan's lips. Ramona's scowl deepened.

Ean addressed his friend. "I take it you've eaten here before." He meant to divide his attention equally between Megan and Quincy, but his gaze lingered on Megan.

"Several times." Quincy sounded preoccupied.

Then why are you studying the menu as though you've never seen it before? And have you always come together? Are the two of you dating? Ean wouldn't ask those questions—even though he was frantic for the answers.

"What would you recommend?" Ean kept his gaze on Megan's bent head.

The differences between Megan and Ramona were even more pronounced as they shared the booth's bench seating. Both women were lovely, but in different ways.

Everything about Megan was understated in comparison to her cousin. She was quietly elegant, with conservative clothes, lack of makeup and minimal jewelry. In contrast, Ramona's expertly applied makeup and thick gold jewelry gave her an exotic appearance.

Megan looked up and her gaze locked with Ean's. She hesitated before answering. "I like their chicken Parmesan. What about you, Quincy?"

His friend peeled his attention from the menu. "I like the New York strip steak and steamed vegetables."

Ramona's grunt was far from ladylike. "If you want a New York steak, you should go to New York."

Quincy met Ramona's gaze without expression. "It's typical of you to criticize something you know nothing about."

Ean stared at Quincy. What was the cause of his hostility?

Ramona leaned into the table and hissed, "I know what a New York steak tastes like." She turned on Ean. "Tell them."

"Ramona." Megan's low voice was a request.

Ean ignored Ramona's command. "Both recommendations sound good. I'll go with the steak, though. I've already had chicken this week."

Ean gave Megan a quick glance. Did she remember their dinner—and the kiss they shared? She looked away. The blush rising beneath her honey brown skin said she did.

Their server arrived to take their drink orders. She appeared young enough to be carded, but must have been a student at Trinity Falls University. Everyone ordered iced tea, except Ramona, who wanted white wine.

Ramona leaned back into her seat. She looked from Quincy, who was diagonally across the table from her, to Megan on her left. "Are you two dating?" The question was tinged with sarcasm.

Ean stilled. He needed to hear the answer. But wouldn't Quincy have said something to him? Wouldn't Megan have mentioned it Thursday night?

"Are you and Ean dating?" Quincy's response didn't relieve Ean's worry.

But why was Ean concerned over whether one of

his best friends was dating his ex-girlfriend's cousin? He wasn't concerned. He was jealous.

Ramona held Ean's gaze. A secretive smile curved her lips as she answered Quincy's question. "I don't know whether or not we're dating again. It depends on whether I can convince Ean to return to New York with me."

Ean wasn't playing this game. "That's not going to happen, Ramona."

Quincy shrugged. His response was swift and satisfied. "It sounds like you have your answer. You're not dating."

Ean frowned at his friend. In high school, Quincy had barely spoken two words to Ramona. That had been bad enough. But now his friend wouldn't stop attacking her. Why?

"Are you really staying in Trinity Falls?" Megan's question redirected the tension.

Ean met her gaze. "I wouldn't have come back if I didn't intend to stay."

He wasn't dating Ramona and he was staying in Trinity Falls. What did Megan think about these things?

Their server delivered their drinks, then offered to take their orders. Ean and Quincy ordered the steak. Megan requested the chicken Parmesan. Apparently, she wasn't opposed to eating the same thing several nights a week.

Then the young woman asked for Ramona's order.

Ramona glared at the menu. "Did you get this salmon fresh?"

"Yes, ma'am." The young woman stood with her pen poised above her notepad.

"How fresh?" Ramona's questions snapped out with a speed and ferocity that would catapult a criminal prosecutor to fame.

"I—I'm certain it's fresh, ma'am." The server seemed taken aback by the cross-examination.

Ean studied Ramona, her tense posture, her strident voice, her lack of eye contact with the server. Had she been this arrogant in high school?

"You don't sound certain." Ramona's eyes remained glued to the menu.

Megan turned to her cousin. "Ramona."

"What?" Ramona snapped the word. "Why are you always whispering my name? That's so annoying."

"Stop it. You're making a scene." Megan spoke through clenched teeth.

Ramona rolled her eyes, then addressed their server. "Are you certain the salmon is fresh—"

Ean interrupted the exchange. "Ramona, she answered your question."

The server's pen began to shake above the notepad. "We get all of our seafood fresh, ma'am."

"Stop calling me 'ma'am.'"

The young woman's eyes grew large. "Yes, m . . . yes."

Quincy's sigh was long and loud. "Mona, do you want the fish or not? If you want it, for the love of God, order it or I'll order something for you."

Ean sat back in his chair. No one had ever spoken to Ramona that way in her life. Of that, he was certain. Even Megan did a slow blink at Quincy's outburst. He prepared himself for the fireworks.

Ramona erupted like Vesuvius. "My name isn't 'Mona.' Don't—"

"People are starving in Third World countries while—"

"—call me that!"

"—you cross-examine our server."

"And you wouldn't dare order my meal!"

Quincy narrowed his gaze. "Test me."

Ean glanced at the nearby tables. People didn't seem to realize he was there any longer. All eyes were on Ramona and Quincy. Considering the circumstances, that wasn't an improvement. Apparently, Megan felt the same. Her cheeks were bright red and she stared at her glass of iced tea as though it could transport her away.

Ramona shoved her menu toward the server in a dismissive gesture, but saved her glare for Quincy. "Get me the salmon. And it had better be fresh."

"Yes, m . . . yes." The young woman took Ramona's menu, then fled the scene.

Ean was certain the outburst would be all over Trinity Falls before he, Quincy, Megan and Ramona left the restaurant.

Megan sat up in her seat and rubbed a hand over her hair. "Now that we have *everyone's* attention, perhaps we can try to act as though we've eaten in formal restaurants before."

Ramona expelled an affronted gasp. "This wasn't *my* fault."

"Nothing ever is." Quincy turned to Ean before Ramona could respond. "So you're here to stay. And what are you going to do?"

Ean took a drink of his iced tea. "Find a job."

He didn't know what bizarre phenomenon had changed his best friend into his sworn enemy. But he was in danger of losing his appetite if Quincy and Ramona continued to act out their hostility.

"What do you want to do?"

In response to Megan's question, Ean shrugged. "For now, I just want a job. There are several companies nearby. I'll apply for work in their legal departments."

Ramona sipped her wine. "You had a job in New York."

"New York wasn't home." Ean set his glass on the table.

Ramona laughed. "Do you really think this town can keep your interest this time?"

Ean shifted his attention to Megan and held her gaze. "Yes, it can."

Megan dropped her gaze.

There, Ean thought, *Ramona and I are done.* He glanced at Quincy. But what was his friend's role in Megan's life?

CHAPTER 11

Ean responded to the summons from his front doorbell, but first stopped to check the security window. What was Ramona doing on his front steps? He thought he'd made it clear that he wasn't interested in reconciling with her.

He pulled the door open and stepped aside.

"Oh." Ramona turned and stepped hastily past him into the foyer. She placed her right hand delicately in front of her nose. "Were you working in the yard?"

Ean glanced down at his sweat-soaked blue T-shirt. "No, I just ran ten miles."

Ramona shook her head. "Ean, it's Sunday morning. Don't you know all roads lead to church?"

"Not for me." Ean locked the front door.

Ramona took another step back. "You're not in New York anymore. People in Trinity Falls will talk if you don't go to church."

Ean led the way to the kitchen. "Since when do you care what people say?" He refilled his glass with ice water from the refrigerator. "Would you like some?"

"When were you planning to take a shower?" Ramona's voice came from the doorway.

"When were you planning to leave?" Ean gulped more water.

Ramona's expression darkened. She lowered her hand. "I came to talk about what you said at the restaurant last night."

"Which was what?"

"You don't remember?"

Ean drained the water, then put his empty glass in the dishwasher. "I said a lot of things."

"You said you weren't going back to New York."

"I've said that before." He turned from the dishwasher and settled his hips against the kitchen counter. "I've meant it every time."

"And I meant what I said, too." Ramona crossed her arms over her chest.

"Which was what?"

Ramona huffed. "That I will *break up* with you if you don't return to New York with me."

Ean gave her a dry smile. "You broke up with me six years ago when *you* left New York."

"And I'll break up with you again."

How would that work? "That's probably for the best."

Ramona worked her mouth several times before words came out. "What do you mean?"

"Ramona, I've changed. I'm not the same guy you dated in high school. We want different things now."

"But you want the *wrong* things."

"They're not wrong for me."

She marched across the kitchen and grabbed his forearms. "You've got to return to New York. With me, things will be different."

Ean pulled free of her hold. "Our relationship wouldn't work, Ramona. We're too different now."

She retreated as she studied his face. "I know my arguing with Quincy made you uncomfortable."

What was behind her sudden change of topic? Ean played along. "Why were you two at each other's throat all night?"

Ramona shrugged. "*He* was arguing. *I* was just defending myself."

Ean looked beyond Ramona's pouty expression to the temper in her dark eyes. "Since when does Quincy argue with you? In high school, he barely spoke with you."

Surprise wiped away Ramona's anger. "I can't believe you don't know."

"What?"

"You *really* don't know?" Ramona rolled her eyes. "Quincy's in love with me. He has been since high school."

"What?" Ean's head spun.

"That's probably why he was angry with me last night. He knows that now you're here, he doesn't stand a chance with me. There's no need for you to feel threatened."

Ean frowned. "I'm surprised, not threatened. Quincy's a good guy. You should give him a chance."

Ramona's eyes stretched wide. "You're *giving me* to *Quincy*?"

"No." Had she screeched this much in high school? No wonder his mother didn't want her as a daughter-in-law. "But you could do a lot worse than Quincy."

Ramona lifted her black purse higher on her shoulder. "Is this some sort of joke? Don't take too long to come to your senses, Ean. You could find that you've lost the best thing that ever happened to you."

Ramona stomped from the kitchen. Moments later the front door opened, then slammed shut.

Ean straightened away from the kitchen counter and strode to the foyer. He locked his mother's front door, then mounted the stairs to the shower. Quincy was one of his best friends; but since Ean had returned from New York, that friendship had been strained. Was Ramona the cause of that? Did Quincy really have a crush on her in high school? Was he in love with her now? If so, why hadn't he ever said anything?

There was only one way to get answers to those questions. He wasn't looking forward to the confrontation.

Hours later, Ean pressed the doorbell to Quincy's two-story townhome. It was like the signal to the second round of a prizefighter's match—the prize being a friendship he valued too much to let go. The first round in Quincy's office hadn't gone well.

He had higher hopes for this morning, especially with the new information.

Quincy greeted him with a scowl that ground his hopes to dust. "Why are you here?"

Not the welcome he'd hoped for. "Are you going to let me in?"

Quincy hesitated before stepping back.

Ean entered the living room. He'd been to Quincy's town house a few times during his brief visits home. The living room wasn't large, but it was comfortable. He crossed the beige Berber carpet and settled onto the thick brown sofa. The honey wood furnishings created a soothing environment, which was at odds for such an angry man.

Across the room, suspended from the wall, was a large, flat-screen, high-definition television. Beside it was a tall matching bookcase crammed with history and professional journals. On the coffee table in front of him lay recent copies of sports magazines.

Quincy propped his shoulder against the archway separating the living room from the rest of the ground floor. "What do you want?"

Ean sized up his witness, from his shaved head to his bare feet, before laying out the evidence in support of his case. "You and Ramona got into it at the restaurant last night."

"Are you here to ask for an apology for your girlfriend?" Quincy wiped all expression from his face.

The former running back used to do the same thing before lining up against their opponent's defense. Quincy didn't believe in giving anything away. So how had Ramona known Quincy had had a crush on her? Was it true or was Ramona speculating?

"She's not my girlfriend."

A flicker of surprise blinked across Quincy's rugged features before he masked it. "If you aren't here for an apology, what do you want?"

"Is it true you've been in love with Ramona since high school?"

Quincy's stunned silence was all the confirmation Ean needed. *How could I not have known?*

"Who told you that?" Quincy's voice was tight.

"She did."

Quincy squeezed his eyes shut. "And who told her?" Every word seemed forced from his lips.

Ean stood, pushing his hands into the front pockets of his gray jeans. "She figured it out."

Surprise, confusion and hurt crossed Quincy's face. "Great."

"Is that why you've been pissed since I came home?"

Quincy paced across the room, stopping in the archway between the living room and the dining area, with his back toward Ean. "I thought you were going to reconcile."

"Q, why didn't you make your move when Ramona returned six years ago?"

Quincy spun to face him. "Oh, so you think I'd have a clear shot, once the great Ean Fever removed himself from the running? Thanks for your permission."

"Man, *she* broke up with *me.*" Why did people keep forgetting that?

"And now you're back."

"But Ramona and I aren't together."

Quincy rubbed a palm across his broad, dark forehead. "Not because she isn't trying."

"What have you been doing to win her over?"

Quincy threw his hands up. "What could I do? I can't compete with you. Besides, you said she knows I'm attracted to her. Well, she never said anything to me. Obviously, she's not interested."

Ean rubbed the back of his neck. "So instead of even trying, you're just going to blame me for your failed love life and end our friendship."

Quincy looked away. "I'm done with living in your shadow."

Ean's eyes stretched wide. "What are you talking about?"

Quincy returned his glare to Ean. "You think you won those high school football championships by yourself? You weren't the only player on the field."

"*We* were the Terrible Trio. No one ever singled me out."

"You were the star quarterback. Everyone wanted to interview you. All the girls wanted to go out with you. Everyone's parents wanted their sons to be like you."

The accusations were so absurd they made Ean's head hurt. "That's not the way I remember it."

Quincy quirked a brow. "Then you're remembering it wrong. Ask Darius."

That scared him. Did Darius harbor the same

resentments toward him that Quincy had? It didn't seem that way.

Ean studied his friend, seeing him with fresh eyes. This wasn't the same guy who'd lined up against much bigger opponents and run through them. "You're a coward, Q."

Quincy's features tightened even as he shrugged. "If it makes you feel better to think so."

"It doesn't. You used to be fearless. You went after whatever you wanted, whether it was a football championship, a college scholarship or a doctorate. When did you lose your nerve?"

"I haven't."

Ean saw the heat of anger in his best friend's eyes. Good. "Or maybe Ramona isn't that important to you. I can understand. I don't know what I saw in her, either."

"Don't blame her for your failures." Quincy's response was swift and vicious.

"Don't blame me for yours." Ean turned to leave. If their friendship was over, he'd accept it. There wasn't anything more to say.

Quincy's voice stopped Ean in his tracks. "Don't insult her just because she dumped you."

Finally, someone believed that Ramona had dumped him—although why that should make him happy . . .

Ean looked over his shoulder. "If you want her, fight for her."

He had enough on his plate without adding Responsible for Quincy's Love Life to it.

Ean walked out of Quincy's townhome,

pulling the door closed behind him. That made two confrontations down—Ramona and Quincy. One to go. But before he dealt with the third confrontation, he needed more information, and he knew just the person to approach for it.

"Can I buy you lunch?" Ean stood on the top step outside of Megan's front door. He held a bag of fast food aloft. The scents emanating from the bag reminded him he'd eaten breakfast almost five hours before, and it hadn't been much of a meal.

Megan's skeptical gaze swung from Ean to the bag. She stepped aside to let him enter her home. "Why don't I make lunch for us?"

A rush of relief eased the tension in Ean's shoulders. He accepted Megan's welcome and crossed into her home. "I thought you liked fast food."

Megan's full pink lips struggled with a smile. Her gaze dipped to the bag. "I draw the line when there's more grease than meat on the sandwich."

Ean looked at the stained bag. "I guess you have a point."

"You guess?" Her chocolate eyes shone with laughter. "I think I'm getting to you just in time to save your arteries."

He followed her across the sunny foyer, past the causal living room, through the formal dining room and into the cozy kitchen. Megan's home woke half-forgotten memories for Ean: meeting Ramona's grandparents and nervously seeking their approval; picking up Ramona for a Saturday night movie.

Megan had changed the rooms a bit, with new furnishings and flooring, but they retained the same warmth and charm. It was a sharp contrast with Ramona's coolly modern condo.

Ean's gaze toured the kitchen's counters and cabinets, comparing his memories to the images around him. The color scheme had remained the same—blond wood cabinets, white-marble counters and pale green walls. But the appliances had been upgraded with a sleek, energy-efficient chrome refrigerator, oven and dishwasher. It was still a familiar, comfortable room—a harmonious blend of the past and present.

He wandered farther into the room and put the fast-food bag into the trash. "The cookie jar is gone."

A quick grin flashed across Megan's lush lips. "Blame that on your mother's baking. Store-bought cookies aren't appealing after tasting your mother's pastries."

The kitchen was crowded with the scents of vegetables and seasonings. Across the room, Megan stirred the fragrant contents of a pot on the stove. The long, neat lines of her slender figure seemed calm and comfortable. She conveyed a serenity that invited him to relax after his contentious meeting with Quincy. "What are you making?"

"Chicken stew."

His mouth watered. If the meal tasted as good as it smelled, he was in for a treat. "What can I do to help?"

Megan inclined her head toward the cupboards beside him. "You can set the table."

Grateful for something to do to keep his mind occupied with thoughts other than Megan's firm curves and long limbs, Ean collected the dishes and silverware for the table settings. He gave Megan two soup bowls before crossing to the refrigerator. He poured two glasses of iced tea and added them to the settings. He also set out a plate of crackers to accompany the stew.

Megan joined him at the table. She offered him one of the bowls of stew before setting hers on the table and taking her seat.

Ean sampled the dish. "Delicious."

Megan's smile mesmerized him. "Thank you."

They ate in companionable silence for a while before Megan spoke. "My grandparents liked you, so you know you're always welcome here. But why are you here?" Her voice was light and teasing, further putting him at ease.

Ean inhaled the warm, savory scents wafting up to him from his soup bowl. "When I first saw you and Quincy enter the restaurant last night, it never occurred to me that the two of you might be on a date."

"That's flattering."

Ean winced at her dry tone. "I'm sorry. That didn't come out right."

"Then try again."

Ean took a moment to collect his thoughts. "The evening with Ramona wasn't going well. I thought inviting you and Quincy to join us would distract Ramona."

"I don't think that worked out for you."

"Not as well as I'd hoped."

"I can't blame a man for trying." Megan seemed unaware of his discomfort. She continued eating her chicken stew.

Ean's eyes moved over Megan's delicate features, her wide chocolate eyes, high cheekbones, long, elegant nose and stubborn pointed chin. The realization that he could watch her all afternoon filled him with a strange restlessness.

"Have you and Quincy ever dated?"

Megan paused. "Why are you asking?"

He shrugged with more nonchalance than he felt. "Curiosity."

"Some would call it nosiness."

A reluctant grin tugged at his lips. "OK. Nosiness. But the two of you would make a good couple." The words didn't come easily. "You're both even tempered. You share similar interests, and you're both intellectually curious."

Megan tilted her head. "You make us sound like brother and sister."

"That's not what I meant." Was he doomed to insert his foot into his mouth each time he spoke with her? Little Megan McCloud had grown into an intimidating woman.

"Would you like to try again?" Megan's calm, steady gaze made Ean feel like an insecure teenager.

He took a deep breath and tried again. "I meant you'd make a good couple because you're similar."

"Yes, like brother and sister. Like you and Ramona." Megan sipped her iced tea.

Ean's brows knitted. "You think Ramona and I are like brother and sister?"

"Especially in high school." She continued eating her stew as though she hadn't just blown his mind.

"How?"

"You had similar interests. You both enjoyed the limelight. You were both popular. And you both defined success as shaking Trinity Falls's dust from your sneakers."

"We had similar goals. That doesn't mean we were like brother and sister—"

She interrupted him. "You were each other's mirror. You didn't challenge each other. You were more like group think."

Ean sat back in his chair. The remainder of his chicken stew cooled in front of him. "Does Quincy challenge you?"

Megan swallowed a spoonful of stew while her big brown eyes seemed to read his thoughts. "Why don't you ask me what's really on your mind?"

He was reluctant to accept her invitation. Instead, he searched for a less incriminating question. "Did you know that Quincy's in love with Ramona and has been since high school?"

Megan's expression told him she knew that wasn't what he'd wanted to ask her. She stood, carrying her bowl to the sink. "I've had my suspicions."

Ean followed her with his own bowl. "Am I the only one who didn't know?"

"You've only been back in Trinity Falls for a

month. Don't be so hard on yourself." Megan scraped the remains of her lunch into the garbage disposal before turning to take his nearly empty bowl.

"How do you feel about Quincy being in love with Ramona?"

Megan hesitated before stacking their dishes into the dishwasher. "What are you asking?"

"I'd think it would be hard if a guy you liked fell in love with your cousin."

The air drained from the room and Megan's lungs. Was he kidding? She straightened from the dishwasher, struggling to draw her next breath. "I'm sure it would be, if I were interested in Quincy romantically."

"Are you dating anyone?"

"Not at the moment."

"Why not?"

He can't be serious.

Megan turned to face Ean. "You sound like my grandmother. She'd always ask me, 'Meg, when are you going to find a nice young man?' And I'd say, 'Gran, they don't make them like Gramps anymore.'"

She still believed that. Her grandparents had been friends and lovers, as well as business partners. They each were everything the other had needed. That's the kind of relationship she was holding out for. The type of relationship she believed she could have with Ean, if only . . .

"I'm surprised there aren't at least a couple of guys trying to get your attention."

Megan maneuvered around Ean to continue clearing the kitchen table. She carried the plate of cracker crumbs and their drink glasses to the sink. "Is that because of your experience with guys breaking down my grandparents' front door in junior high school and high school?"

Ean stepped out of her way to allow Megan access to the sink. "It's more about the person you've become. You're successful, which is appealing. You're smart, which is very sexy, and you're—"

"Stop right there." Megan held her palm out. "If you're going to complete the terrible three, I don't want to hear it."

Ean frowned. "What 'terrible three'?"

Megan held up a finger for each feature. "Successful, smart and a good personality. Whenever a friend or neighbor wants to set you up with someone who meets those qualifications, it usually means he has some sort of fatal flaw, like a horse laugh or poor grooming habits."

"I wasn't going to say that you have a good personality."

Megan turned from the sink and settled her hands on her hips. "Why not?"

"You're too bossy."

Megan's jaw dropped. "No, I'm not."

"And too confident. You border on arrogant. Men find that intimidating."

Megan arched a brow. "Maybe weak men."

He stepped in closer, giving her a slow, sexy smile. "I've never considered myself weak, and you've had me shaking in my shoes since I came back."

His voice was too low, casting a spell on her. Megan could smell him—soap and musk. His scent made her stomach muscles quiver. His warmth wrapped around her. Megan gripped the counter behind her to keep from swaying into him.

Who's shaking now?

CHAPTER 12

"Maybe you're not as strong as you think." Megan cleared her throat.

It was hard to concentrate with Ean's body so close to hers. *Step back*, her mind shouted at him. Her eyes widened as he drew even closer instead. It was as though he'd read her mind and chose to defy her.

Ean lowered his head. "Maybe you're stronger."

She'd have to disagree. Right now, with Ean's body heat slipping into her clothes, she had as much strength as a newborn baby. Her body was so limp, she was in danger of melting into the ground.

"You don't need to stand this close to hear me." What happened to her voice? She could barely hear herself.

But she could hear her heart, slamming against her chest. Hear the warnings, screaming in her head. *Run before you do something stupid like kiss him back if he kisses you.*

Oh, please let him kiss me!

"But I need to stand this close to taste you." The intensity in his olive gaze pinned her. His rough voice made her body ache.

Megan's breath left her in a gasp. She opened her mouth to speak, and Ean sealed her lips with his.

The man knew how to work his tongue. He slid into her mouth and explored every inch of that erogenous zone. Megan's pulse beat fast and hard. The combination of his smell, his touch, his taste, made her mind spin. He stroked the sides of her mouth, teased her tongue. He tasted wonderful. He felt great. She wanted more.

Ean wrapped his arms around her and pulled her closer. Megan moaned as he pressed his chest to her breasts. Her nipples tightened. An urgency grew in her. Ean's big hands traced her back. He traveled the curve of her waist to her hips, then cupped her derriere. Her core burned hotter. Megan's hips jerked against him.

Ean deepened their kiss. He drew her even tighter against him. She felt the throbbing between his legs against her. It echoed her pulse. His right hand followed her curves back up to her left breast. His big hand gently squeezed its weight. The tip of his finger traced the nipple, circling it until Megan wanted to cry from the sensations tightening inside her body.

Her breath drained from her lungs. Was she having an out-of-body experience? She wanted more. She needed more. She had to . . .

. . . pull back. Megan bit her lower lip.

Ean's unfocused gaze found hers. "What is it?"

Megan's pulse still raced. Her body throbbed in places with an intensity it never had before. She took a deep breath, then another. "Ramona."

Ean's breathing was still ragged. "She broke up with me. Remember?"

"I don't want to be your rebound romance."

Ean expelled a rough sigh. "It was six years ago. I've rebounded."

Megan examined his dark, chiseled features—his irritated olive eyes, his thickly knitted brows and his full, sensuous lips, which had once again pulled her hidden desires to the surface.

"I had a crush on you in junior high school." Why had she blurted that out? What had she been thinking?

"Really?" Ean's eyes twinkled and his sexy smile stretched his lips.

Megan circled him to put distance between them. "If you didn't return for Ramona, then why did you come back to Trinity Falls?"

Ean held her gaze for several silent seconds before turning his broad back to her. Her eyes traced his wide shoulders, then lowered to his tight buttocks. She should have removed his shirt when she'd had the chance.

Ean dragged his right hand over his close-cropped, tight curls. "Something happened to me after my father died. My job, the firm, New York didn't hold any interest for me anymore. I felt disconnected."

All thoughts of stripping off his shirt vanished from Megan's mind. Empathy replaced lust. "That's part of your grieving process. Give yourself some time."

He turned to her. "It's been almost a year."

"It takes as long as it takes."

"It's not about time. I need answers, Megan."

Her heart clenched at the pain in his voice. "To what?"

Ean paced the length of her kitchen, past the table and back. The hurt in his voice hinted at the torment in his eyes. "Why didn't my mother call me as soon as my parents found out my father had cancer?"

Megan didn't want to betray a friend. At the same time, she didn't want her friend to be blamed for something that wasn't her idea.

She wandered to her blond wood table and lowered herself into the closest chair. "Your father didn't want her to."

His shock slammed into her from across the room like a body blow. "How do you know that?"

Megan looked up at him. Ean was so still. "It's the only thing that makes sense. Your mother would have told you about your father's illness—unless he specifically asked her not to."

He started his uneasy pacing again. "You're speculating. When I asked her why she hadn't told me about Dad's cancer right away, she said there wasn't anything I could do but worry."

Megan tilted her head. "Doesn't that sound more like something your father would say?"

Ean stopped, staring at the faux-stone flooring.

"Why wouldn't she just tell me Dad didn't want me to know?"

"Doreen wouldn't want you to be angry with your father, but I don't want you to be angry with her."

"It doesn't matter that he didn't want me to know. If the situation had been reversed, I would've told her."

Megan's voice softened. "You don't know that. Until you've walked in her shoes, you don't know what you would have done. And I hope you never find out."

Ean turned away. Silence stretched between them. Megan considered his back. What could she do to ease the tightness in those broad shoulders? She wanted to touch him, but would he rather have some space?

He rubbed the back of his neck. "What do I do now?"

"Talk with her. As you said, this is all just speculation. If you confront her with it, she won't lie to you."

Ean faced her. "It won't be easy. The last time we talked about Dad, it didn't go well."

"You said you came back for answers. This is your chance."

Ean nodded, staring into the middle distance. A soul-deep sigh lifted his chest. He exhaled before pinning her with his olive gaze. "What about us?"

Her heart tripped, then continued a steady beat. "We'll talk after you speak with Doreen."

* * *

The next day, Ean slowed to a walk when he reached his mother's house at the end of his morning run. He strode to the corner as part of his cooldown. Megan hadn't been on the jogging trail this morning. Was she avoiding him?

"Ean, how was your run?"

He looked up at Ms. Helen's house. She'd stepped out onto her porch. The older woman was nearly lost in the oversized purple winter coat. Whose coat was it?

"It was fine, thank you, Ms. Helen. How's your magazine?" Ean crossed the street. He nodded toward the women's magazine she held against her chest.

"I just got to the column on personal revelations. This young actress is talking about her big reveal."

"Sounds interesting." Ean glanced at Ms. Helen's sesquicentennial banner.

"When are you going to have your big reveal, Ean?" Ms. Helen held the door open so he could join her inside.

"Excuse me?" He shed his jogging shoes before crossing her threshold.

Ms. Helen smoothed her graying hair back toward the thick bun at the nape of her thin neck. "Now, I don't mean to pry into other folks' business."

It was a struggle not to laugh. "I know, Ms. Helen."

"But you've been back more than a month now. When are you going to start looking for work, son? I know you didn't come home to live off your mama."

Ean smiled at her chastising tone. "That's not my intention at all."

"I knew that. Your parents brought you up right." Ms. Helen nodded as though satisfied that he'd confirmed her opinion of him. "So what are you going to do, young man?"

Ean had been wondering the same thing. "That's what I'm trying to figure out, Ms. Helen."

Her frown deepened the wrinkles across her brow. "What's there to think about? You've got to find a job. And you should find another place to live, too. Your mother has needs, and having a grown son living at home with her probably isn't helping her to meet those needs, if you get my meaning."

Ean's gaze dropped to the publication in Ms. Helen's hands. What was in that magazine? "I'm trying to decide where to apply for work."

Ms. Helen grunted. She settled into the teak-wood chair in front of her window. "Seems to me you would've given some thought to that before you came home." Her tone was dry enough to start a campfire.

"I did, ma'am. But to tell you the truth, my priority was coming home. I knew I'd figure out everything else later."

"Later is now, Ean. What have you figured out?"

Not much. In fact, he had more questions now than before he'd come home. "A lot of the bigger companies that would have law departments are headquartered farther away than I'd want to drive."

She snorted. "The way I've heard it, people in New York are used to traveling long distances to work."

Ms. Helen had always had a way of dismissing excuses.

He nodded. "That's true."

"Besides, what makes you think you'd have to travel?"

"There aren't any law firms in Trinity Falls."

"So what?" Ms. Helen kissed her teeth. "Does that mean people in Trinity Falls don't need lawyers? There are businesspeople here who have contracts you can charge them to read. People need wills. Are we supposed to drive into the city just to pay you to write them for us?"

"You shouldn't have to." The lightbulb was flickering on. He was an idiot for not realizing it sooner.

"You don't have to work for someone. So there aren't any law firms in Trinity Falls. Start one yourself. And we'd trust you to do a good job for us and not rip us off."

"Ms. Helen, you're a genius."

She sucked her teeth again. "Tell me something I don't know."

Her voice was gruff, but Ean saw the blush of pleasure on her thin cheeks.

He rose from the chair. "Thanks for your help, Ms. Helen."

"You're welcome, baby. But don't forget, you've got to move out of your mama's house. Get your own place—the sooner, the better. I don't mean to embarrass you, but a woman has needs."

Ean waved as he let himself out of her house, then put his shoes back on. He didn't want her to embarrass him, either. Ms. Helen meant well, but he didn't want to discuss his mother's needs. A conversation like that would scar him for life.

CHAPTER 13

Ean entered his mother's house. He removed his running shoes before walking to the kitchen. He filled a glass with cold tap water and drained it in one long gulp. He refilled the glass and drank it more slowly as he padded up the stairs. His thoughts raced with Ms. Helen's suggestion that he start his own law firm. There was office space for rent in the Trinity Falls Town Center. He'd contact the center's rental office after breakfast.

Twenty minutes later, showered and dressed, Ean jogged back downstairs. In the threshold, he stopped short at the sight of his mother sitting at the small honey wood kitchen table. She was reading the paper and sipping coffee. A red velour robe was wrapped around her. Fluffy brown slippers protected her feet.

How much longer could he delay a confrontation about his father's illness? He'd wanted to ask her last night, but couldn't find the courage.

"Good morning. Did you sleep well?" Ean walked to the fridge and pulled out the pitcher of ice water.

Doreen lowered the newspaper. "Yes, I did. How was your run?"

"Good." Ean refilled his water glass. Was it his imagination or did their conversation sound stilted? "Can I make you breakfast?"

Doreen's eyes widened. "I'd like that."

"Don't look so shocked." Ean tossed her a wry smile. "It's not as though I've never cooked for you before."

"And every time is a pleasant surprise." Doreen shifted in her chair to face him. "Do you need any help?"

"No, thanks." With his back to her, this seemed like the perfect time to introduce a difficult conversation. "Mom, Dad told you not to tell me he was dying, didn't he?"

Silence dropped into the room. He felt Doreen's tension beating against him like a blast of frozen air.

"What makes you ask that?" Her tone was brittle.

Ean pulled the pans from one cupboard and ingredients from another. "Why did you let me blame you for not telling me?"

Doreen was silent for so long, he thought his mother would ignore his question. "Your father and I had been together for more than forty years, you know."

"I know, Mom." Ean worried at the husky note in her voice. Was she going to cry? If she did, then so would he.

Doreen exhaled a shaky breath. "He meant everything to me. He gave me everything I needed to be the person I wanted to be."

Memories of his parents talking, laughing and dancing to music only they could hear played across his mind like a favorite film. He recalled their public displays of affection that had grossed him out as an adolescent and had filled him with envy as an adult.

"I know, Mom." Ean poured a glass of ice water from the refrigerator and offered it to his mother.

"Thank you." Doreen's voice was a whisper.

His throat was too tight to respond. Maybe this wasn't a good idea, after all. Ean gulped his own drink.

Doreen continued. "We were lovers, spouses, parents, friends." She hesitated. Her voice grew huskier. "The hardest role I had to play was caregiver."

Ean returned to the stove and set his glass on the counter. He lifted an egg, intending to break it into the pan, but he couldn't do it. He set the egg back into the carton.

"Why didn't he want me to know he was sick?" He spoke with his back to his mother.

"Watching him die was unbearable for me. I tried not to let him see how much I was hurting—for him, for myself, for you. But he knew. And it was intolerable for him. He didn't want you to go through that."

His eyes stung, thinking about the two people he loved most in the world in so much pain. He turned to face Doreen. "But I should have been there with you."

Doreen raised her gaze to his. Her eyes were wet with unshed tears. Her voice was raw with sorrow. "This wasn't about you or me, Ean. This was your father's dying wish. And as much as it hurt me, I respected that."

And he had to respect it, too. That didn't mean he had to like it. "I didn't get a chance to say good-bye." The cold water did little to ease the burning in his throat.

"Yes, you did. Every time he spoke with you, you ended the call with 'I love you.' What more was there to say?"

How was he to know that, to his father, "I love you" meant "good-bye"?

"He'd sounded so weak and tired on the phone. I kept asking him about it. He said he would be OK."

"He is." The muscles in Doreen's throat worked as she drank more water. "It gives me comfort knowing he's in a better place—that he's not in pain any longer."

"I'll have to take comfort from that, too." How much longer before that comfort replaced his guilt and grief? Ean carried their empty glasses to the sink. "I'm sorry I blamed you, Mom."

"Better that you were angry with me than your father. We have the time to reconcile. Your father didn't."

He washed the glasses and set them on the drain to dry. "I understand why Dad made his choice, but I still don't like it."

Doreen stood. "I would be upset, too."

Ean crossed to her, wrapping her in his embrace. "I wish I'd been there with you, Mom."

She hugged him tighter. "You were, baby. You were with me when I needed you most, and I'm glad you're here with me now."

And he'd continue to be there with her, giving her the love and support she'd given him all of his life. Now that they'd cleared the air, they could start this new phase of their relationship—whatever it might be.

CHAPTER 14

Quincy tensed when Ramona took the stool beside him at Books & Bakery's food counter early Tuesday morning. Thinking about his last exchange with Ean almost cost him his appetite. How long had Ramona known he'd been in love with her? Why hadn't she ever said anything? Why, after fourteen years, couldn't he fall in love with someone—anyone—else?

"Good morning, Quincy." Her greeting was like salt in a wound.

"Ramona." He kept his attention on his breakfast of scrambled eggs, turkey bacon and wheat toast. If it killed him, he'd act as though nothing had changed.

Ramona leaned into the counter to see Darius seated on Quincy's other side. "How are things at the paper, Darius? Still making up what you don't know?"

Darius chuckled. "Why don't you tell me what I got wrong, Mayor?"

"You didn't get anything wrong, Darius." Quincy's protective reflexes, honed since their days on their elementary school playground, kicked in. "But it sounds like you hit a nerve."

Ramona turned on him. "Do you even know what you're talking about?"

Quincy steeled himself to meet her ebony eyes. "Do you?"

Ramona narrowed her gaze. "This doesn't concern you."

That's where she was wrong. If it involved one of his friends, it definitely concerned him. "Why are you here, Ramona, at eight in the morning? You're not usually an early riser. Is your conscience giving you a hard time?"

Looking into Ramona's seductive eyes while speculating on her sleeping habits was a mistake. His body temperature spiked. In his peripheral vision, he caught the stares of the other breakfast patrons. Quincy feigned disdain as he returned his attention to the safety of his bacon and eggs. He took a deep breath to calm his pulse and drew in the warm, mouthwatering fragrance of baking bread wafting from the bakery's kitchen. And Ramona's perfume beside him.

"You have a point, Quincy." Darius's tone was taunting. "What part of my ace reporting caused you to lose sleep, Mayor?"

"This blowhard doesn't know what he's talking about." Ramona jerked her head toward Quincy. Her voice tightened, an indication that her renowned temper was about to snap.

"Blowhard." Quincy shook off the inappropriate images her insult brought to mind. "If Darius's reporting had been inaccurate, you'd have confronted him in his office at a much more convenient time for you, like noon."

Ramona pointed a finger at Darius while the dark inferno of her gaze scorched Quincy. "His irresponsible reporting implied that I was raising fees and taxes on the stores in the shopping center to run them out of business. That sort of reckless writing will hurt my reelection campaign."

Darius turned away from his plate of steak and eggs. "That reckless reporting came from your quote. You said you were hoping to attract higher-end businesses to the vacant stores in the center."

Ramona inclined her head. "Yes, that's what I said. But you took that statement out of context. The way you positioned it in your article made it seem as though I chased those stores out. I didn't run them out. They left."

"You're splitting hairs, Ramona." Darius shrugged. "Those businesses left because the town's increased fees and taxes amounted to extortion. You should have thought about how that would play during the election before you asked for the increases."

Quincy sipped his coffee. "But since she's running unchallenged, she doesn't have to worry about how her decisions will affect her reelection."

"I'm not doing this to hurt the town. I'm trying to help the town." Ramona spoke as though she believed what she said. "It's not my fault the original center owners defaulted on the loan the town granted them. Those increased business taxes will generate more revenue for Trinity Falls."

"Revenue for what?" Megan joined the discussion. She greeted Quincy and Darius as she strode past them to stand behind the counter. "What will the town do with the money?"

"We haven't identified the use yet." Ramona flipped her heavy raven locks behind her shoulder.

Quincy recognized the gesture as one she often used when she was uncertain. He softened his response. "That's backward, isn't it? You raise taxes to generate revenue for something. You don't tax your constituents just because."

Ramona stood, sharing her glare equally with the other three people at the counter before resting it on Darius. "If I can't get you to curb your reckless reporting, I'm sure your publisher will."

Quincy watched the irritated swing of her firm hips as she stormed out of the bookstore. Was she on her way to talk to *The Trinity Falls Monitor*'s publisher? "Do you think Susan Liu will listen to her?"

Darius grunted. "Liu doesn't listen to anyone."

Megan caught Quincy's eyes. "Why don't you tell her how you feel?" Her question was just above a whisper.

CHAPTER 15

Quincy looked over his shoulder, surprising several other breakfast patrons, who promptly glanced away. He turned back to Megan. "How many people know?"

Darius swallowed a bite of steak. "Who doesn't? Your inner twelve-year-old takes over whenever you're around her. What I want to know is what do you see in her?"

"She's smart."

"She's conniving."

"I like her sense of humor."

"She has one?"

Quincy scowled at him. "Do you want an answer to your question or not?"

Darius held up both hands in a gesture of surrender. "Sorry."

Quincy tipped back his head, staring at the off-white ceiling. What was there to love about Ramona? A woman who couldn't see beyond her own reflection, who used his feelings to taunt him with her other men and who'd barely acknowledged his existence in fourteen years. Why was he lost in love with her?

He must be a masochist.

Quincy addressed Megan. "She makes me feel protective. There's a vulnerability about her."

Darius's eyes widened. "She's a shark."

Quincy opened his mouth to blast Darius. Megan's hand on his shoulder quieted him.

"Ramona and I don't always see eye to eye, but I agree with everything Quincy's said." Megan squeezed Quincy's shoulder before releasing him. "Darius, you've obviously never been in love. Sometimes you can't explain your feelings. You just feel."

Quincy couldn't have put it any better.

"I wish I could stop feeling." He offered Megan the bill and his credit card, then followed her to the cash register. "I hope the University of Pennsylvania offers me that faculty position."

Megan ran his credit card through the card reader, then returned it to him with his receipt. "It's been six years since Ramona and Ean broke up. Why haven't you asked her out?"

Quincy was shaking his head before he heard the end of Megan's question. "I'm not competing against Ean. I don't want to be the runner-up."

"You're right. You're not competing against him. You're competing against yourself." Megan held his gaze. "Give yourself a chance, Quincy. Give Ramona a chance."

* * *

Megan glanced at Wesley Hayes, one of her part-time assistants, who walked the aisles of Books & Bakery with her as they closed the shop Thursday night. The high school junior was a great employee—smart, efficient and dependable. She started to tell him that when the chime above the store's front door interrupted her.

"I'll be right back."

"All right, Ms. McCloud." Wesley's response was preoccupied.

Megan checked her red Timex as she hurried to the front of the store to greet the last-minute patron. It was five minutes to eight. Why would someone arrive so late? Everyone in town knew the store closed promptly at eight P.M. during the week.

Her steps faltered when she recognized Ean strolling forward. She hadn't seen much of him since Sunday. She'd begun to think the last kiss they'd shared had never happened. His loose-limbed grace drew her eyes to his faded denim jeans and his long, strong thighs underneath.

Megan jerked her gaze upward. "We're closing in a few minutes. Is there something I can help you find?"

"No, thanks. I've already found her." Ean tossed her a boyish grin.

Did he think those pretty words and that sexy grin would make her forget his five days of silence? He was right.

She returned his smile. "Did you come to walk me home?"

"Yes."

Megan blinked. She'd been joking, but he looked serious. "Ean, that's very kind of you, but I'll be fine on my own."

"I know, but I'd like to walk with you tonight." His casual words played with her heart.

Megan glanced around. If she looked at him too long, his hypnotic olive eyes would claim her soul. "It'll take me a while to get ready. We're making sure everything's in order before closing the store."

On cue, Wesley emerged from one of the aisles. His blue button-down shirt was slipping free of the waistband of his navy pants again.

"Ms. McCloud, I've straightened the shelves in the back." The seventeen-year-old jerked a thumb over his shoulder. "I'm going to . . . Hey! Aren't you Ean Fever?"

"Yes, I am." Ean extended his right hand. "Who are you?"

"I'm Wes Hayes. I play ball for Heritage High." A broad grin lightened Wesley's usually solemn features. His lanky body vibrated with excitement. "I want to be just like you one day. Leave this place behind and make a name for myself in the big city."

Ean shot a glance toward Megan, releasing Wesley's hand. "Keep your grades up. Not everyone makes it in the pros. I didn't."

Wesley shook his head. His thin brown braids swung above his shoulders. "No, but you were making serious jack with the law firm. I wanna do that."

"How are your grades?"

"They're all right." Wesley shrugged, still staring at Ean as though the lawyer was a pop star.

Megan smiled at Wesley's modesty The high school junior was taking Advanced Placement classes and his grade point average was almost a perfect 4.0.

Ean knitted his brows. "Your grades will have to be better than 'all right' if you want to get into a good college and law school."

"Yes, sir." Wesley's grin remained in place. "Maybe you could give me some tips. I'd like to attend the schools you went to."

"Sure. Since we're going to be neighbors, you can stop by my office anytime. It's just a few doors down." Ean nodded to his right.

The air drained from Megan's lungs. *"Your office?"*

"Cool! Thank you, Mr. Fever." Wesley's brown features glowed with joy. "See you later, Ms. McCloud, Mr. Fever."

Megan regained her breath. "Your office?"

Ean watched Wesley jog from the store, closing the door behind him. "Does he remind you of me when I was his age?"

"No." Megan turned toward her own office. She knew he would follow. She was right. "Wes has a quiet intensity. He thinks things through. You were much more outspoken. You said whatever was on your mind, always assuming you were right."

"I usually was."

"Or so you thought." Megan rolled her eyes, even though Ean couldn't see her.

Why wasn't he answering her questions? What did he want? And why was he renting office space in the Trinity Falls Town Center?

"If I was so obnoxious, why did you have a crush on me?"

Megan stopped mere steps from her door. Why had she armed him with that information? Ean bumped into her from behind, causing her to stumble even closer to the threshold.

"I have no idea what I was thinking." Megan began the ritual of leaving for the evening. "Are you really renting office space in the center?"

"Yes. I'm opening a law practice." Ean turned away from her to examine the bookcase across the room.

Megan contemplated his broad shoulders, covered in his gray London Fog jacket. He reached out to handle the framed photograph of her and Ramona posing with their grandparents and a children's book author. It was the closest Ramona had gotten to reading that summer.

"Why?" She turned back to her desk and logged off her computer.

Ean returned the picture to the bookshelf. "Trinity Falls could use a local lawyer."

"And you're going to fill that role?" Megan collected her purse from her bottom desk drawer and shrugged it onto her shoulder. "For how long?"

Ean turned to her. "How can I convince you I'm home to stay?"

"You'd have to stay." Megan led Ean from the

room and turned off the lights. "Even then you'd have a credibility problem because your goal in high school was getting out of Trinity Falls and never coming back."

"I'm not in high school anymore."

Megan locked her office door. "Trinity Falls wasn't able to hold you fourteen years ago. What's changed?"

"I have." Ean paced beside Megan as she strode to the store's front exit.

Megan set the alarm before joining Ean outside. Was he really home to stay? That couldn't be possible. A longer visit—he'd already been back for more than a month—was more plausible. He'd reconcile with Ramona and then they'd both return to New York. That was a scenario she could believe. She was far more familiar with people leaving than with people actually wanting to stay.

Then why was he opening a solo practice and claiming his relationship with Ramona had ended? Ramona probably would have something to say about that.

Megan joined Ean on the sidewalk. "Did you ask Doreen about your father's illness?"

"You were right. It was his idea not to tell me he was dying."

She turned toward home. "So now you have the answers you were looking for."

Ean shoved his hands into his front jacket pockets. He kept pace beside her. "I'm beginning to think you don't want me here."

"I don't believe you want to be here."

His chuckle was dry. "Because when I was eighteen, I wanted to leave. I'm thirty-two now."

"And you now know that you no longer crave the bright lights of the big city. After fourteen years, you've finally realized that you're a small-town boy at heart."

"That's right."

Megan smothered a sigh of frustration. Were all men this difficult to communicate with, or was Ean a special case? They walked for several blocks in a preoccupied silence. The evening breeze carried a sharp chill. Megan pulled her overcoat tighter around her body.

Another peaceful night in Trinity Falls. It was only a little after eight o'clock, but already the streets were empty of traffic. Their footsteps echoed against the redbrick pavement. A few townspeople were gathered in quiet conversations in front of darkened storefronts. The intermittent streetlights kept the deepest shadows at bay.

Megan inhaled the clean, crisp fall air. If she stood still and closed her eyes, she could imagine she was the only person on the planet. She'd attended the University of Illinois and had experienced what the big city had to offer in Chicago. The noise, congestion, sirens, shortened tempers. Chicago, New York, Philadelphia—they could all keep their cultural attractions, nightlife and skyscrapers. She was more than happy with the peaceful solitude of small-town life, thank you very much.

But what about Ean?

"After seven years in New York, what made you decide to come home?"

Ean's introspection ended with Megan's quiet question. She was persistent. He'd give her that. And she didn't shy away from confrontations, another formidable trait. But why didn't she believe him?

He looked at her cool chocolate eyes beneath her knitted brows. "Why are you angry?"

Megan didn't hesitate. "I'm not angry. I'm concerned. I don't want Doreen—or the town—to be disappointed when you return to New York."

"I won't." What about her? Would she be disappointed if he left?

"Then explain why you've come home to stay after achieving your dream in New York."

Ean would have laughed if the statement hadn't been so absurd. The dream had become a nightmare. "I hadn't realized my father was dying. What does that say about my dream life in New York?"

"That your priorities were wrong."

Ean flexed his shoulders, trying to dislodge the tension growing there. "I got tired of the rat race. In seven years, I was home a total of six weeks. That's less than a week each year."

"I remember how disappointed your parents were when you stayed only two or three nights."

That didn't make him feel better. It only added guilt to the anger and resentment he still felt toward the demands of his previous job. Ean drew a deep breath. The scent of burning wood sweeping out of the nearby chimneys settled him. It was a marked contrast from the stench of trash and exhaust that had assailed him in his former New York neighborhood.

"I worked every waking moment, but still couldn't keep up. I made partner two years ago. But when I realized I'd been billing hours for the firm instead of spending time with my dying father, I knew I'd made a mistake." Even as he spoke the words, he knew he'd failed to mask his resentment.

"Your father was proud of you, Ean." Megan's tone had softened.

Ean closed his eyes briefly. She felt sorry for him now. That was worse. "I was using my law degree to find loopholes for companies to get out of lawsuits and government investigations. That's not something to be proud of."

"He was proud that you'd achieved your dream of becoming a lawyer and working in New York."

"It was a mistake." Ean's tone was flat. "I should have stayed in Trinity Falls. Here people care about me as a person rather than a legal weapon."

"Are you saying, 'There's no place like home'?"

Streetlights lit the small smile hovering around Megan's full lips and the twinkle in her chocolate eyes.

Just like that, Ean's tension dissipated. "I guess I am."

The silence between them was comfortable for several minutes. Ean still hadn't seen an automobile drive down the quiet neighborhood street. But several townspeople walked past them—elderly couples enjoying an after-dinner stroll, teenagers hurrying home after hanging out with friends, families on their way back from the local ice-cream parlor. Ean exchanged greetings and withstood curious stares from all of them. He hadn't missed the nosy neighbors. How long would it take before everyone in Trinity Falls knew Ean Fever had walked Megan McCloud home from work?

Megan pulled her key from her purse as they neared her home. "I understand why you're upset. But if you hadn't accomplished your goal, you would have had different regrets."

He couldn't argue with that. "You're right."

"Doreen must be very happy that you've decided to stay. She didn't like your being so far from home." Megan adjusted the shoulder strap of her purse.

Ean noted the gesture and studied her posture. She seemed uncomfortable. Why? "Mom seemed happier when she learned I was getting my own place."

"Really?" Megan tossed back her head and laughed. Her demeanor relaxed.

Ean remembered the conversation he'd had with Ms. Helen. For both his mother's and his sake, he was glad he'd taken the older lady's advice.

He smiled at the amusement on Megan's honey-toned features. "Coach George was coming over for dinner when I left."

Some of her amusement faded. "Ean, you've got to give Leo a chance."

"I will, but not tonight." Ean followed Megan up the winding walkway to her front door. "Anyway, I found a town house in Quincy's complex. I'm moving in tomorrow."

"You have been busy." She sounded impressed. Her reaction meant more to him than winning any of his multiple high-profile corporate cases.

"Do you believe me now?"

"We'll see." She tossed him a grin that warmed his body. "Is that the reason you came to the store today? To tell me you've moved out of your mother's house?"

Ean took the keys from her. He was getting used to her sense of humor. Ignoring the question in her gaze, he unlocked her front door. "Not exactly."

"Then why exactly?" She spoke over her shoulder as she preceded him into her home.

Ean scanned the foyer, noting the corner light she'd left on again. He locked the door and gave Megan back her keys. "I signed the lease on the office space Tuesday and the rental agreement this morning."

She hung her coat on the coat tree in the corner of the foyer and held out her hand for his. "You've gotten a lot done since I last saw you."

Ean shrugged out of his jacket and hung it beside hers. "That proves I'm here to stay." He fisted his hands in the front pockets of his jeans. His palms were sweating like a nervous adolescent's.

"I hope you are."

Ean searched her features for a sign that she was wavering in her disagreement. He found nothing. "I want to explore this attraction between us."

Megan's breath caught in her throat. She coughed to dislodge it. "That's direct."

Ean's features eased into his smile. "I thought you'd prefer that."

She wouldn't bother to deny their attraction. They'd both know she was lying. Megan led them from the bright foyer to the deeper shadows of the living room.

She settled onto the sofa. "It's never been only a question of when you were leaving. I also don't know whether Ramona will be able to let you go."

Irritation creased his brow. "She walked out on me." Ean sat beside her. "We'd been living together for less than a year before she told me she was returning to Trinity Falls with or without me."

Megan shifted on the cushion to face him. "I'm really not sure, Ean. If Ramona still has feelings for you, I don't want to get in her way."

Which was much more loyalty than Ramona would ever show her. So why did she care? Because when she'd needed Ramona, her cousin had stayed. And when the town had needed her, Ramona had stayed longer.

Ean shook his head in disgust. "The only thing Ramona wants from me is a New York address. I've told her the same thing I've told you—I'm staying in Trinity Falls."

Megan's pulse beat harder. She stood and crossed the room, hiding her reaction to his words in deeper shadows. "But your being here may have brought back her feelings for you."

Ean's touch on her shoulder startled Megan. She hadn't heard him approach. She turned to face him and was caught by the intensity in his olive eyes.

"I don't want Ramona. I want you." Ean lowered his mouth to hers.

CHAPTER 16

His taste was more than fourteen-year-old Megan could have imagined. Mysterious and dark, tempting her curiosity. Open and bright, sharing all that he was. Megan leaned closer, taking the kiss even deeper. Her control was slipping away. She wanted to get closer. She needed to taste more. She hooked her arms behind his back, pressing her breasts harder against his chest. She sent her tongue after Ean's, showing him what she wanted—his touch, his heat, his essence.

Ean tightened his arms around her waist, pulling her body to his. He plunged his tongue into her mouth, stroking her moist cavern with a suggestive pulse. Megan groaned deep in her throat. She'd dreamed of this. Her hips picked up their rhythm, moving against him with her own demands.

Ean shifted his hands lower to her hips, taking hold of her buttocks and raising her against him. Even with the layers of clothes between them, the sensation of his desire pulsing against the apex of her thighs set Megan's body on fire. She tore free of his lips and threw back her head with a gasp. Her muscles ached. Her nipples tightened. She wanted more. She drilled her fingers into his shoulders.

Megan's eyes popped open at the feel of Ean's knit sweater beneath her hands. "Off."

He froze, loosening his hold on her. "What?"

"Your sweater. Off." Her words croaked.

Ean smiled as he set her free. He stepped back and, with his left hand, pulled off his sweater, letting it drop to her carpet.

His body was a masterpiece. Broad, molded shoulders, sculpted pecs and hard, flat abdominals. Dark hair lightly covered his chest, leading a tempting trail to the waistband of his denim jeans. She could stare at him all night. She'd rather lay with him, instead.

Megan lifted her gaze to his. She cleared her throat. "Your body . . . It's incredible."

The look in Ean's eyes made her damp. "Your turn."

"Yes." She raised her arms to unbutton her suit jacket.

Ean stepped forward and nudged her hands aside. "Let me."

"All right." Her voice trembled. Was it nerves or need?

He took hold of her jacket. His fingers lingered on the bottom button. He leaned closer to her, pressing his face against her hair.

"I love the way you smell." His voice, low and husky, shared a secret in her ear.

Oh, God. This *was seduction.* She'd never experienced it this way before. "It's soap." Her heart was beating too fast. She could barely speak.

"It's you." His breath was warm against her neck.

The first button came free. Megan swallowed. Ean's finger traced her exposed skin. Her stomach muscles fluttered. The jacket tugged slightly as he released the second button. Two more to go. *Hurry! Hurry!*

Ean planted a butterfly kiss behind her ear. "Your skin is so soft."

Megan sighed. The third button came undone.

He stroked his tongue along the side of her neck. "You taste so sweet."

Megan moaned. The fourth button released. Ean trailed kisses to the curves of her breasts. As he peeled the jacket from her, her bra snapped free. How . . . ? Who cared?

Ean kissed and licked his way across her breasts, then opened his mouth and took her nipple.

Megan gasped. The fire at her core burst into an inferno. She cupped Ean's head closer to her as his teeth grazed her nipple. His tongue licked. His lips tugged. The pull carried deep inside her to echo between her legs. She needed to end this pressure. She wanted to feed this ache. She offered her other breast for Ean's attention. Her hunger swelled.

"Ean." She panted his name. "Protection?"

Ean raised his head. Through the fog of her

desire, Megan noted his tense expression and the glow in his olive eyes. He was hungry, too.

"My wallet."

"Get it. Now. Please."

He'd been confident. Thank God.

They made quick work of kicking off shoes and stripping the rest of their clothes. Megan was mesmerized by the strength of Ean's passion. Her nipples tightened. Her body moistened in response.

Ean took the condom from his wallet with hands that weren't quite steady. He turned to her. He wanted to take it slow. He wanted this to be a night to linger. He ached to touch and taste her . . . everywhere. He wanted to learn what she liked. He wanted to deepen her pleasure. But he didn't think he could last that long. Just looking at Megan's long, graceful figure drew him to the edge. He loved her small, perfect breasts, her hands, her feet. But it was her eyes that drew him. He could gaze into those large chocolate pools for an eternity.

Megan took the condom from him, then dropped to her knees. Ean's eyes widened. He'd never expected this. His pulse quickened. His muscles grew even more tense. With her gaze locked with his, Megan guided him into her mouth. It was hot and wet. And hot. Megan's tongue slid along his length. A tremor rolled from his toes to the top of his head. Straining for control, Ean closed his eyes and leaned his head back. He needed to rest his hands on her shoulders to steady his shaky legs. His body moved as she drew him into a rhythm with her lips and her tongue. Her hot, wet tongue. His breathing became ragged. His body began to burn.

No! Not yet. Ean forced himself to step back, freeing himself from her mouth. "No more." His words were a desperate gasp for control.

Megan stood and grinned at him. "Can't you handle it?"

Ean was surprised he could laugh. It helped him gain some control over his arousal. "I want to come inside you." He took the condom from her, then lifted her into his arms. "But not yet."

"Where are we going?" Megan glanced around as he carried her toward the staircase.

"That floor doesn't look all that comfortable for what I have in mind." Although it was torture, holding Megan naked in his arms when he was fully erect. He should have thought of that before he'd let her make love to him with her mouth. Ean groaned.

Megan kissed his neck and whispered into his ear, "What do you have in mind?"

"I'll show you." Ean mounted the staircase.

Megan chuckled. "Lucky for you, my room is right at the top of the stairs."

"Thank God."

Ean released her beside her bed, letting her skin rub against his. Megan climbed onto the mattress, drawing him with her. Ean lay beside her. He touched each breast, then trailed his fingers down her abdomen to her hip. "You are so beautiful. Perfect."

"I want to touch you." Megan raised her arm.

"Not yet." Ean caught her wrist and drew her arm above her head.

He lowered his mouth to graze and suckle first one breast, then the other. Megan squirmed beside him until he stopped. Ean rolled away, quickly securing the condom before returning to her side.

His hand hovered above her nest of curls. Ean traced his index finger through the soft patch, pressing against her core. He fed on each gasp and moan as he explored her. Each tremor.

Megan spread her legs wider. "Ean, come in me."

"Soon." He kissed each nipple again, then slid down her body. With his eyes holding hers, Ean separated her folds, then he licked her treasure.

Megan's hips shot off the bed. "Ean!"

He kissed her deeply. And continued kissing and licking her as her muscles grew tighter and tighter in the palms of his hands. Her hips pumped in his grasp. A fine sheet of sweat glistened on her naked body. Her breaths panted. Her body twisted. Her passion flowed. Ean's erection hardened to an almost painful point. When her body began to shake, he sought his own release. Ean raised himself above her, then slid deep inside her core. Megan gasped. The sound surrounded him.

Ean groaned, hanging his head as he braced his weight on his arms. *She feels. So. Damn. Good.* He savored the feeling washing over him. It was what he'd been looking for. What he'd been wanting. Home. He'd never made that connection during lovemaking before. Somehow he knew he never would again. Ean raised his head to meet Megan's gaze. The wonder in her chocolate eyes told him she'd felt it, too.

He picked up their pace, arching his back to sink farther into her damp secrets. Megan pressed her hips against his, harder, matching him thrust for thrust. She wrapped her legs around his waist to hold him tighter, still. Her eyes closed. Her cheeks flushed. Ean dipped his head and suckled a pebbled nipple into his mouth.

Megan stiffened. Her muscles tightened around his erection. Ean felt her quivering deep inside as her pleasure burst. She pressed her head back into the pillow and screamed. He cut off the sound with a deep, hungering kiss. Ean gathered her close as the waves crashed over them.

Much later, Megan lay on her back in the bed, pressing the comforter to her breasts. She met Ean's gaze as he sat on the edge of the mattress. His magnificent body was clothed again—more's the pity. He set his palms on either side of her shoulders.

"No regrets." His rough voice sent shivers down her spine.

Megan traced the chiseled lines of his cheek, then let her hand drop. "Only that you're leaving."

He touched his lips to hers, hard and quick. Too quick. "I don't want people talking about us, at least not yet."

She arched a brow. "You don't think they'll know what we did tonight?"

Ean stood. His movements were gratifyingly

reluctant. "If I leave now, they'll wonder. If I spend the night, they'll know."

"If you say so." Megan tossed off the comforter and rose from the mattress. The chill air puckered her nipples. "I'll walk you out."

She stretched her arms above her head and arched her back.

"You're killing me." Ean sounded as though he were choking.

His reaction wasn't a surprise. She'd wanted it. Megan glanced over at him. His hot, hungry gaze followed the profile of her figure. Her skin burned where his eyes touched her.

"You don't have to leave."

Ean pivoted from her and crossed to the door. "Yes, I do."

Stubborn man.

Megan grabbed a robe from her closet and hurried after him. Ean was shrugging into his coat when she entered the foyer.

"What time are you moving into your townhome tomorrow?"

"First thing in the morning." He pulled her close to kiss her again.

It was an urgent meeting of tongues. A touch to remind them of the hours they'd just shared. A taste that would sustain them throughout the rest of the night. Megan groaned low in her throat. Why wouldn't he just spend the night? To hell with chivalry. She'd tried reasoning with him earlier, but his mind had been made up by the time he'd rolled out of her bed.

Ean stepped back. "I'd better go."

"Don't expect me to dream about you." Megan crossed her arms under her breasts and pouted. "I guess, then, I'll probably bump into you sometime tomorrow."

Ean gave her a half smile. "I'll cook dinner for you."

She gave him a dubious look. "Takeout?"

He laughed. "I can cook."

She poked his flat abs. "You're on."

"Sleep well." He pulled the front door open and started down the stairs.

"You too." Megan locked the door and leaned against it. Regardless of what she'd told Ean, she would dream of him. Hopefully, she'd have many more opportunities on which to base her dreams . . . even long after he'd left Trinity Falls.

CHAPTER 17

"Does Quincy know you're his new neighbor?" Darius grunted.

Ean glanced briefly at his friend as Darius helped him carry his black leather sofa into the tan-and-white living room of his new town house Friday afternoon.

"I didn't tell him." Ean wiped the sweat from his brow and straightened away from the furniture. It looked good in its new surroundings. What was even better, he'd only had to keep the furniture he'd brought from New York in storage for just over a month.

"Are you going to tell him?" Darius dropped onto the sofa.

"I'm sure we'll run into each other sooner or later." Ean sank onto the sofa's other end.

He and Darius had been working, more or less nonstop, since seven o'clock that morning. It was close to lunchtime, and they were almost done.

Darius rolled his head on the sofa's back to face

Ean. "What are you going to say to him when that happens?"

Ean swung his right ankle onto his left knee. "It's not as though Trinity Falls has a lot of housing options."

"That's true. You had only two choices—my condo development, where there's no drama, and Quincy's townhome complex, where you'll have nothing but drama."

Ean spread his arms. "What's he going to do? Have the management office kick me out because I broke up with the woman he's in love with?"

Darius shook his head. "It would go better if you confront the situation, instead of waiting for Quincy to trip over you."

"I'll take that under advisement." Ean stood. "We're almost done. Let's get the rest of the stuff so we could finish before lunch."

Darius pushed himself off the sofa. "Now remind me again how this works? *I* take the day off from work to help you move your stuff, and you take *Megan* to dinner. Do I have that right?"

Ean ignored Darius's tone. "Who helped you move in and out of your dorm every year?"

"That was ten years ago."

"My back has never been the same." Ean led Darius outside to the driveway and well-manicured lawn. "But what are friends for?"

"I could at least get an invitation to dinner."

"Three's a crowd."

"Has anyone told Ramona you've moved?" Darius bent his knees to lift his end of the coffee table.

Ean carried the table's other end. "I'm not worried about Ramona."

Darius grunted. "Maybe you should be."

As he guided Darius back into the town house, he wondered whether his friend was right.

When Ean opened his front door later that afternoon, he found his mother on his doorstep.

Doreen lifted the bag of fast food and a drink carrier with two containers. "I come bearing gifts. Have you eaten?"

With a grin, Ean stepped back to allow his mother to enter. "Perfect timing." He locked the door behind her before escorting her farther into his new home.

Doreen slowed to consider the newly furnished living room. The black leather sofa's dominance was rivaled only by the large flat-screen black television.

His mother nodded toward the TV. "That's new."

Doreen's voice wasn't as disapproving as he'd expected. Ean's parents had discouraged watching television. When he was growing up, his family's set had been so small, if he'd actually wanted to *see* a televised sporting event, he'd had to go to Quincy's house.

Ean rubbed a hand over his mouth to mask a smile. "You're welcome to come over to watch a football game anytime."

She inclined her head. "I may take you up on that."

Ean's jaw dropped. Was she serious? How should he respond? He was still thinking about that when she walked away.

His mother circled the heavy mahogany coffee table. She traced the matching end table beside the sofa. Its twin stood on the opposite side. Each table supported stone lamps in modern designs.

His parents had helped him pick out his living-room set from a furniture store in Long Island. His father had saved him from his mother's selections. Every set she chose had screamed, "My mommy decorated my condo." Was she remembering that day? He'd never forget it.

Ean cleared his throat. "That was a good day."

"Yes, it was." Doreen gave him a soft smile over her shoulder. "Your things suit your new home perfectly."

"Yes, they do." It was as though he was meant to be here.

Doreen wandered toward the dining room and another furniture set on which he and his father had outvoted her. She unpacked the fast-food bag onto the table. "I brought your favorite—burger, fries and soda. Although, how you can eat this stuff and not get fat is beyond me."

He held the chair at the head of the table for his mother, then sank into a seat on her right. "I exercise. Besides, I don't eat like this every day."

Doreen's gaze remained fixed on her burger as

she unwrapped it. "I'm concerned that you may have felt forced out of the house. You didn't have to leave, if you weren't ready."

Ean released his still-unwrapped burger and covered her hand with his. "I was ready, Mom. I'm thirty-two years old. I need a place of my own."

And so did she. Ean had heard footsteps creeping down the stairs the previous night after he'd settled into bed.

"Are you sure?" Doreen's brown eyes were dark with concern.

"Positive."

A smile touched her eyes. "Good, then I can enjoy my meal."

Conversation about his move into the town house, her morning at Books & Bakery and the paperwork he needed to complete to establish his law practice carried them through their meal.

"Another reason I like fast food." Ean stood and crushed the remains of their lunch into the restaurant's paper bag. "No dishes."

He crossed to the kitchen, which was a cozy nook beside the dining room, and stuffed the garbage into the large, black heavy-duty bag he'd designated for his move-in–day trash.

Ean turned back toward the dining room—and paused. He rested his shoulder against the threshold between the kitchen nook and the dining area. He studied his mother, who was still seated at the table. "Mom, I'm glad you asked about the reason I moved out."

"So am I, Ean." She shifted in her chair to face him.

Doreen looked as though she'd turned back time. Her dark brown hair's soft-layered cut highlighted her classic features. Her wardrobe—hot pink jersey, light blue jeans and powder white sneakers—was even more youthful.

He took a deep breath; then he realized he was stalling. "I don't like this awkwardness between us."

"Neither do I."

She sensed it, too? Was that bad or worse? "How do we get past it?"

Doreen sighed. "It'll take time, Ean. Frankly, your moving out will help. We haven't lived together in fourteen years. You were a kid when you left home. You're an adult now. We have to become reacquainted."

Ean's eyebrows shot upward. "'Reacquainted'? I'm your son."

Doreen smiled. "We were bound to have some conflict simply because our relationship will have to change now that you're older."

Ean leaned more heavily against the wall. "I guess some changes aren't so bad. I hadn't realized when I returned to Trinity Falls, I'd open a practice here. I think it was the right decision."

"I agree."

Was there reticence in her voice? Ean swallowed his disappointment. He pushed away from the wall to sit beside her again. "Then why do you sound like you don't?"

"Ean, I *am* happy for you. But you don't need me anymore. Your father's gone. What's next for me?"

The sadness on his mother's face stabbed him in his heart. "What do you mean?"

Her tormented brown eyes stretched wide in frustration. "I'm single again after more than forty years. That's a lifetime. All of the decisions I used to make were as part of a couple. Now I have to make them by myself. I don't know who I am anymore or what I want to do. I'm still trying to figure out my next step. And the biggest decision—what do I want to do with the rest of my life—I thought I'd already made. I wanted to spend it with Paul."

Doreen buried her face in her hands and dissolved into muffled sobs. Ean was undone. He sprang to his feet and frantically scanned the area. He hadn't unpacked. He didn't have any tissues. What should he . . . ?

Ean jogged into the bathroom and returned with the liberated roll of toilet paper. "I'm sorry."

Doreen accepted his offering with both hands. "This is fine. I don't even know why I'm crying." She used the quilted tissue to dry her eyes and blow her nose. "Your father and I built a good life. We raised a wonderful son." She squeezed his arm and gave him a watery smile as he towered above her. "He's not in pain any longer. I don't have any reason to be sad."

Ean dragged his chair closer before sitting. He took both of his mother's hands in his. "You're crying because you miss him. I miss him, too."

Doreen drew one hand from Ean's grasp and cupped the side of his face. "He was so proud of you."

"And I'm proud of both of you. Look at what you've already accomplished, Mom. The bakery's a huge success."

"A bakery is a thing, Ean. It doesn't need me. If I walked away from it tomorrow, no one would notice."

Ean disagreed. A lot of people would notice. But he didn't think his mother wanted to hear that now. Instead, words from his childhood returned to him. "Whatever you decide you want to do, Mom, I'll support you."

"That sounds like something Paul would say." Doreen's chuckle was unsteady.

"He did. On more than one occasion."

Doreen squeezed his hand. "Thank you. I really needed to hear that now."

Ean kissed her cheek. "You'll figure it out."

"I have to." Doreen's chin trembled once before she controlled it. She checked her wristwatch. "I'd better get back to work."

Ean escorted her to the driveway. "Thanks again for lunch." He helped her into her car.

"You're welcome."

Ean straightened to watch his mother drive away. He wished he knew how to help her. But as she'd said, it was her life and she needed to make her own decisions. All he could do was support them.

CHAPTER 18

The back door's bell summoned Ean from the books he was stacking onto his dining-room bookcase. He straightened from his crouched position and crossed to the door.

"Ramona?" Ean couldn't believe his eyes. Her presence at his back door seemed surreal. "How did you know where to find me?"

"It's a small town, Ean. You know that." She adjusted her shoulders under her winter coat. The material hung in fluid lines over her curves to her midcalf. "May I come in?"

Ean stepped back. "I don't have any refreshments to offer you. I haven't made it to the grocery store yet."

Ramona strutted across the dining room. "It's kind of small."

Ean locked the back door. "It's bigger than your condo."

Ramona stopped in the center of the living room

and looked around. "It probably seems that way because you have two floors."

It seems that way because it's true. Ean followed her into the living room. "What are you doing here?"

Ramona turned to face him. "I brought you a housewarming present. Me."

She unbelted her coat and allowed it to fall to the ground. Ramona was barely clothed in matching skimpy, see-through smoky black bra and panties, that left nothing to the imagination. Her figure was even more enticing today than it had been seven years before. But Ean preferred to make love to the person, not the body. And Ramona didn't appeal to him as she once had.

Ean met her gaze. This was awkward. "I'm flattered by your offer, but no, thank you."

A myriad of reactions chased across Ramona's fair features—confusion, disbelief and shock—before she settled on anger.

"What?" Her octaves could peel the paint from the walls. "I'm not offering you cheese."

"I'm aware of that."

"I don't think you are." She twisted open the front clasp of her bra, then peeled the cups apart. Her creamy breasts bounced free. Ramona allowed the scrap of fabric to land silently on the ground.

"Put your clothes back on."

She stepped forward. "Make me."

Ean clamped his hands around her upper arms and held her still. "I'm not playing games, Ramona. You and I are through."

"No, we're not. You came back to Trinity Falls for me."

"No, I didn't." What made her think that?

"You may not realize it yet, but you did. I know you were lonely in New York. I never should have left you. But we can go back together and you won't be lonely anymore."

Ean stared at her. "Ramona, I don't know how you made those conclusions. I came back to Trinity Falls because it's my home and I'm staying here. If you want to move to a big city, talk with Quincy. He's interviewing for a job in Philadelphia."

"What is wrong with you?" Ramona ripped free of Ean's grasp. "Why are you throwing away everything that we had? Who cares about *Philadelphia*? We were going to make it big in *New York*."

Ean crossed his arms over his chest. "I've accomplished all I needed to in New York. If you'd like a shot at the city, be my guest. But I'm *not* going with you."

Her eyes flared with fury. "You don't have anything to keep you here. Your father's dead and your mother's sleeping with your high school football coach."

Ean hung onto his tattered temper with both hands. "Get dressed. And get out."

He held Ramona's glare with his own until she broke eye contact and snatched her coat off his carpet.

With stiff movements, Ramona put on the coat and belted it. "You're a fool."

"Are you done?" He couldn't take seriously criticism from a woman without the courage to go for her own dreams.

Ramona tightened the belt around her waist. "You'll never be happy here. You can't be. Trinity Falls couldn't hold you when you were eighteen. What makes you think you can come back to it now?"

When Ean didn't respond, Ramona shoved past him. The gesture didn't even rock him on his heels. He tracked Ramona's progress to his back door. She slammed the door so hard, he wondered it didn't crack the window beside it. With any luck, this would be his last awkward encounter with her. *And, hopefully, she'll set her sights on someone else.* Quincy might be just the calming influence she needed.

"It smells wonderful." Megan didn't try to hide her surprise. She leaned against one of the counters in Ean's kitchen, sipping iced tea with plenty of lemons, just the way she liked it.

"Thanks." Ean smiled over his shoulder. Her heart sighed.

"Are you sure you don't need any help?"

"I've got it."

Fine. Then she'd just enjoy the view, which was also very fine. Muscles moved across Ean's broad back under his black jersey as he stirred the pasta sauce. The image reminded her of the feel of his strength under her fingers last night.

Her gaze trailed down his back to his tight waist

and taut buttocks. Megan's palms itched at the memory of those hard muscles as well. Her study continued to his long, lean legs covered in coffee-colored khakis. Last night, she'd wrapped her limbs around his legs and drawn him tighter to her. She bit back a moan as those memories flooded her body. How would tonight end?

Megan took a long drink of her iced tea to ease her dry throat.

She wandered into the living room. "How's your unpacking going?"

"Faster than I'd thought." Ean's voice carried into the other room. "I'm ready to get on with my life now that I finally know what I'm doing."

That was Ean. He wasn't impulsive, but he'd always been impatient—to grow up, to move away, to move on. Was he really going to settle down in Trinity Falls? If so, with whom?

Megan crossed back into the dining room. "We'd love to have you as a member of the Trinity Falls Town Center Business Owners Association."

"Have you ever considered shortening that name?"

"If we did, would you join the group?"

"What does it do?" He measured spaghetti into the pot of boiling water.

Just the sight of his large hands brought back memories of last night. She sipped more iced tea. "We promote the town center, address its maintenance and resolve any other issues."

Ean turned away from the stove. "'Issues'? Like the town council putting the center on the market?"

She had his undivided attention. His olive eyes

regarded her with interest. It took a moment to collect her scattered thoughts. "And Ramona's plans to gentrify the center."

"How's she going to do that?" Ean's expression was part amusement, part confusion.

Megan spread her arms. "Even she doesn't know. But we're concerned for our businesses. We're also concerned for the town."

"Why?"

"If the council members change the character of the town center, what types of stores will they bring in? Will those stores still meet the town's needs?"

"Those are very good questions."

Megan waited for something more than Ean's verbal pat on the head. "Did you read Darius's article?"

"Yes." He took two dinner plates from an open packing box on the marble-tiled flooring to wash and dry them.

She swallowed her exasperation. "Do you agree that there's a cause for concern?"

"Definitely." Ean placed the plates on the counter beside the stove.

Megan waited. "And?"

"What?" Ean pulled silverware from another packed box and cleaned them.

Was he being deliberately obtuse? "Would you like to be a member of the business owners association?"

"Sure." Ean shrugged. "It sounds like an important group."

Megan shook her head and swallowed a laugh.

After all that prodding, Ean made the decision to join the business group seem like a no-brainer. They spent the rest of the pasta preparation talking about the association, Books & Bakery and the tasks Ean had to complete before officially opening his practice.

Their conversation continued through dinner. She helped him clear the table, but Ean insisted on loading the dishwasher and scrubbing the pots and pans himself.

Megan wandered over to his narrow maple wood bookcase and scanned the titles. "When did you develop an interest in biographies? You used to love science fiction."

"I like a lot of different genres—mysteries, classics, nonfiction. I still read sci-fi."

"No romance?"

He chuckled. "No."

Megan looked toward the doorway, surprised that Ean had approached without her hearing him. She pulled a book from one of the shelves. "Did you like *The Odyssey*?"

"Very much."

She returned the novel to the bookcase. "Then you enjoy romance."

He walked over to her and stood so close. "I never said I didn't *enjoy* romance."

His voice was low and rough and elicited a reaction from her she couldn't put into words. It was a feeling she'd never had before.

Megan swallowed to ease the tightness in her throat. "Can you take anything seriously?"

"Let's see." He lowered his mouth to hers.

Megan sighed. This was what she'd been waiting for all evening . . . all day. Her eyelids drifted closed and she inhaled deeply. Ean's scent—musk and soap—clouded her judgment. His taste thrilled her—pasta and spice. His corded arms wrapped around her, pulling her closer to his long, lean warmth. Megan was on sensory overload. She pressed even harder to Ean, pushing her breasts against his muscled chest.

Ean lifted his head, then trailed hot kisses down the side of her neck. "Is this serious enough for you?" His voice was a powerful aphrodisiac.

"Oh yes." Megan could barely breathe much less talk.

He chuckled deep in his throat. The sound vibrated down her body to her thighs. Megan traced his ear with her tongue, then bit its lobe. Ean's lips traveled farther down her neck. He licked her collarbone and Megan shivered from the inside out.

She tipped back her head and breathed slowly. Megan dragged her fingers across the vast expanse of his shoulders. Her nipples tightened as his heat burned her through his black jersey. She followed the rigid line of his spine, until she found the waistband of his khakis. She needed to feel his skin against hers, nothing in between them.

Megan tugged Ean's jersey from his pants and slipped her palms up his back. His muscles quivered beneath her touch. Her mouth went dry. Memories of last night made her damp and hot.

Ean swept her into his arms. Megan's eyes popped open as he carried her to the sofa in two long strides.

She looked up at his sharp, tense features. "I could have walked."

His gaze scorched her. "This was faster."

Ean toed off his shoes and lowered her to her feet. Megan stopped him before he moved them to the sofa. Wordlessly, she helped him pull off his jersey. The sight of his bare burnt sienna chest made her swallow. She trailed her fingers through the light layer of crisp hairs that covered his pecs and led into his waistband. Holding his gaze, Megan tugged off his belt and popped open the button of his pants.

Ean lay on the sofa, luring her down on top of him. Megan didn't take much coaxing. She was so hot—she could have burned to ashes. He drew her head down to his. Megan parted her lips for their kiss . . . but a deeper shadow on the beige carpet in front of the mahogany coffee table snatched her attention.

She pulled away from Ean. "What's that?" A warning stirred in the back of her mind.

"What?" Ean sounded as though he was still in the moment.

Megan stretched down to rescue the flimsy, see-through material. She straddled Ean as she held the bit of cloth in front of her. Megan had never seen the bra before, but she knew instantly to whom it belonged. Ean's expression of surprised dismay confirmed her fears.

"How could you?" Megan hadn't felt so inadequate since she'd been fourteen and had opened her bedroom door to find Ean and Ramona kissing in the hallway. She struggled to get away from him.

Ean clamped a hand on her left leg. "Megan, wait a—"

"Don't touch me." She snarled like a wounded wild animal and flung Ramona's bra in his face. Ean dropped his hand and she scrambled off him.

Ean rose to his feet beside her. "Megan, will you please wait a minute?"

She spun toward him. "You knew I didn't want to get involved with you until you broke up with Ramona."

"We have broken up."

"Really?" She snatched Ramona's bra from the carpet and shook it under his nose. "Then whose *bra* is this, and *how* did it end up beside the very same sofa on which we were *making love*?"

Ean cupped her fist. "I didn't invite her here. I didn't invite her to take off her clothes, either."

"Oh, my God." Megan wrenched her hand free. She spun on her heel and marched to the coat closet near the front door.

Ean followed her. "Megan, nothing happened."

"Oh, I'm sure." Megan closed her eyes and shook her head to rid her brain of the image of that bit-of-nothing black bra. "My cousin came to your townhome, took off her clothes in front of you, re-dressed, then left—*without anything happening*. But somehow she left her *bra* behind, right next to your sofa." She yanked open the closet door, shrugged into her coat and snatched her purse. "That sort of thing happens to *everyone. All the time.*"

Ean pressed the heel of his right hand against his front door seconds before Megan tugged on its doorknob. "I'm telling you the truth."

Megan stared at his large hand pressing against the door above her head. If only Ramona had kept her clothes on, Ean's hand could have been on her, instead. *It still could,* a voice whispered in her ear.

"Let me out."

A beat of silence passed before Ean dropped his hand. Megan pulled the door open, then shut it quietly behind her. She glanced down at herself to make sure her clothes were in order. That's when she realized she still clutched her cousin's bra. Megan jammed the underwear into her black handbag.

She strode to her Honda Accord, parked in front of Ean's town house. Megan strapped herself into the driver's seat and pulled away from Ean's home. She knew someone who was missing the bra's support. But she would wait until she'd calmed down before returning the lingerie to its rightful owner.

CHAPTER 19

Bright and early Saturday morning, Megan pounded on the front door of Ramona's condo, then leaned on the doorbell. She kept up the racket for a good seven minutes before her cousin finally answered her summons.

Ramona stood in the doorway, her right hand braced on the knob, the other pressed against the threshold. An ice pink silk robe wrapped her figure, baring her from midthigh. "What the hell is the matter with you?"

Megan plucked the flimsy black garment from her purse. She shook it out and waved it. "You left this behind."

Ramona gaped. She dragged Megan across the threshold with one hand and slammed the door shut with the other. "Have you lost your mind?" She snatched the bra from Megan and stuffed it into the pocket of her robe.

"No, but you've lost yours."

Ramona narrowed her eyes. "Well, listen to the little mouse roar."

Megan ignored the taunt. "Why did you take off your clothes for a man who has no interest in you?"

Ramona planted her fists on her hips. "Of course he's interested in me."

"Then why did he tell you to leave?"

Ramona's lips were tight with temper. "Aren't you full of questions? I have one. Where did you spend last night?"

"Alone in my bed, wondering why I was allowing you to hijack my happiness again." Megan shed her winter coat. Ramona had a penchant for keeping her thermostat at desert climes.

Ramona snorted. "*Hijack your happiness?* That's rich. The town may be buzzing about how much time he's spending with you, but Ean's not yours." She strutted barefoot across the white carpet and into the living room. "He may have returned to Trinity Falls, claiming that he's here to stay, but that doesn't mean you have what it takes to satisfy him any more today than you did when you were fourteen."

Ramona's words delivered a sucker punch to her self-confidence. Megan ignored it.

She slipped off her walking shoes and followed her cousin, still in attack mode. "Did you ever care for Ean? Or did you chase after him only because you knew I had a crush on him?"

Ramona spared Megan a disdainful look over her shoulder. "I've never chased after anyone. I've never had to."

"Did you ever care about him?"

"He was exciting, if you know what I mean." Ramona's grin was wicked. She settled onto her overstuffed white armchair and crossed her legs.

Megan did know what Ramona meant, and that enraged her. "You went after him because you knew I liked him. The same way you stole my toys and my clothes. Why?"

"Poor little orphan Megan. Our grandparents' favorite."

Ramona's words confused Megan. "Our grandparents didn't have favorites."

"Easy for you to say." Ramona's tone was dry. "You couldn't do anything wrong in their eyes. *Miss Perfect.*"

"Why do you say that?"

"You never got dirty, never stayed out past curfew, never did poorly in school."

"You chose to do those things. No one made you do them. But our grandparents still loved you."

"But I wasn't you, was I, Megan?"

"No, but you weren't orphaned, either. Both of your parents were alive." She hated reliving this painful past.

"But they didn't dote on me the way our grandparents doted on you." Ramona's tone was tense.

Was her cousin actually envious of her? She couldn't grasp that concept. Ramona had everything: career success, social success, confidence and beauty. Why would Ramona possibly envy her?

Megan sank onto the sofa. "Your Heritage High graduating class was right when they voted you most likely to succeed. You have a successful business *and* you're the town's mayor."

"But you're trying to turn the town against me." Ramona folded her arms.

"Because you're trying to put us out of business." Megan sighed. "We were never in competition, Ramona. I thought you realized that when you decided to stay with me after Grandpa died."

Ramona relaxed her arms and straightened in her chair. "You thought I stayed because of *you*?"

"We're the only family we have left. Why else would you stay here rather than go back to New York and Ean?"

"I don't have to explain myself to you." Ramona looked away.

"No, you don't. But you should at least understand the reason yourself. Why did you come home?"

Ramona's café au lait cheeks flushed. Her lips tightened. Megan remained still and quiet, waiting her out.

Finally Ramona crossed to the far side of the room, facing the fireplace. "I wasn't ready."

"For what?"

Ramona hesitated. "The demands of Ean's career. He was working all of the time. I barely saw him."

It sounded like a plausible explanation. Ean's career was very demanding. That was the reason he hadn't been able to come home more often or stay for longer visits. Still, something in Ramona's voice made Megan realize her cousin wasn't completely forthcoming.

"That didn't mean you had to leave New York."

Ramona turned to her. "I didn't have anyone else in the city."

"Neither did Ean."

Ramona shrugged a shoulder. "He survived."

Megan's lips curved in a slight smile, as proud as though she had a right to be. "He did more than survive. He thrived."

"And then he came home." She gave Megan a considering look. "Is there any truth to Quincy getting a job in Philadelphia?"

Megan's brows jumped up her forehead. "Why? Are you looking for another ticket to a big city?"

Ramona returned to the armchair. "I'm just curious."

Megan gave her a hard stare. "Ramona, don't play games with Quincy."

"What? Are you his mother?"

Megan stood. "You should know that some people are tired of your self-serving antics, including me. Ean made his choice and he chose me."

Ramona angled her head. "Are you actually color blind?"

Megan lowered her brows. "What?"

Ramona gestured toward Megan's outfit. "Your pantsuit is very nice. It flatters your figure. But that's a god-awful ugly color."

Megan spoke through clenched teeth. "Stop chasing after Ean. He's mine."

Megan left Ramona's condo feeling like the strong, assertive woman Ean saw whenever he looked at her. She should have drawn the line for her cousin years ago.

What was behind Ramona's crack about my clothes? Megan shelved the mystery for another time.

She exhaled as she climbed into her car. Guilt at the possibility Ramona had given up her life in New York to stay with her in Trinity Falls had made her the passive one in their relationship. Ramona claimed that wasn't the reason she'd stayed. Megan didn't believe her. Nevertheless, she was done being the doormat. Today she'd fought for her man. Tomorrow she'd fight for her bookstore.

CHAPTER 20

Later that day, Ramona paused outside of Quincy's office. He was right where his neighbor had said he would be when she'd gone to his town house first. Why was he working on a Saturday? She'd much rather have entertained him in her condo or his town house. Having this conversation in his office was the reason she was out of sorts. It wasn't because of nerves. Why should she be nervous? She was about to make Quincy's day—his year. Ramona patted her flowing brown hair into place again and adjusted her formfitting emerald dress.

She stepped into view and knocked on his open door. "Am I interrupting?"

Quincy eyed her with suspicion. He laid his pen and papers on his already cluttered desk. "Are you lost?"

Ramona forced a laugh. It cracked in the middle. "I guess I can't say I was in the neighborhood." She leaned a shoulder against the doorjamb with studied nonchalance. "It doesn't take long to get anywhere in this town, not even the college."

"It's a university, Ramona. We offer graduate courses here. You're an alumna. You should know that."

"That's right." Why did he always have to be so superior? "It was a slip of the tongue."

The silence grew brittle as Ramona searched for a better conversation topic. Quincy wasn't offering any help. The least he could do was stand. Chivalry was dead and six feet under the ground.

She stepped farther into his office and looked around. She'd never been here before. She didn't see much to talk about, though. Just a couple of bookcases crammed with stuffy books, a bulletin board littered with boring memos and the tiniest coffeemaker she'd ever seen.

She pointed at it. "Do you know how many pots I'd have to make with that, just to get through the afternoon?"

That comment earned her a smile that was gone in a blink. "Why are you here?"

Ramona spied his family photos beside a picture of the young Terrible Trio on a shelf above his desk. Inspiration struck. "How's your family?"

Quincy's coal black eyes narrowed. It was a good look on him, very virile. He often looked at her that way. "What do you want?"

It took Ramona a few seconds to shift her focus from his expression to his words. When she did, her anger stirred again. "I want to know how your family is doing."

"Cut the crap, Ramona. We've known each other for more than twenty-five years. When have you ever asked about my welfare or my family's well-being?"

He was a bit sarcastic, a little amused. She'd heard that tone from him before. But it had never seemed as naughty as it did today. What had changed? Her? Was she manufacturing an attraction to him to make her plan easier?

"I'm interested now." She couldn't help her defensive voice. Her mind was spinning too fast for a more sincere tone.

"Why?" He waited for her answer. When she didn't respond, he picked up the papers he'd been reading before she'd arrived. "I've got work to do, Ramona. Close the door on your way out."

He was serious!

Ramona stared at the top of Quincy's bent bald head. No one had ever dismissed her before. No one. In her entire life. But Quincy had the obnoxious habit of treating her unlike anyone else. He frequently disagreed with her. He challenged her. He chastised her—in front of other people. And now he was dismissing her.

She stood for several moments in uncharacteristic indecision. Their encounter wasn't supposed to happen this way. Quincy should have been surprised, happy and excited to see her—like other men were. He wasn't supposed to send her home. She needed to be more direct.

Ramona cleared her throat. "I've been meaning to ask if the rumors were true."

"What rumors?" His tone reeked of manly exasperation. Kind of cute.

"Ean told me that you'd interviewed for a faculty position with the University of Pennsylvania."

Quincy was silent for so long, she didn't think he'd heard her.

"He's right." Quincy's response was flat. Why wouldn't he look at her?

"Well, congratulations." She tried a trill of laughter. It sounded better than her first attempt. "We should celebrate."

"'We'?" That made him look up.

Ramona wanted to trace his arched brow. "Let me take you to dinner."

"Isn't that premature? They haven't offered me a job, only an interview."

Ramona dragged her hand through her hair, a nervous habit she still couldn't break. "But you know that they will. So you should celebrate this opportunity."

More silence. Quincy's dark gaze was steady and demanding on hers. "Why?"

Ramona's mouth opened and closed like a suffocating fish. Why was he making this so hard for her? "Because this is a momentous occasion. It's life changing. You're leaving Trinity Falls."

"That's the real reason you're here. Because you think I'm leaving town."

"Of course." Her cheeks stung with heat. "I'm going to miss you. Everyone will miss you. Really badly. I just want an opportunity to let you know that."

"Because we've meant so much to each other for so long."

"Yes." *Oh, God, is he buying this?*

"Bullshit."

That answered her question. But he didn't sound angry. Was he laughing at her? Again? "You don't believe me?"

Quincy lowered his papers and pen once more. "You've known for years how I feel about you, yet you never said a word to me. Do you expect me to believe that my leaving town just happens to coincide with your sudden attraction to my magnetic charisma and movie star good looks?"

He *was* laughing at her. His cheeks creased with his smile. His eyes danced with humor as he stared up at her from the seat behind his desk.

Ramona's palms itched with the urge to smack him, but she also was inexplicably turned on. "It's like you said, Quincy. We've known each other for a long time."

Surprisingly, she was telling the truth. They'd known each other since the first grade. Except for those years he'd spent away at college and graduate school, he'd been a fixture in this town. The town would feel his absence—including her. This all came as a surprise. How was she supposed to react to this?

Quincy leaned forward. "You probably thought your dinner invitation would make my day, if not my entire year."

Ramona's eyes stretched wide. Could he read her mind? "Of course not."

"Really?" Quincy sat back in his chair and crossed his arms. "What would you say if I told you I'd turn down the University of Pennsylvania if they offered me the position?"

"But you won't."

"I might. I'm kind of fond of Trinity Falls."

Ramona spread her arms. "What's keeping you here? Your parents and sister moved to Florida years ago. This is a wonderful career opportunity for you. It's more money, a bigger more prestigious university. Why wouldn't you go?"

"Trinity Falls is my home. I'm happy here." His smile drained from his eyes. "If you're unhappy, you should leave. But do it on your own. Stop attaching yourself to men's coattails."

Ramona gasped. "How dare you!"

"When you were eighteen, you hitched yourself to Ean's ride. Now you're thirty-two. Instead of making your own opportunities, you want to tag along with me. That's pathetic, Ramona."

"You're grossly mistaken." Ramona's temper snapped. "I wouldn't hitch myself to your ride, as you so crudely put it, if you were the last man on earth." She spun toward the door and strode across Quincy's office.

"Does this mean you won't be taking me to dinner?" Quincy's voice taunted her.

Ramona ground her teeth. Without breaking stride, she gave him the one-finger salute. Quincy's laughter followed her down the hall.

CHAPTER 21

"Shouldn't we wait until I'm open for business before you write about my practice?" Ean straightened from his crouch, allowing the tape measure feed to snap back into its case. He tried to ignore Darius as he recorded the measurement of his office's width.

His stomach growled again. It was almost 1 P.M. on Saturday, but he wanted to finish this last room before he and Darius broke for lunch.

"You'll be open in a couple of weeks." The reporter spoke from his perch on the office's bay window. "Besides, your practice will be old news if I wait until it opens. So quit the bullshit and give me a quote, asshole."

Surprised laughter burst from Ean. "Do you get a lot of interviews with that attitude?"

Darius gave him a reluctant smile. "This article will be free publicity for you, man. What's the problem?"

"It's easier to talk about cases than myself."

Ean crouched again. This time, he measured the room's length. "What do you want me to say?"

"Just answer my questions—"

"First answer mine." Quincy's voice interrupted them.

Ean rose, turning to face the university professor. He ignored the temper snapping in Quincy's eyes. "Hey, Q. What brings you to my humble office?"

Quincy stepped forward. "Why did you tell Ramona that I'm going to Philadelphia?"

"Because you are," Darius answered. "Penn is going to offer you its faculty position. If you're smart, which you are, you'll accept it."

Quincy scowled at the reporter before meeting Ean's eyes again. "Were you trying to set me up with Ramona?"

Darius laughed. "Ean wouldn't do that."

Ean spoke over the other man. "Yes, I was."

"What? W-why?" Darius stuttered.

"Because he's the great Ean Fever." Quincy sounded as though he was chewing glass. "No one measures up to him. He's too damn perfect. He has no choice but to help us mere mortals because we could never be as perfect as he is."

"Quincy, you know damn well that's not what I was thinking." Ean pulled a hand through his close-cropped hair.

"Grow up, Q." Darius turned to Ean. "Dude, what were you on?"

Ean cast his gaze around the freshly painted white walls before meeting Quincy's snapping eyes. "Ramona and I broke up six years ago. You had all that time to make your move. Why didn't you? Are you that big of a coward?"

Quincy's scowl darkened. "Who the hell do you think you are?"

"Your friend."

Darius rose from the bay window ledge and put a hand on Quincy's shoulder. "Only a friend would tell you the truth. And the truth is, Q, you've been a gutless wonder with Ramona. I should have told you that six years ago."

Quincy shrugged Darius's hand from his shoulder. "You're one to talk. Do you think people don't realize why you sneak over to the next town every weekend? You're dating some woman over there because you don't want her to meet your family."

Darius's expression tightened. "You'd hide your dates, too, if you had my family."

Quincy lowered his head and braced his hands on his hips. "I'm sorry, man. That was uncalled for."

Darius shook his head. "No harm, no foul, brother."

"So what's the problem, Quincy?" Ean crossed his arms over his chest. "Why haven't you tried to get something going with Ramona?"

Quincy paced the empty room, from the bay window past Darius and Ean, to the far wall and back. His movements were stiff and abrupt, as though he was debating with himself.

The professor finally stopped in front of the window, his back to the room. "I don't like to lose."

"Who does?" Ean glanced at Darius. What did that have to do with anything?

The former running back turned from the view outside the office and held Ean's eyes. "If Ramona turned me down, it would mean that you won and I lost."

"Ramona isn't a trophy we're competing for." Ean's voice snapped.

Darius scratched his chin. "I thought you liked Ramona."

"I love her." Quincy spoke as though forcing out the words.

Darius's frown deepened. "If you love her, ask her out."

The conflict in Quincy's eyes added to Ean's frustration. "In your mind, you've worked me into this perfect person who's really popular and never wrong. I don't know where that came from."

Darius shrugged. "It's bullshit."

Ean spared the former tight end a glance but otherwise ignored him. "It's not true. I don't even see myself that way."

Darius shook his head. "Neither do I."

"Ask her out." Ean clamped a hand on Quincy's shoulder. "Even if she says no, you wouldn't have lost."

Quincy snorted and turned away. "That's what you think."

His friend's reluctance was a wall Ean couldn't break through. "How do you know if she could love you if you don't give her a chance?"

Quincy quirked a brow. "Since you told her I'm

leaving Trinity Falls, how do I know whether she loves me or the idea of moving to Philadelphia?"

Good question.

Ean exhaled as memories returned. "When Ramona left New York, I realized she never loved me. She loved the dream of living in New York. I was just a part of that dream."

Quincy pulled his hands over his clean-shaven head. "Why did you tell her about the Penn interview?"

"Let it go, Q." Darius leaned back against the bay window's ledge. "This is Trinity Falls. It's not like she wasn't going to find out."

"Philadelphia gives you an in with her." Ean propped his shoulder against the room's far wall.

Quincy grunted. "New York didn't help you keep Ramona."

Ean shrugged. "I didn't love her, either. We were too much alike, like brother and sister."

Darius looked closely at Ean, as though seeing him from another perspective. "I'd never thought of that."

Ean hadn't, either, not until Megan had pointed it out—Megan, who'd stormed from his town house Friday night. What would it take to convince her he hadn't slept with her cousin?

Darius turned to Quincy. "Ean's right. Use Philly to get Ramona's attention. What do you have to lose?"

"Everything." Quincy's answer was bleak.

"If you love her, it's worth the risk, Q." Ean spoke

from the heart. He was just beginning to realize he was falling fast and hard for Megan McCloud.

As though his thoughts had conjured her, Megan appeared in the office doorway, cradling a potted plant. She wore blue jeans and a black jersey, with the image of a green bookworm reading a brown book.

She smiled and the room was warmer, brighter. Her laughing eyes moved from Ean to Quincy to Darius on the far side of the office. "You guys look so serious."

Darius stood away from the window. "Quincy and I were just leaving."

Quincy looked startled. "No, we weren't."

Darius placed a hand on his friend's back and propelled him forward. "Are you sure you have an advanced degree?"

"Why are you always questioning that?" Quincy's voice carried a wealth of irritation.

Their quarrelsome exchange faded as they left the office suite.

Ean sighed. "They're like grouchy old men. I'd forgotten that."

Megan turned away from the door. "I think you're all like brothers."

Indeed, they were. They didn't have real brothers. Darius and Ean were only children, and Quincy had an older sister.

Ean held his breath as their eyes met. "You haven't returned my calls."

Why had he said that? He sounded like a sulky

child. Not the image he wanted to project to the person with whom he was falling in love.

Megan came closer. "I'm sorry. I reacted . . . just reacted yesterday. After I calmed down, I knew you were telling me the truth."

"How?" Ean glanced at the plant—bamboo shoots—before looking into her melted-chocolate eyes again.

Megan drew her right hand through her dark hair. "You wouldn't have made love to me if you were still attracted to Ramona."

Ean felt as though she'd kissed him full on his mouth. He licked his lips. The movement drew Megan's gaze. Her eyes darkened. Ean's body heated.

He pushed away from the wall and came closer to her. He brushed her hair back, smoothing the wavy locks she'd tousled. The pulse in the base of her neck fluttered like a hummingbird. His fingers itched to touch it.

Ean inclined his head toward the potted plant she held. "What's that?"

Megan blinked down at her arms as though she'd forgotten she was carrying anything. "Bamboo shoots." She extended the plant toward him. "They're an office-warming gift for you."

"Thank you." Ean accepted the gift. He examined the simple pale green ceramic planter, which held the four leafy stalks.

"Sure." Megan cleared her throat. "You're welcome."

"No one's ever bought me a potted plant before."

Ean carried the planter to the bay window. He placed it on the center of the ledge and stepped back to look at it. It seemed lost on the shelf by itself.

"They're for good luck."

Ean laughed. "I can use some of that."

"You don't have anything to worry about. You're going to be a success."

"I hope so." Ean faced Megan. His gaze dropped to the image of the somber-faced bookworm on her T-shirt. It's head rested against her breasts. Lucky bookworm. "This practice was Ms. Helen's idea."

Megan chuckled. "Then you know it will succeed."

Ean slipped his hands into the front pockets of his blue jeans. "How does she know so much about what's happening in Trinity Falls? I've never seen her leave that porch."

"She makes it into the bookstore now and again." Megan wandered the office, seemingly engrossed in the nothingness all around them. "I returned Ramona's bra to her this morning."

Ean raised his brows. "How did that go?"

"About as well as you'd imagine. She didn't appreciate my confronting her."

Ean crossed his arms over his chest. "She's not used to you standing up to her."

"*I'm* not used to my standing up to her." Megan laughed.

"Then why did you?"

Megan stared out the bay window. "I was tired.

Tired of her bullying me, pushing me around and taking what I wanted."

Ean's heart skipped. "Me?"

Megan met his gaze over her shoulder. "Yes. I wasn't going to let her take you from me."

His heart sped up. "What did she say?"

"She seems to think I don't have a prayer of holding on to you."

Surprised laughter burst from Ean's throat. "She's wrong."

A playful smile curved Megan's generous lips. "That's nice to hear. She also asked about Quincy moving to Philadelphia."

"What did you say?"

"I thought that was a strange question." Megan faced him. A look of suspicion sparked in her eyes. "Do you know anything about her sudden interest in Quincy's plans?"

"I might, but I'll let Quincy tell you about it."

Megan's eyes stretched wide with amazement. "Ean Fever, you're playing matchmaker. I never imagined you as a romantic."

"Maybe you're changing me." Ean stepped closer to her.

She laughed. "I'm not a romantic."

"Then maybe we're changing each other." He drew her into his arms.

Megan tilted her head and searched his eyes. "For the better, I hope."

"Would either of us have it any other way?"

CHAPTER 22

Megan surveyed the packed assembly hall as yet another Tuesday-night town council meeting came to an end. She shifted closer to Ean and lowered her voice to a whisper. "There are even more people here tonight than usual. It's surprising this close to Thanksgiving."

The room teemed with town center business owners and their families, and neighbors who hadn't attended a council meeting in at least four years.

Ean whispered back. "Makes you wonder if they're here for the issues, or because they expect you and Ramona to give them a show."

Megan's stomach muscles knotted. "Thanks a lot."

"Just wondering."

Town council president CeCe Roben banged her gavel for attention. Her pale blue eyes watched Megan as she addressed the audience. "Are there any questions or statements from the public?"

A murmur rippled through the audience. Megan returned the other woman's gaze without shrinking. Ean was probably right. Her neighbors were expecting a show. She wasn't looking to accommodate them, but she couldn't speak for Ramona.

Megan strode to the podium. Her knees were solid. Her pulse was steady. She'd found the confidence to confront Ramona about Ean. Facing her now to protect Books & Bakery and the Trinity Falls Town Center was a breeze in comparison.

She squared her shoulders and looked Ramona in the eye. "Mayor, the members of the Trinity Falls Town Center Business Owners Association are still waiting for details regarding your plans for the center and future businesses."

Megan ignored the murmurings around the assembly room, as well as Ramona's cold stare. Other members of the association, including Ean, were behind her, literally and figuratively. The cause uniting them was too important. She wouldn't back down. She wouldn't let them back down, either.

Ramona pulled her microphone closer. "The idea for the upgrade isn't just mine. It's also the idea of the entire council."

Megan doubted that. She studied the uneasy council members seated around tables arranged in a U-shape. One by one, their eyes shifted away from her.

She returned her attention to Ramona. "What's your goal in searching for a high-end real estate broker?"

Ramona folded her arms on the table. "You

don't expect us to locate individual businesses, do you? We're putting out an announcement for an individual broker who will attract the right businesses for us."

A chunk of ice the size of a fist settled in Megan's gut. So her cousin really was moving forward with her plan, even though it would destroy the bookstore, which had been in their family for generations.

The audience's murmurings were a distracting buzz in Megan's ears. "When?"

"We don't have an exact timetable, but we're intending to fast-track the bids."

"Why are you doing this?" The question shot from Megan's lips before she'd realized she was going to ask it.

Ramona smoothed her salon-styled hair. "This was a decision the council made in consideration of the best interests of the town."

"Exactly how will this benefit Trinity Falls?"

Ramona's gaze wavered. "Being able to offer trendier shops will raise the town's profile and attract more tourists."

Megan frowned her confusion. "To shop? When people plan shopping vacations, they think of New York, Chicago, Los Angeles. Not Trinity Falls, Ohio."

Ramona looked down her nose at Megan. "They would consider the town if we had the shops."

"You can't be serious." Megan shook her head. "You don't really have a plan for bringing upscale businesses to Trinity Falls, do you?"

"Of course I do."

"We're waiting to hear it." Megan gestured to include the residents in the audience.

Ramona smoothed her hair again. "The town needs to change with the times."

"Our businesses are thriving. Obviously, the community sees a need for us."

Ramona jerked her head toward the council members. "The community elected us to represent their interests. We've decided it's in the town's interest to bring in new, trendy stores."

Megan felt her blood boil. "Trinity Falls isn't a room you can redecorate on a whim. It's a community of people. The town center businesses are vital to this community."

She looked over her shoulder at the center's business owners: Grady Weatherington, Belinda Curby, Vernon Fox, Tilda Maddox and Ean. She'd known these people all of her life. She'd shared their struggles and triumphs, just as they'd shared hers and her family's.

Her gaze met Ean's. Was that admiration in his eyes? With that look, he'd given her a much-needed boost of energy.

She faced the council and Ramona again. "We organize annual fund-raisers for school supplies and college scholarships. I benefited from one of those scholarships. You did as well, didn't you, Councilwoman Roben?"

CeCe smiled. "Indeed, I did."

Megan continued. "We've also led the charge when the elementary school needed money for renovations and computers, as well as when the local clinic needed medical equipment. Would chain businesses without ties to this community have that same commitment?"

A rumbling chorus of agreement rose behind Megan like an unstoppable wave.

Ramona banged the gavel as she glowered at the audience. "Quiet! Any more disruptions and the meeting will come to an end."

Megan stared down her cousin. "Give us answers, Mayor."

"I've given you answers." Ramona's response was brittle.

"And we've given you ours. We won't sit on our hands as you bring New York lite to Trinity Falls."

The reaction of the audience was even louder this time—cheers, applause and foot stomping.

Ramona banged her gavel again. "I warned you, didn't I? I warned you. This meeting is now adjourned."

Megan watched her cousin push away from the table and stalk from the assembly room via the rear exit. She returned to her seat to collect her handbag and coat. The hand that came to rest on her arm was Ean's. She'd know his touch forever.

Ean's palm slid from her shoulder to cup her elbow. "You were fantastic."

Megan shook her head, nearly shaking with frustration. "No, I wasn't."

"The crowd disagrees with you. Did you hear them?"

"I didn't get any answers. Instead, I brought the meeting to an end." Megan blew out a breath.

"Ramona ended the meeting because she couldn't handle you." He used his hold on her arm to draw her closer to him and away from pedestrian traffic.

Darius shoved his pen and reporter's notebook into his backpack. "Ean's right. You had her on the ropes. This will make the front page of tomorrow's *Monitor.*"

"Great." Megan's sarcasm was a mask for her unsettled nerves.

"I'm impressed." Ean's grin lent a mischievous light to his olive eyes. "You're a natural leader."

She blinked at him. "I don't know about that, but you might be onto something. Maybe what we need is a better leader."

Darius arched a brow at her. "What do—"

"Excuse me, Megan." CeCe Roben's voice interrupted them.

Megan gave her a questioning look. "CeCe, are you sure you're allowed to fraternize with the enemy?"

CeCe's chuckle sounded uncomfortable. "I don't think of you as the enemy, Megan. I hope you don't consider me one, either."

Megan faced the councilwoman. She took a moment to regret the loss of Ean's touch as his warmth dropped from her elbow. "You and the rest of the council are threatening my livelihood. How am I supposed to consider you?"

"I don't agree with Ramona's plan. I'm not the only council member who feels that way, either." CeCe looked around as though searching for someone in the crowd. Was she worried Ramona had reentered the room?

CeCe's confession didn't make Megan feel better. "We elected you to represent *our* interests, CeCe, not to cave in to Ramona's demands."

"It's not that easy." CeCe's blue eyes searched for understanding.

Megan didn't give her any. "Why not?"

"Ramona is socially connected. If we cross her, she could use her connections to hurt our careers."

"If you disagree with Ramona's direction for Trinity Falls, why don't you run against her?"

CeCe looked horrified. A blush warmed her translucent skin. "I couldn't do that, Megan. I need my job. Serving on the council doesn't pay enough to support me and my family. I'm truly sorry."

Megan watched CeCe walk away. "I'm ashamed to admit that I understand CeCe's reluctance to stand up to Ramona."

Darius grunted. "So do I. She can be a bitch when you cross her."

Ean helped Megan with her coat. "You found the courage to break the story about her plans for the center."

Darius feigned a nervous shiver. "And I needed Quincy's protection from her wrath."

Megan settled the strap of her black purse onto her shoulder. "Ramona's term is up next year. Maybe we can find someone to run against her."

"Why don't you?" Ean took her elbow to escort her from the hall.

Megan almost tripped over her feet. "Me?"

Ean steadied her. "Like I said, you're a natural leader."

She'd never considered herself a leader. She'd found the courage to push back against Ramona's bullying. But leading a town? Was that something she could do? Was it something she wanted to do?

Tension was an uninvited guest seated at the tables with the Trinity Falls Town Center Business Owners Association members the Wednesday night before Thanksgiving. Megan had expected their unease after last night's council meeting.

She opened her mouth to start the discussion, but Tilda forestalled her with her question for Ean.

"How much are you paying in rent for your office space?" The elderly owner of Gifts and Greetings pinned Ean with a shrewd look from her sharp gray eyes.

Megan stiffened at the older woman's tone. This was Ean's first meeting. But his wasn't one of the new businesses Ramona wanted to bring in. Did the other members realize that?

"Tilda, that is so rude." Belinda drank some coffee. The voluptuous owner of the Skin Deep Beauty Salon had almost choked on a bite of biscotti at Tilda's question. She'd selected the pastry from the snacks Megan and Doreen had provided from the association's petty cash fund.

"Why?" Tilda's frown deepened the fine lines on her thin pale face. "He has the newest lease among us. If we don't ask, how will we know whether they're raising the rents on the stores?"

"She's right." Grady Weatherington, owner of Fine Accessories, cast a dubious eye toward the biscotti. He picked up a chocolate chip cookie instead and pointed it toward Ean. "What are you paying?"

Ean named a figure that made Grady cough. Megan caught her breath.

Vernon Fox's bushy brows shot to his thinning red hairline. "I guess that answers the question of whether they're going to raise our rents. They are." The owner of Are You Nuts?, the nuts and candy store, lowered his coffee mug.

Ean exchanged a concerned look with Doreen. "I hadn't realized the rent was higher than what everyone else was paying."

Doreen waved a dismissive hand. "How could you know that?"

Vernon turned to Megan. "I can't afford to pay a higher rent."

"None of us can." Belinda pushed her perfectly styled raven hair from her forehead with her well-manicured mahogany fingers. "Can't you talk to Ramona?"

Megan shook her head. One more worry to add to the list. "You were there last night, Belinda. You heard how Ramona reacted to my attempts to reason with her."

Belinda waved her biscotti. "I don't mean as business owner to mayor. I mean as cousin to cousin. Use the bookstore's roots to appeal to her. They were her grandparents, too."

Megan squelched her frustration. "I've tried that. Ramona's not going to give me special treatment just because we're cousins."

Tilda grunted. "There is no reasoning with Ramona. She's a soulless bitch."

"No, she's not." Megan pinned Tilda with a look. Regardless of how angry she made Megan, Ramona was still family. "Ramona's goals are different from ours. Since we're unable to change her mind, I think it's time we try to get another mayor elected."

Doreen tapped the table with her fingertips. "That's a great idea. Make her a one-term mayor."

"Who are you going to get to run against her?" Grady cast his gaze around the table as though prodding the other members' memories. "That's how she got elected the first time, remember? And that's how the mayor before her got elected. Twice. No one ran against them."

Ean glanced at Megan before turning to the others. "I think Megan would make a great mayor."

Megan's stomach dropped. "No, I wouldn't."

Tilda gestured toward her. "See? You won't even run against her."

"She's my cousin." Why had Ean brought this up?

"Why are you giving her special treatment?" Tilda mocked Megan's earlier words.

Megan looked at each member in turn. "I'm not a leader—"

Ean interrupted her. "Yes, you are. You've taken the lead on this issue with the center."

Megan spoke in a firm tone. "This is the first time I've ever been active on a government issue. I can lead an organization. I can run a business. But leading a town, balancing the needs of hundreds of people within a budget, is a completely different set of skills. We have to find someone else."

"I don't know who." Doreen sounded disappointed.

Megan blinked. Doreen had been active in community organizations all of Megan's life. Had their future mayor been sitting among them this entire time?

CHAPTER 23

The bell above the front door to Ean's business suite chimed Monday afternoon. He straightened from the box of office supplies he was transferring into his supply closet and stepped into the hallway. He froze when he saw Leonard George standing in his waiting area.

"Your office looks good." The older man shoved his hands into the pockets of his winter coat as he glanced around.

"Thanks." Ean had arranged a couple of chairs and a corner table with current magazines in the waiting area.

Leonard met Ean's eyes. "Are you busy?"

They'd just spent Thanksgiving together. What did Leonard want now? Ean glanced over his shoulder toward the supply closet. He resisted the temptation to further delay their conversation. Coach George had always been persistent.

Ean gestured Leonard into his office and followed him. "It can wait."

Leonard settled into one of the black leather chairs in front of the large mahogany desk. "I like this furniture."

"Thanks." Ean circled his desk and lowered himself into the matching executive chair.

He sensed the other man's discomfort, which meant they had something in common besides affection for his mother. Neither of them wanted this meeting.

Leonard's shoulders lifted and settled in a deep breath. "I care about your mother."

"I know." Ean's tension rose in the beat of silence that followed his response.

"I mean . . . I'm not . . . using her."

Ean really didn't want to have this conversation. "My mother wouldn't allow anyone to use her."

Leonard gave in to a short laugh. "That's true. It's one of the things I admire about her. Dorie is a strong woman."

Dorie. Ean cringed on the inside. "Yes, she is."

Leonard shifted in the visitor's chair. "Look, Ean, I know you're not happy about my dating your mother. I don't understand why. I'm not trying to replace your father. You just said you know I'm not using your mother. Then what is it?"

Ean studied his high school football coach while he tried to put his feelings into words. "I'm having trouble adjusting to the change in your relationship with my mother."

"Is that really the problem, or are you wondering whether your mother and I were together even before your father died?"

Ean tightened his grip on the arms of his chair. His former coach was coming too close to the line. "My parents loved each other very much. Neither would ever have been unfaithful to the other."

"But you didn't know how sick your father was or for how long. It's natural to wonder what else you didn't know."

It was a struggle to control his temper. "Maybe *you'd* wonder, but I don't have to."

"Then what would it take for you to accept my relationship with your mother?"

Ean wanted to rewrite the past to prevent this relationship from ever coming to fruition. But that wasn't possible. Barring that, "Time. I need time to adjust to my mother's new life."

The chime distracted Ean from the anger boiling in his blood. He rose from his chair when Megan moved into his office doorway.

Her smile faltered when she saw Leonard seated across from Ean. "I'm sorry. I didn't mean to interrupt."

Leonard stood. "Don't worry, Megan. I was just leaving."

Megan sent a look at Ean—part concern, part accusation—before returning her attention to Leonard. "Please don't leave on my account, Coach. I'll come back later."

"No, it's fine." Leonard turned back to Ean. "I'm glad we cleared that up, Ean. I'll see you later."

Megan frowned at Ean again as she switched

places with Leonard. "Coach, I know a lovely lady who's free for lunch."

Leonard paused in the threshold. A grin brightened his still-youthful features. "That's good to know. It was nice talking with you, Ean."

He hadn't enjoyed their conversation and couldn't bring himself to lie. "I'll see you around, Coach."

Megan sank into the seat Leonard had vacated and started unpacking the picnic basket. The chime of the bell above the front door as Leonard left seemed to loosen her tongue. "Your mother likes Leo. That alone should convince you to be nice to him."

"Why do you think I wasn't being nice?"

Ean looked at the food she was unpacking. All healthy stuff—salad, fruit, soup and what appeared to be chicken sandwiches—without cheese or mayonnaise. Who ate like that?

"When I arrived, I could cut the tension in your office with a knife." She lifted two cartons of plain milk onto the table.

Plain milk. Ean smothered a groan. "I'm not used to my mother having a boyfriend."

Megan closed the picnic basket and looked him in the eye. "She has a boyfriend. Get used to it."

Ean fought a smile. She was delicate on the outside, but a bully on the inside. "I'm trying."

Her fierce expression eased slightly. "Coach was a very good friend when Doreen needed one."

Ean's humor faded. "I should have been here when she needed someone."

Megan stood, circled Ean's desk and settled onto his lap. She twined her arms around his neck. "You're here for her now. She's still adjusting to her life without your father. She'll need your encouragement and support."

"She'll have it."

"I'm still trying to figure out my next step." His mother's words made him think of his own future. He knew his next step. But would the woman sitting on his lap be willing to take it with him?

CHAPTER 24

Ean left Books & Bakery on Wednesday morning after breakfast with Megan, his mother, Quincy and Darius. A smile lingered on his lips. Brisk strides carried him through the cold December wind that was blowing across the town center's courtyard. His smile faded and his pace slowed when he saw Ramona waiting in front of his law office.

She balanced on navy leather stiletto boots. Her faux-fur coat covered her from neck to midthigh. Her teased raven tresses danced in the wind.

A glance at his bronze Omega wristwatch showed nine o'clock. This couldn't be good. "Isn't this early for you?"

Ramona ignored his question. "So you're a member of the town's business association now."

He was right. This wasn't going to be good.

Ean pulled his keys from his jeans pocket and gestured toward his office door. "I suppose you want to come in."

"That would be very gracious of you." Ramona's

gloved hand clutched the high collar of her coat closer to her neck.

Ean led her into his office and waved her toward the same black leather visitor's chair Leonard and Megan had used two days previously.

"What's on your mind?" Might as well get to the point. Ean shrugged off his fleece winter jacket and hooked it onto the coatrack.

Ramona handed him her coat before settling into the seat. "You can't possibly agree with Megan's plan to allow the center to stagnate."

"It's not stagnating." Ean sank into his executive chair and propped his elbows on the armrests.

Ramona flung an arm toward the bay window. The view overlooked the center's courtyard. "The same businesses have been in this center since we were in elementary school."

"They've continued to thrive and meet Trinity Falls's needs. That's something to be proud of."

Ramona crossed her legs, smoothing the skirt of her navy blue power suit. "This center could be so much more. The town's people deserve so much more. And I want you to help me get it for them."

"Get what for them?"

"I want to modernize the entire town, not just the center. Think about it." Her face glowed and her voice sang with enthusiasm. "If Trinity Falls were more sophisticated, I wouldn't have to move to New York. I could stay here with you, and we could become the town's power couple."

Ean didn't want any part of her plans. "I like Trinity Falls the way it is."

"It can be better." Ramona was insistent.

"Has anyone asked you to change the town's shopping options?"

"No, but—"

"Then it's only your opinion that the center needs more sophisticated shops."

"Yes, but—"

"Your opinion isn't the only one that matters."

"Would you stop interrupting me?" Ramona snapped the command. "People don't understand what they're missing. Not everyone has lived in New York like we have. When they see the sophisticated, trendy shops we bring in, they'll be so much happier."

"What about the businesses you'll be displacing? What about your family's bookstore?"

"It's called 'progress,' Ean."

"Not to the center's business owners." Ean stood as his irritation rose. "I have a lot of work to do today."

Ramona looked up at him, stunned. "You're not going to help me?"

"No, I'm not." Ean crossed his arms over his chest. "Nor will I be one half of your power couple. I'm already in a relationship with Megan."

Ramona stood. Her surprise morphed to deep displeasure. "You're compounding one mistake with another. With my connections, I can make or break your practice."

Ean's lips curved in dark amusement. "I'll do fine on my own."

"Go ahead. Laugh." Her voice was ragged as she

glowered at him. "You're standing in the way of progress. When it runs right over you, we'll see who laughs last."

Ramona spun on her heels, snatched her coat from his coatrack and stomped from his office.

The slamming of his front door sounded like a cannon blast from the opening salvo of a battle—loud, long and threatening. Ean returned to his seat.

Ramona was determined to change the business makeup of the town center. The business association appeared to have two choices: elect a new mayor or buy the center from the town. They were running out of time for the first, and they didn't have money for the second. Was there a third option?

CHAPTER 25

Later that afternoon, Ean looked up from reading *The Trinity Falls Monitor* while waiting to have lunch with Megan at Books & Bakery.

Tilda and Belinda settled into the table beside him before Tilda spoke. "Saw Ramona leaving your office this morning. What was she doing there?"

In his peripheral vision, Ean saw Megan enter the bakery section of the bookstore. The other women weren't aware of her approach.

He took in the pugnacious angle of Tilda's chin and the suspicion in her gray eyes. "You sound as though you already know the answer."

Tilda laughed without humor. "Going to play that game, huh? Well, I'll tell you what I think. I think you're in cahoots with her. I think you're helping her to undermine the rest of us."

Megan came up behind the older woman and took the chair beside Ean. "Why would he do that?"

Tilda's expression remained combative. "Ramona

and Ean have hated our small-town ways since they were kids."

He couldn't let that comment go unchallenged. "I never hated Trinity Falls. I was born here. I grew up here. At the time, I thought I wanted more than the town had to offer. Now I realize it has everything I'll ever need." Including the woman he was falling deeper in love with every day.

Tilda's rough voice cut across his realization. "You came back to Trinity Falls with your New York ways. Now suddenly Ramona wants to bring big-city stores to the center. That can't be a coincidence."

"This isn't sudden." Megan's voice was cool and measured, but Ean sensed her tension. "I have a feeling Ramona started planning this the moment the original center owners defaulted on the loan."

Belinda flipped her glossy mane behind her shoulder. "I agree. Ramona's crafty that way. And we never saw it coming. That's a kick."

"Then why was Ramona in his office this morning?" Tilda pointed at Ean. Her voice reeked of spite. "Rekindling old flames?" The old woman was determined to cause trouble.

Ean struggled to match Megan's cool. "You're right, Tilda. Ramona did ask for my help with her plans for the center—"

Tilda sprang from her chair. "You see? I told you!"

Ean ignored her interruption. "I turned her down. I also told her, I wasn't interested in being the town's power couple with her." He couldn't read the look in Megan's eyes.

"'Power couple'?" Belinda blew out a breath. "Girlfriend has a lot of balls. No offense intended, Megan."

Megan's inscrutable gaze remained on Ean. "Thank you for letting us know about your conversation with her."

Tilda reclaimed her seat. "How do we know we can trust him?"

Megan experienced another stir of irritation. Tilda's negativity had hindered the association almost since Megan had formed the group.

"Ramona has been in all of our stores. Should we start suspecting each other?" She gestured toward Belinda. "Are we going to question Belinda whenever Ramona buys a product from her salon?" She inclined her head toward Tilda. "Should we worry about you whenever Ramona buys a birthday card?"

Tilda scowled. "I've lived my whole life in this town."

Megan's voice hardened. "Ean wouldn't sign a long-term lease and pay exorbitant rent just to help Ramona take apart the town center."

Tilda gave Megan a grudging look. "I suppose you have a point."

Megan was more than happy to change the topic. "Instead of wasting our time suspecting each other, we have to identify a candidate to run against Ramona in the next election. That person has to register in two weeks."

Belinda waved a mahogany hand between Megan and Ean. "Why don't one of you run?"

Megan looked at Ean. "What about it?" She liked

the idea of Ean as mayor. For one thing, it meant she'd know how long he would stay in town. "With your legal background, you'd be a strong candidate."

Ean was shaking his head even before Megan finished speaking. "I'm starting a law practice. It's going to take all of my time to get it off the ground."

Megan looked away to mask her disappointment. Was his business the only reason Ean wouldn't run for office?

"What about you, Megan?" Tilda's tone made the question an accusation. "You started the association. You'd be the best person to represent our interests to the council."

Megan glanced over her shoulder toward the bakery's counter, where Doreen shared a pastry with Leonard. "The mayor needs to represent all of the town's interests, not just the association's. We need a candidate who can speak intelligently to all of the community's needs."

"Who would that be?" Tilda sounded frustrated.

Megan turned back to the group. "I can think of one or two people."

"Who?" Ean sounded intrigued.

Megan shook her head. "Let me speak with them first."

She suspected Ean wouldn't support her idea, but she couldn't allow that to dissuade her. The candidate to run against Ramona for mayor was about more than Ean. It was about the good of Trinity Falls—and, maybe, the good of the candidate.

* * *

Quincy adjusted his hold on the Trinity Falls Cuisine take-out bags and waited for Ramona to open her front door. When she did, Quincy had to remind himself to breathe. She always looked so beautiful. Like art. Just being near her disrupted his complex and noncomplex brain functions.

As usual, Ramona looked ready for a fashion photo session. Tonight she wore a long-sleeved bronze jersey, which flowed over her sensuous curves. Her black skinny pants showcased her dancer's long legs. His eyes traced the limbs to her bare feet, accented with bronze toenail polish the exact color of her jersey.

"I asked, what are you doing here?" Ramona's ebony eyes twinkled with humor.

She'd had to repeat herself. Quincy battled back a blush. Thirty-two-year-old men should never blush. "You offered to help me celebrate the possibility of my new job."

Ramona's smile broke free. She crossed her arms and cocked her right hip. "And you turned me down."

Keep breathing. Start talking. Don't stare. "I changed my mind." He nodded toward the paper bags in his arms.

Ramona's arched brows lifted. "You brought me takeout from the Trinity Falls Cuisine?"

"That depends. Are you going to invite me in?"

Her cheeks flushed beneath her perfect makeup. Ramona stepped back. "Of course."

Quincy had never been to her home. He crossed the threshold and entered a world of perfect white. He hesitated, then toed off his shoes, using his feet to tuck them into a corner together. "Nice place."

Ramona watched his movements with an approving expression. Quincy's confidence increased. He peeked into the rooms they passed as he followed her down the hallway to her kitchen. It didn't strike him as an accidental oversight that Ramona, the granddaughter of bookstore owners, didn't have a single bookcase in her home.

"What made you change your mind about celebrating with me?" Ramona stood too close to him as he unpacked the bags, placing the covered to-go dishes and plastic ware on the dining-room table.

It was scary, feeling this vulnerable. It was worse than lining up against a defensive lineman on the football field; worse even than his first day of class as a university professor.

"I thought you deserved a second chance." Quincy finished arranging the table, then held a chair for Ramona as she sat.

She uncovered her dish. The fragrant scents of lemon, herbs, fish and fresh vegetables escaped into the room. "Salmon. Thank you."

Quincy settled into the seat across the table from her and uncovered his steak, potatoes and broccoli. The surprised pleasure in her voice was more gratifying than a touchdown. "And it's fresh. I asked three times."

Ramona's startled laughter held a hint of embarrassment. Her elegant café au lait features grew pink.

They ate in silence for a time before Ramona spoke. "It took me a while to realize that your mean comments to me were the grown man's version of a little boy tugging the pigtails of the girl he liked."

He had to swallow his bite of steak twice. "Is that so?"

"You know it is." Ramona sent him a coquettish look. "It's been six years. Why haven't you asked me out?"

"Would you have agreed if I had?"

"No." Apparently, she didn't have to consider the question.

Quincy's lips curved in a wry smile. "Then you have your answer." Being right wasn't always a good feeling.

Ramona shrugged one sexy shoulder. "You still could have tried. That's another thing. Why are you attracted to me? I mean, I know men find me attractive, but why do *you* find me attractive?"

He'd often wondered the same thing. "I don't know."

She waved her fork. "We have nothing in common. You're a university professor. I've always hated school."

"We both went to college."

"I love going to Broadway plays and concerts. Your idea of a cultural experience is preordering the next hardcover release of one of your favorite authors."

"We both have a connection to bookstores."

Ramona sighed. "You never lose your temper—

except with me. Some people have said I have a short fuse."

"Those people are right."

She feigned a frown, but Quincy saw the laughter in her eyes. "So why are you attracted to me when we're both so different?"

Quincy claimed a broccoli spear with his fork. "I don't think we are." He held her gaze while he chewed and swallowed the vegetable.

"I'm serious, Quincy. I really want to know."

So did he. "All I know is that when you walk into a room, my common sense walks out. You're the reason for my insomnia. And the thought of seeing you is enough to give me a stroke."

Ramona frowned at him in silence for several long seconds. "Are you trying to be romantic? Those are all bad things."

"Those words didn't make your heart flutter?"

"Not in the slightest."

He took his courage in both hands and laid his heart bare. "You stayed in Trinity Falls after your grandfather died so your cousin wouldn't be alone. You ran for mayor because no one else would. You hired a drunk to read stories to a group of children because he said he needed a job. And when he used the money to get drunk, you did the reading, then drove him home."

Ramona's shocked expression wasn't encouraging. "I don't know what to say."

"Not only are you smart, beautiful and ambitious, you have a big heart. I don't know if that's why I . . . I'm attracted to you. I can only tell you that I am." His stumble over the *L*-word almost triggered a heart attack.

Ramona blinked. "Then why are you leaving Trinity Falls?"

Every muscle in his body tensed. "Is there a reason for me to stay?"

Ramona lowered her gaze to her half-eaten salmon. "I don't know."

Ean and Megan arrived outside her home. He could see the lights she'd left on in her foyer so she wouldn't return to a dark house at the end of the day. They glowed in her front window, making the structure appear to have two eyes staring fixedly from her house.

Megan had been darting glances at him throughout their walk from Books & Bakery. Somewhere along the way, she'd linked her arm with his. Had she felt his tension?

They hadn't talked about what he really wanted to know—Megan's true reaction to Ramona's trip to his office. Instead, they'd spent the last thirty minutes dissecting every inane topic he could introduce: work, what they'd accomplished, their to-do lists for the rest of the week.

He couldn't stall any longer.

Grow a pair, Fever.

"Thanks for defending me to Tilda this afternoon."

Megan released his arm to cup the side of his face. Her touch was so soft. "Is that what's been bothering you tonight? Don't worry about Tilda. She gets paranoid. I usually ignore her. But we can't have her distracting other members of the group with her theory that Ramona is looking for allies."

"So you don't believe that I'm working with Ramona to drive the businesses out of the center?"

Megan led him up the winding walkway to her front door. Her voice snapped with irritation. "Of course not. That was a totally baseless accusation."

Emboldened by relief, he continued his questions. Ean stopped on the step below her. "And you know that Ramona and I are never getting back together?"

"Oh yes." Megan's eyes shone under her porch lights. "I've known that for a while."

The early December evening was cold. A crisp breeze ruffled Megan's hair. He reached up and tucked the tormented strands behind her right ear. "Do you finally believe I've returned to Trinity Falls for good?"

Megan smiled. "Let's say I'm willing to consider the proposition."

He was two for three. "Maybe this will help convince you." He drew her into his embrace and lowered his mouth to hers.

CHAPTER 26

Megan's keys fell onto the steps. The sound pulled Ean back to his senses.

"I'm sorry." He crouched to pick up her keys, then straightened to open the door.

"I'm not." Megan led him into her home. She locked the door and tossed her keys onto the chaise lounge on the far side of her foyer.

That surprised him. He hooked his jacket onto her coat tree. "Anyone could have seen us, kissing on your doorstep."

Megan stripped off her coat and hung it beside Ean's. "Ean, by now, everyone knows we're sleeping together. If they don't, they're just fooling themselves."

"Is that right?" Ean crossed his arms as he tried to get a read on Megan. She'd been cool and professional during the association meeting, quiet on the walk home. Now she was playful. Why?

"Um-hmm." She stepped closer to him. "And I'll tell you something else. You can't kiss a woman senseless, then apologize and try to change the subject."

Ean's body responded to the heat gathering in Megan's eyes. "Is that what happened? I kissed you senseless?"

Megan unfolded his arms. "You know you did. Would you like to do it again?"

Ean didn't need to be asked twice. She met him halfway, her mouth parted, lips moist. He swept his tongue inside and felt her sigh. Her body melted against his. He pulled her closer, wrapping his arms around her slender waist. Seconds—or was it minutes?—later he felt her tugging at his clothes.

He stepped back and pulled his sweater off, letting it drop beside their feet. Megan reached for his belt buckle. Something between a chuckle and a groan rumbled in his chest. "Do you need help?"

"I don't think so." Her voice was shaky.

"Then let me help you with yours." Ean pulled her sweater over her head, then kissed her deeply as he slipped two fingers into her waistband to unbutton her pants. Her stomach muscles fluttered beneath his touch.

They kissed and stripped their way to the staircase. Ean paused to take the condoms from his wallet. By the time they reached Megan's bedroom, they were naked and thoroughly aroused.

Megan pressed Ean onto her mattress, then straddled him. She arched a brow. "I hope you brought more than one condom tonight."

"Big talker." Ean handed her the unopened packets.

She sat up, stretching her lithe, nude body toward her nightstand, tossing the packets onto the surface. Ean's mouth watered.

He reached out to trace her hip. "I love watching you, with or without your clothes."

"I love watching you, too."

His smile faded as she traced his erection. She leaned closer to kiss him. Ean caressed her breasts, loving the feel of the soft, warm weight in his hands. He caressed their curves and she moved against him. He pinched their nipples and she pressed closer to him. His erection flexed into her stomach.

Ean held her tighter, shifting on the mattress to put her beneath him. They explored each other, tracing pulses and pleasure points. A kiss, a touch, a taste. Foreplay that carried them to the edge of the tide.

"Are you ready for me?" Ean's throat was dry. He slipped a finger inside her.

"Yes." Megan sighed.

Ean reached for a condom on her nightstand. He felt Megan's small hand clasp his manhood and guide him into her mouth. Her maneuver caught him off guard.

"Just making sure you're ready for me." She held his gaze and licked her lips.

"I'm ready, wicked woman." Ean sheathed himself with the condom.

Megan reached for him. He wrapped her in his embrace, pressing her back into the mattress. He worked his way down her body, pausing to kiss her breasts, lick her torso, tease her navel and caress her hips. He loved the warmth of her body beneath his lips. He could grow drunk on the sweet, soft taste of her flesh. Her moans and sighs encouraged him. She was so responsive to his touch. Megan made him feel needed, as well as wanted.

Ean stopped at the juncture of her thighs. He looked at her again. Her cheeks were flushed. Her eyes were closed. A dreamy expression had settled on her lovely features. Ean lay between her legs, cupped her hips and raised them to his mouth. He worked her sensitive spot with his tongue, starting slowly, then speeding up. He kissed her deeply, then with quick nips. Megan reacted with gasps and pants and moans of pleasure, which fueled his desire. Her body moved in time with the speed he set. Ean drew back, caressing her gently with a soothing touch. He pulled himself up and over her, leaning in to kiss her. Catching him off guard again, Megan pushed him onto his back and straddled his thighs.

She was hungry for control. She wanted to give free rein to the desire that was always just under the surface when she was near Ean. He looked at her and she grew warm. He smiled and she wanted to jump his bones.

She leaned forward to position Ean's erection at her entrance. Her breasts hovered just above his lips. Ean raised his head to take one into his mouth.

Megan gasped at the feel of his tongue circling her nipple, his teeth grazing the hardening nub.

She straightened away from him. "Don't distract me." Her words emerged on puffs of breath.

Ean's smile turned into a groan as she lowered herself onto his erection. "You're so hot, so wet."

Megan inhaled sharply. "That's what you do to me."

Ean's hands moved over her body, caressing her breasts, tracing her hips, gripping her thighs. Megan alternated her rhythm—slowing down to savor his every inch, moving faster to bring him more pleasure. Loving the feel of him inside her.

She leaned forward to cover his mouth with hers. She stroked his tongue, teasing it and sucking it. She moved her lips to his neck, licking and tasting his skin. Ean held her hips, moving her closer, faster. His breaths came in pants.

Megan was close, but she wanted it to last longer. "Not yet."

And then he touched her, slipping his finger between their joining. Her hips quickened on their own. Megan heard her pulse pounding in her ears. Her blood swept through her veins. Her back arched. Her breasts strained toward the ceiling. She gasped as her muscles flexed and burned. Ean drove into her, lifting her higher and higher as he kept pace with her urgency. Drawing closer and closer, pulling tighter and tighter. Then her pleasure crashed over her, shaking her body from the inside out.

Ean thrust one last time and found his release.

His body bowed and shuddered. She collapsed onto Ean's chest. His strong arms came around her, holding her closer as their bodies shook together.

"That was cheating." Megan made the accusation to Ean's neck.

"That wasn't cheating. It was strategy." Ean used the same response she'd given him when he'd accused her of cheating during their foot race.

Megan chuckled. "Well played."

She rolled off of Ean and curled up beside him. Already half asleep, she felt Ean tuck her closer to him. She was safe and sated in his arms. Could they make this last forever?

"Whose idea was this five-mile run?" Megan picked up the pace to keep up with Ean.

"Yours." Ean tossed a smile her way before wiping the sweat from his brow.

"It had seemed like a good idea at the time." That was before she realized the former college quarterback could outrun her on one leg.

The trail was getting brighter as the sun rose above the park. The cool air was perfect for their Thursday-morning jog, during this first week of December. Who knew how many outdoor runs she'd have the rest of the year?

"Do you need me to slow down?"

Did she detect a taunt in Ean's question? "No, I'm fine. Don't speed up." Pride goeth before a fall—or a total collapse.

He chuckled. "I promise."

They jogged in silence for a while. The scent of morning dew, fresh earth and pine trees were some of the reasons she enjoyed running in the morning. She also loved the scenery along the winding path, thick old trees and lush bushes.

"I had an idea about the town center." Ean interrupted her musings.

"Yeah? What?" She could barely puff out her responses.

A drop of perspiration trailed the side of Ean's chiseled features and slid along his sharp jawline. Megan wanted to trace its path with her fingertip. She resisted the urge. Barely.

"Why doesn't the Trinity Falls Town Center Business Owners Association buy it?"

They looped the halfway point of their run and started back toward Megan's home. The end was near. Thank goodness.

She dabbed perspiration from her upper lip with the back of her wrist. "Considered that. Couldn't afford it."

Ean seemed to slow his pace. "But there are six of us now."

"Some of the owners are struggling to pay their rent." Megan drew in a deep breath. "It would be too much of a hardship. Our best chance is a new mayor."

"But not you."

"Not me."

"You'd be good at it."

Megan liked the way he saw her, even if his vision was skewed. "I can lead a group, not a town."

"So you say." He didn't sound convinced. He didn't sound winded, either.

They slipped into another comfortable silence as their steady strides carried them up the winding path.

"What about you? You won't reconsider?" Megan glanced at Ean. Was this run even challenging to him?

"My future isn't in politics. Who else can we consider?"

"I have an idea."

"So you've said. Who?"

"Doreen." Megan braced for Ean's reaction.

"My mother? Why?" He didn't sound ready to jump on Doreen's campaign train. Megan hadn't thought he would.

"She's helped affect changes in a lot of community services—local schools, the volunteer fire department." Megan took a moment to catch her breath. "Ramona takes credit for the lights along this trail, but they were your mother's idea."

"Ms. Helen told me about that." He still didn't sound convinced. "I don't want my mother involved in politics."

"Why not?"

"I don't want the people of this town calling open season on my mother's personal life." There was anger around the edges of his voice. His pace increased. "I don't want her to be the subject of rumors, gossip and innuendos. She's a good person. She deserves her privacy."

He was right. Still . . . "Isn't this Doreen's decision?"

Ean started to speak, then stopped. "You're right."

"I'll ask her today."

"Fine. She won't agree."

"We'll see." Megan smiled.

That sounded like wishful thinking on Ean's part, but he'd had to contend with a lot of changes in his mother's life—her new boyfriend, her new job. How would he handle his mother's role as mayoral candidate?

"You don't stand a chance running against me for mayor. You know that." Ramona's overly confident words came from Megan's bookstore office doorway Thursday afternoon.

Megan lowered her pen and looked toward her cousin. "What makes you think I'm running against you?"

"That's your plan, isn't it?" Ramona strode into Megan's office. The ankle-length skirt of her emerald green business suit hugged her slim hips and thighs under her faux-fur coat. "You think that electing a new mayor will save the center."

"How do you know that?" Megan searched her mind for the source of Ramona's intel.

"Come on, Meggie."

"Don't call me that."

Ramona shed her coat. She sank into the teal blue upholstered chair in front of Megan's mahogany-laminated desk. "No one in Trinity Falls can keep a secret. You know that."

"Who would have shared that particular secret with you?" Only members of the business association knew their plan to identify a challenger for Ramona.

"Does it matter who told me?"

Yes, it does. "No, I guess not. But what makes you think your reelection is guaranteed?"

Ramona hugged her coat in her lap like a pet. "The people in this town won't vote against me. They're afraid of what I can do to them socially."

"They should be more concerned with whether you'll serve a full term. The fact that you're planning to leave Trinity Falls at your first opportunity is not a secret, either."

Ramona's self-assured smile faded. "Leave the town politics to me. You'd be better off figuring out what to do about the bookstore."

"You mean *our* bookstore? Our grandparents left it to both of us. Why are you trying to destroy it?"

Temper flared in Ramona's eyes. "I'm not. I'm trying to improve the town."

Megan studied her cousin in silence. "What is it that you want, Ramona? To run the town or leave it? You can't have it both ways. Trinity Falls needs a mayor who'll stay."

Confusion nudged out irritation in Ramona's dark eyes. Her gaze shifted. Did she even know what she wanted? "I have plans for this town—"

"How long will you be here to enjoy them?" Megan relaxed back into her seat, enjoying her cousin's discomfort. It was nice to turn the tables on Ramona.

"Are you going to make loyalty your campaign platform?" Ramona cocked her head. "I don't think that will go over well, considering you're my cousin. That's taking family feuds a bit far, don't you think?"

Just that quickly, Megan's enjoyment faded. "We may not be close—"

"No, we aren't."

"But you're my cousin." Megan ignored Ramona's interruption. "I care about you. And I care about Trinity Falls. If you were honest with yourself, you'd admit that you're not making changes to the center for the town's sake. You're doing it for yourself."

Ramona managed to cross her legs, despite the tightness of her skirt. Impressive. "From where I stand, you're the one being selfish. You care more about the center than the town."

"Ramona, if you're not sure what you want to do, take some time to figure it out."

"I know exactly what I'm doing. I'm making this town a better place to live."

"In your opinion." Why couldn't she get through to her cousin? "Most of the people in this town don't agree with you."

"They'll come around, once they see that I'm right."

Megan thought of the business owners who were struggling with the increased rent and faced an uncertain future for their businesses. "You're gambling with their livelihood."

"Well, instead of worrying about my campaign,

you and your friends should figure out what you can do to help your businesses."

"We already have. We're going to find someone to run against you."

Ramona narrowed her eyes. "You won't win, Megan."

"We aren't children any longer, Ramona." Megan swallowed back her temper. "If you break your toy, you can't take mine. Books and Bakery isn't just *my* livelihood. *You* draw an income from it, too."

"I've got a job. My interior-design firm, remember? I have two, if you count this mayoral gig." Ramona shrugged a shoulder. "The town center is in my way. You can't stop progress, Meggie."

"Stop calling me that." Megan sat back in her chair.

"What's different about you?" Ramona's scowl cleared and a smile slowly curved her full, red lips. "You're wearing makeup. And you bought new clothes. That sweater's not your usual drab color. Trying to hold on to your man?"

Megan ignored her. "Why didn't you stay in New York? What happened?"

Ramona's smile vanished. She rose from her seat. "I've told you before. I wasn't ready to stay in the city then."

"Are you ready now?"

Ramona didn't answer. She just turned and walked out of Megan's office, leaving behind a cloud of Chanel No. 5.

Was Ean just biding his time with Megan until he and Ramona could return to New York?

The question was a poisonous whisper in her mind. No way could Ean make love to her as he did last night if he was still interested in Ramona. She knew the two of them would never get back together. And she was starting to believe Ean would not return to New York. Then where had those doubts come from?

Doreen rushed into her office, distracting Megan from those worries. "What did Ramona want? We saw her walk into the store as smug as the cat with the canary. Now she looks like I could fry an egg on her head."

Megan kneaded her shoulder with her right hand, trying to work out the knots of tension. "She warned me against challenging her in the election."

Doreen frowned. "Did you tell her you weren't running against her?"

"I didn't see the point. Just because *I'm* not running doesn't mean I don't want someone else to."

"Like who?"

"How about you?" Megan watched Doreen closely for her reaction.

Doreen's eyes grew wide. She gripped the back of the visitor's chair. "You think *I* should run for mayor?"

"Why do you sound so surprised?" Megan wrapped her hands around her mug of coffee. It was cool to her touch.

Doreen's mouth opened and closed several times

before words came out. "It's just not something I ever considered."

"Would you consider it now?"

Doreen looked shocked, but she didn't seem as though she'd refuse the proposition. She sank into the chair and was silent for several moments. Finally she raised her head and met Megan's gaze. "Let me think it over."

Megan's shoulders relaxed. "Of course. But keep in mind that the deadline for challengers to register is Monday. December ninth is ninety days from the primary."

"All right." Doreen rose. She fussed with her clothes unnecessarily. "Do you think I'd make a good mayor?"

Megan smiled. "I do. If I didn't believe that, I wouldn't have asked you to consider running."

Doreen's face glowed with pleasure. "Thank you, Megan. That means a lot to me."

Megan watched her friend walk out of her office. There was a spring in Doreen's step, an extra energy and confidence in her carriage.

She hoped her friend decided to run for office. She also hoped Ean supported his mother's decision. If not, regardless of whether Doreen won the election, Megan feared both mother and son would lose.

CHAPTER 27

Doreen led Leonard into the family room Thursday evening. She settled onto the thick rose-colored sofa, but it was hard to remain still. Her muscles trembled with excitement.

"Tell me about your day." She watched him set the tray with their mugs of hot tea and cookies on the coffee table. How would he react to her news? Would he pepper her with questions? Wrap her in a bear hug?

Leonard was a tall, fit man. Her muscles quivered again when she thought of where their evening could lead after her announcement.

He settled beside her. His brown eyes twinkled, deepening the creases around them. "You're the one who's glowing. What's going on?"

Doreen's grin sprang free. "Megan suggested I run for mayor. Can you believe it?" Her voice rose to a squeak of excitement.

Leonard's dark eyes clouded with confusion. "But you don't have any experience in office."

Hmmm . . . she hadn't expected that response. *What's the phrase kids are using these days? "What a buzzkill."* "But I do have experience volunteering on community boards and working to get legislation passed."

Leonard angled his body to face her on the sofa. "That's different."

"How? Because I didn't get paid?" She thought he'd be excited for her. Why was he so condescending?

Leonard shook his head. "That's not what I mean."

"I've lived in Trinity Falls all of my life, and that's about how long I've been actively involved in community issues. My parents were volunteers. My father was a two-term council member."

Leonard raised both hands, palms out. "All I'm saying is that volunteering is very different from actually serving in office."

Doreen crossed her arms and legs. "Would I have learned more if I'd drawn a paycheck?"

"Dorie." Leonard spoke her name on a sigh. "You've supported a lot of changes that benefited the community. But as mayor, you have to consider both sides of an issue, not just the one that benefits you."

"Do you think I can't do that?" Doreen pushed herself from the sofa.

Leonard returned his mug of tea to the serving tray and stood. "I'm not undermining what you've done. All I mean is that your running for mayor is a bad idea."

Doreen's eyes widened. "Why?"

Leonard hesitated. "The campaign will give everyone an excuse to invade your privacy."

Doreen cocked an eyebrow. "We live in Trinity Falls. No one here has any privacy."

"People will gossip about you. They'll speculate about our relationship."

"They're already speculating about our relationship."

"What about me, Dorie?"

"What about you?"

Leonard planted his hands on his hips. "You have a full-time job running the bakery. It takes a lot of your time. What if you win this election? When will you have time for me?"

Doreen studied Leonard's closed expression. "You're worried that I won't have time for you?"

"Why do you need another job?"

"*You're* asking me that? You're a math teacher *and* a football coach."

"Coaching isn't a yearlong position."

Doreen ground her teeth. She didn't have to justify herself to anyone. "I don't *need* this job. I *want* it."

Leonard turned away, pinching the bridge of his nose, and paced. "Where does that leave us?" He faced her from across the room. "I'm going to retire in a few years. I was hoping we could spend more time together."

Warning bells sounded in Doreen's ears. He wasn't implying marriage, was he? Proceed with caution. "I enjoy spending time with you, Leo. But this is an opportunity that I don't want to dismiss. I promised Megan I'd think about it."

She'd hoped Leonard would be her sounding board. Instead, this discussion had been all about his feelings. He'd never once asked her why she wanted to run for office. To say his reaction was a disappointment would be an understatement.

Leonard's sigh lifted the broad shoulders she'd wanted to hold tonight. "Well, I hope you reconsider your decision."

"I won't."

He didn't respond.

Doreen followed Leonard to the coat closet. She waited while he shrugged into his parka. His movements were slow. She could sense his reluctance to leave. But, after his reaction to her news, she didn't want him to stay.

"Good night, Leo."

Leonard hesitated before letting himself out. "Good night."

Doreen exhaled. She locked the door behind him, pressing her hand against the cool maple wood. This wasn't the way she'd imagined the evening would end.

"Mom didn't mention that you'd suggested she run for mayor." Ean leaned back against Megan's white-marble kitchen counter Thursday evening.

Megan handed him a mug of green tea, with fresh lemon juice. The hot brew seemed just the thing to make them feel better after their cold walk home from the bookstore. The walks had been so much more enjoyable in the fall.

"She'll probably tell you tomorrow. She wanted to think it over tonight." Megan linked her arm with his and walked with him to the living room.

Alicia Keys sang softly on Megan's stereo system. Low light spilled in through the far archway leading to the foyer.

"How did she seem when the two of you talked?" Ean sank onto her fluffy coffee-colored sofa.

Megan sat beside him. "Excited." She smiled at the memory. "I wish you'd seen her."

"Do you think she'll do it?" Ean drank his tea as his olive green eyes searched hers.

"I hope so." She slid out of her black pumps and curled her legs under her.

"I'm still not sure this is a good idea."

"Why not?" Megan sipped the hot tea. The lemon juice was tart against her taste buds.

Ean shrugged. "The campaign itself will be stressful and demanding, not to mention the job."

"Doreen can handle it. She raised you. I'm sure that was stressful and demanding." Megan sipped more tea. Delicious.

"I'm serious."

"So am I." Megan sat up, lowering her feet to the cream Berber carpet. "She's not going to be the mayor of a large metropolis. She's going to lead a town with less than fifteen hundred residents. And she won't be running it alone. She'll have the entire town council helping her."

"But she's sixty years old. Don't you think it's time that she started slowing down?"

"Your mother? No." Megan cradled her mug of hot tea and drew another sip. She loved the way he loved his mother—as long as he didn't smother her. "There are people running this *country* who are a lot older."

"Doesn't it concern you that, if she wins the election, she'd have to split her time between the mayor's office and your bakery?"

Megan hid her smile behind her mug. Was that his attempt to sway her to his side of the argument? "Ean, would you feel this way if Doreen wasn't your mother?"

He set his mug on a coaster on her coffee table and stood to cross her living room. "But she is my mother and I can't separate that. I realize she's changed while I was in New York. But I don't want her to change any more. Is that wrong?"

"Yes, it is. Whether your mother changes, and how much, is not your decision."

A quiet contemplation seemed to drape over Ean. Megan studied him, standing across the room with his head bowed and legs braced. His dark gray Dockers hugged his hips. His broad shoulders stretched his burgundy sweater. She wished she could convince him he wasn't losing his mother. Doreen had been, and always would be, there for him. She didn't know any other way.

"She didn't want me to go to New York." Ean spoke with his back to her.

"I know." Megan sipped her tea.

"She didn't want me to marry Ramona, either."

"That I didn't know." Megan had never guessed that Doreen hadn't wanted Ramona for a daughter-in-law. In fact, her friend had seemed concerned when Ramona had left Ean in New York and returned to Trinity Falls.

"She never tried to influence me in either direction on those things. She let me make my own decisions." Ean faced her once more.

"That sounds like Doreen."

"I can't tell her what to do, but I don't have to like it."

"Fair enough." Megan finished her tea and set the mug on the coaster. Ean seemed a million miles away. "Why did Ramona leave New York?"

"I don't know." He didn't seem interested in the reason, either.

"Could you tell that she wasn't happy there?"

Ean returned to sit beside her. "Ramona had spent her whole life in Trinity Falls, so I knew New York would be an adjustment."

"You adjusted."

"The transition wasn't as hard for me. Remember, I went to college in D.C., then law school in New York. Ramona went to Trinity Falls University."

Megan still wasn't buying that. "But she didn't stay in New York for even a year."

"I was surprised, too."

Megan regarded him in silence for a moment. "Did the two of you have a fight?"

Ean's olive gaze was steady on hers. "I wasn't unfaithful, if that's what you're asking."

"I told you, I know you're not a cheater."

"Most women think all men cheat."

"I'm not most women, and you're not all men."

Ean rewarded her with his sexiest smile, the one that creased his dimples and sparkled in his eyes. "Thank you." He leaned forward.

Megan caught her breath and met him halfway. "You're welcome." She breathed the words against his lips.

Their mouths touched, at first testing and teasing each other. Megan slid her hands up Ean's arms toward his shoulders. She felt his muscles, enjoying their strength and power. She paused to linger over the shape and hardness of his biceps. Megan shifted closer to him and deepened their kiss. Ean tightened his arms around her. Megan sighed into his mouth. This was where she wanted to be. Forever.

Then she realized the buzzing in her head wasn't blood rushing through her veins or her pulse galloping in her ears. It was her front doorbell. She opened her eyes and pulled away from her lover's embrace.

Ean caught her. "Where . . . ?"

"Someone's at the door." Megan stood.

She smiled at the obscenity Ean bit off as he followed her into the next room. "Who the hell is it?"

Megan blinked a few times in the brighter light of the foyer. She stood on tiptoe to check the peephole. "It's Leo."

"What's he doing here?" Ean asked the question

that came to Megan's mind. There was a hint of concern in his voice.

Megan unlocked the door. She stepped back, bumping into Ean as she pulled it open. "Hi, Leo. Is something wrong?"

Leonard stepped into her foyer. His gaze went briefly to Ean before returning to Megan. "Yes, there is."

"What is it?" Megan locked her front door, trying but failing to ignore her unease.

"Is it my mother?" Ean's question was sharp.

Leonard's hard eyes turned to Ean. "Did you know she was planning to run for mayor?"

"I knew she was thinking about it." The tension had left Ean's voice.

"Well, she's made up her mind. She's going to do it." Leonard turned his anger to Megan. "And I was told that we have you to thank for that."

Megan's gaze shifted between the two men. "You're both very welcome."

Leonard scrubbed his face with his palms. His voice was tired. "I was being sarcastic."

"I know." Megan regarded the older man with bewilderment. "What I don't understand is how you, of all people, could be opposed to Doreen becoming mayor."

"What do you mean, me, 'of all people'?" Leonard sounded defensive.

"You know how many boards Doreen has served on in Trinity Falls and how passionate she is about the issues concerning the town."

"Which just proves my argument." Leonard

spread his arms. "She doesn't have to become mayor to make a difference in Trinity Falls. She can just keep doing what she's doing."

"Leo has a point." Ean inclined his head toward his high school coach. "Why can't Mom just keep volunteering? It's a lot less responsibility."

Megan blinked. Were they serious? "I can't believe you don't understand the difference between serving in a legislative office and volunteering for an issue-based organization. Doreen's work isn't a social-studies exercise. She's serious about helping her neighbors and making Trinity Falls stronger."

Leonard rubbed a hand over his forehead. "But she's doing that now. Why does she have to run for office? It will take up a lot more of her time and attention."

"There's a big difference between being an advocate for an issue and being the executive who can actually enact the change." Megan threw up her arms and returned to the living room.

Leonard followed her. "Why did you talk her into this? Why is it so important to you?"

"Why *isn't* it important to you?" Megan collected the two empty mugs from the coffee table. She left the coasters behind.

"What does that mean?" Leonard's tone was impatient.

She turned and found Ean and Leonard standing behind her. "This is important to Doreen. She didn't make this decision lightly. You both care about her—so why isn't this important to either of you?"

Leonard rubbed his forehead again. "*She's* important to me. Not the town center. I don't want her to take on this additional responsibility and pressure. It isn't necessary."

Ean nodded. "She doesn't have to be mayor to serve the community. It's just more work and aggravation for her."

"This is Doreen's decision." Megan continued into the kitchen and loaded the mugs into the dishwasher.

"But it was your idea." Leonard followed her. "You talked her into it. You can get her to change her mind."

"She'll listen to you," Ean added. "You could suggest she reconsider her decision."

No way. Ean and Leonard apparently thought they could gang up on her. Maybe they could have pressured the old Megan, but recent events had shown her she could stand up for herself.

"I'll do no such thing." She walked past the two men on her way back into her living room.

"Why not?" Leonard's question was plaintive as he continued to follow her around her home.

With regret, Megan stopped her Alicia Keys compact disc and turned off her stereo. "I didn't coerce Doreen into making this decision. She made it on her own." She turned to face Doreen's son and boyfriend. "Listening to your complaints, it sounds to me that you're more concerned with how Doreen's new career will affect you rather than what this opportunity will mean to her."

Leonard and Ean exchanged looks before Ean responded. "That's not true."

Megan looked at Leonard. "You said the mayor's position would claim a lot more of Doreen's time and attention."

"It would." The older man spread his arms.

"Time and attention that would be taken away from you, right?" Megan asked the rhetorical question before leading both men to her front door.

"But that's not the reason I don't want her to get involved in politics." Leonard's stubbornness sounded close behind her.

"Isn't it?" Megan had her doubts. "Doreen has spent most of her adult life putting other people first, giving them her time and attention." She addressed Ean. "She was at every one of your games."

"I know." Ean put emotion into those two words.

"She made a home for you and your father." Megan added before turning to Leonard. "And, Leo, when your wife died, the town rallied around you. But they let you put the pieces of your life together the way you saw fit. How could you do any less for Doreen?"

"That's not what I'm doing." Leonard was adamant, but he was wrong.

"Yes, it is. You're trying to tell her what's important to her and what she can do. Those are absolutely her decisions." Megan unlocked her front door. "I want you gentlemen to consider what we just talked about. But do it from the other side of this door."

The two men exchanged another look. Ean

moved first. He stepped in front of Megan and cupped his large hand around her upper arm. "Good night."

Megan nodded, unable to speak. Heat radiated from her arm across her breasts and deep into her abdomen. She sighed inwardly when Ean released her.

Leonard paused before her, too. "I'm sorry I interrupted your evening."

"So am I." She meant it to the bottom of her soul.

Megan locked the door after them and exhaled. She pressed her hand against the cool maple wood. Damn, this was not the way she'd envisioned her evening ending.

CHAPTER 28

Megan walked into the bakery's kitchen early Friday morning to find Doreen kneading dough at the table. The room already was full to bursting with warm, mouthwatering scents.

Her friend glanced up. "Nice suit."

"Thank you." Megan glanced down at her woolen turquoise skirt suit. It was another successful find in her efforts to bring her wardrobe from the darkness into the bright.

"You're here early. Paperwork?" Doreen's greeting lacked its usual energy.

Not surprising. Megan wasn't very energetic this morning, either. Flashes of her argument with Ean and Leonard had kept her awake last night. She swallowed a sigh of regret over the previous evening.

Megan sank into the chair near the corner table, the same chair Ean had used when she'd first seen him again. "I was anxious to check on you this morning. I should have called you last night."

"Why?" Doreen seemed distracted. Her movements were unusually tentative as she manipulated the dough. Was that because of her argument with Leonard?

She studied the older woman's profile. "Leo came to my house last night."

"Oh, Lord." Doreen froze, squeezing her eyes shut.

"He accused me of coercing you into running for mayor."

Doreen's eyes snapped open. "Does he think I'm your puppet?"

"Of course not." Though Megan could understand how Doreen had come to that unflattering conclusion.

"You just told me, he said you put words in my mouth." Doreen's temper was building steam.

"That's not what he said, Doreen." Last night, Megan had wanted to slap Ean and Leonard until they came to their senses. This morning, she was working overtime to defend them.

Doreen persisted. "He asked you to get me to change my mind, didn't he?"

"They're concerned that you might be taking on too much."

"They? Was Ean there? Did he want you to get me to change my mind, too?"

Megan hesitated. "Yes."

"What did you say?"

"I told them that whether you run for office is your decision. No one could make it for you."

"Thank you." Doreen tried a smile. She failed. "Why can't Leo and Ean understand that?"

"In fairness, Doreen, Ean returned to Trinity Falls to find his football mom had become a career woman, with a boyfriend and political aspirations. That's a big adjustment."

Doreen seemed to relax by degrees. "You have a point."

Megan crossed her legs, adjusting her skirt. "I think it's understandable that Ean would feel a little unsettled."

Doreen went back to kneading the dough. "When I was younger, my greatest satisfaction was making a home and raising a family. Now my son has a life of his own and my husband is dead. I need to find out what the next chapter of my life is supposed to be."

"Do you really want to run this town?"

Doreen picked up the rolling pin and began flattening the dough. "Yes, I do. I'm going to file my application Monday morning."

Megan wanted to jump from her seat and cheer. Instead, she stood and contented herself with a satisfied smile. "We'll work on your campaign talking points."

Doreen grimaced. "I've got a lot of ideas, but none of them would sound interesting in a fifteen-second sound bite."

Megan crossed to her friend and wrapped her arm around her shoulders. "Don't worry. I'll call Darius about an interview with you for the paper.

We'll schedule it for after you file your application. There's no sense to do it beforehand."

"An interview?" The look of horror that crossed Doreen's still-youthful face was priceless.

Megan let her arm drop. "You're in the big time now. Imagine. This town will have a choice between two candidates for mayor this election. Trinity Falls hasn't had that in eight years. Darius will be so excited."

"I'm glad someone will be." Doreen sniffed as she flattened the dough.

"Don't worry about Ean and Leo. They'll come around." Megan hoped.

Tuesday morning, Doreen smiled at Darius as she rose from her seat behind Megan's desk. "That wasn't as bad as I thought it would be."

Her friend and employer had encouraged Doreen to use her office for the newspaper interview. Doreen had appreciated the privacy. Armor-clad butterflies had been battling in her stomach since she'd filed her application yesterday to get on the ballot for the mayoral election next November. They'd settled down midway through the interview, though.

Darius turned off his audio recorder and stood. "You did well, Ms. Doreen." He closed his reporter's notebook and capped his pen. "I'll probably leave out the part about you playing the judge in Ean, Quincy and my mock court, though."

Doreen saw the twinkle in his dark eyes and

laughed. "You were only nine years old. I think people would understand."

Darius shook his head. "I'm glad the town will have two qualified candidates to choose from for mayor this election." He opened the office door and stepped back to allow Doreen to precede him. "This should be interesting."

Sporadic chitchat about the day and the weather kept them occupied as they crossed the short hallway to the main bookstore and bakery.

"Would you like another cup of coffee before you leave for the newspaper?" Doreen asked as Darius walked beside her.

"If you add a slice of hot apple pie, you've got a deal."

"Didn't I serve you breakfast before our interview an hour ago?"

"I always have room for pie."

Doreen grinned at Darius's playful tone. The reporter had been susceptible to her pies since he was six.

Her smile froze when she saw Ramona seated at the counter. The mayor rarely came into the bookstore this early. Stares from the few customers at the bakery tables, including Darius's parents, warned Doreen that any words she and Ramona exchanged would be all over Trinity Falls before noon. She made a mental note to prepare for a large lunch crowd.

Doreen squared her shoulders. "Good morning, Ramona. What can I get for you?"

Animosity gleamed in the younger woman's

ebony eyes. "An answer. What makes you think you can beat me in the election?"

Doreen tried to keep her voice down. "I'm more in tune with the needs of the town than you are."

"Oh yeah?" Ramona folded her arms on the counter. The volume of their conversation didn't appear to concern her. "What are you going to do about those needs, especially since we don't have any money?"

Darius shrugged off his jacket and hung it on the chair beside Ramona's before folding his tall frame onto the seat. "What have you done during your four-year term to raise money, Mayor?"

"Ramona's done a good job for this town, Darius." Darius's father, Simon, spoke from one of the tables.

Seated beside her husband, Ethel nodded. "Doreen, you should be grateful for all Ramona's done, instead of running against her."

Doreen struggled not to let her jaw drop. Didn't this same couple criticize Ramona's first term in office just two months ago? Now that she was within earshot, they were giving her their full support.

Doreen filled a mug of coffee and offered it to Darius. "If the people of Trinity Falls are satisfied with Ramona's performance, we'll have four more years of the same. If they're not, then they can vote for me." That was pretty much what she'd told Darius during her interview.

"I'm sure you'll do your very best, Doreen." Ramona leaned into the counter. "The problem is, running a town is a little harder than running a bakery."

Simon's guffaws almost drowned out his wife's twittering giggles. Doreen sensed the customers straining to hear every word that passed between her and Ramona as they lingered over their pastries and drinks. She wished she could respond to Ramona in kind. However, Doreen had never been one to deliver denigrating comments.

But she could learn.

She gave her young opponent a cool look. "We both know I have more to offer Trinity Falls than my business experience. After all, during your term, the town council enacted several of my suggestions for improvements."

Ethel again came to Ramona's defense. "That's part of being a good leader, knowing when to take ideas from other people." The bakery's silence seemed to drain her confidence. She looked to her husband. "Isn't that right?"

Ramona's expression tightened. "You may be good at coming up with ideas to *spend* the town's money, but how are you at coming up with ideas to *raise* money without raising taxes?"

"We won't find out until next January." Megan stopped beside Doreen.

"Don't you think you should wait for the election before predicting Doreen's win?" Ramona's voice was cool, but Doreen thought she saw a flash of hurt in the younger woman's eyes.

"No." Megan's gaze moved from Doreen to Darius. "How did the interview go?"

Doreen marveled that her friend could appear so calm while she felt as though her nerves were about to snap. "It went well."

Darius's dark eyes danced with amusement. "The article should make the front page of tomorrow's *Monitor.*"

Ramona's cream skin flushed pink. "The town's losing its tax base because people keep leaving."

"People like you?" Megan asked.

"I'm running for reelection." Ramona's voice was tight.

Megan lowered her voice to a barely audible whisper. "But will you serve all four years?"

Doreen held her breath for Ramona's response. The other woman's face flushed darker. Without a word, she rose from her chair and marched from the bookstore.

Doreen watched her leave. "Was that a 'yes' or a 'no'?"

Megan crossed her arms. "It was a 'no.' But I don't think my cousin realizes that yet."

Darius lowered his mug of coffee. "Do you think she'll realize it before the election?"

"For her sake, I hope so." Megan lowered her arms and turned to Doreen. "You did a great job holding your own against Ramona. You'll do well during the debates."

"'Debates'? Plural?" Doreen swallowed. "Do we have to have more than one?"

Megan turned to leave, waving a hand over her shoulder. "You're in the big time now, Doreen."

CHAPTER 29

What jackass is leaning on my doorbell at seven-thirty in the damn morning?

Ramona flung her sheets off and threw herself from the bed. She wrenched her robe from the closet and shrugged into it as she stomped down the hall to her front door. She braced her fingertips on the cold blond wood and rose up on her bare toes.

Quincy, that vindictive psychopath!

Ramona jerked the door open. "What the *hell* is your problem?" When he didn't immediately respond, she stomped her bare foot. "Well?"

"You look so much younger without any makeup."

That growling was coming from her throat. "What do you want, Quincy?"

He lifted a copy of *The Trinity Falls Monitor* chest high. "You're free to leave Trinity Falls now."

Ramona snatched the newspaper from him. "Take off your shoes if you're coming in."

She turned and marched into her living room. A photo of Doreen smiled up at her beneath the headline FEVER ENTERS RACE FOR MAYOR.

"Do you always wake up in such a bad mood?" Quincy's words followed her.

Ramona spun on her bare heels. "Do you always lean on people's doorbells at such an ungodly hour of the morning?"

Her gaze dropped to Quincy's feet. He'd better have taken off his shoes before he'd lumbered across her white carpet. She relaxed as she noted his long, narrow feet covered in black dress socks. It was a sexy look for the bookish professor. Ramona pulled her gaze up past his black pants and gray jacket over a white dress shirt and black tie.

"It's after seven o'clock in the morning." Quincy walked farther into the room. "Most people are on their way to work, if they haven't already arrived."

"I'm. Not." Ramona froze with the sudden realization of just how scary she must look.

She wasn't wearing makeup. And she was certain her hair was matted and pointed in all different directions like a weather vane in a storm.

She closed her eyes. This was her worst nightmare. She dragged her fingers through her tangled hair and scrubbed a hand over her face.

In contrast, the university professor looked as though he'd been up for hours. His rugged features were clean-shaven. And his business clothes loaned his tall, bulky form the scary elegance of a Chicago mobster. Ramona's body heated.

"How would I know your sleeping habits, Ramona?" Quincy's voice had deepened. Its texture stroked her skin.

Ramona raised her eyes to his darkened gaze. She knew how he felt about her. Was that the reason she was responding to him? How much of what she felt was wishful thinking, and how much was the pull of his masculinity?

"Why did you say I was free to leave?" Her question was meant to remind him of the supposed reason for his obscenely early visit. She exhaled when he broke eye contact with her.

Quincy gestured toward the newspaper. "Last time, you ran unopposed for the mayor's position. If Doreen's willing to take on the job, you don't have to run at all."

Ramona regarded him through narrowed eyes. "You don't think I should run for reelection? Has my performance been that bad?"

Quincy frowned. "That's not what I'm saying."

"What *are* you saying?"

"You don't want to live here. If you campaign again, you'd be tied to Trinity Falls for another four years."

Ramona tossed the paper onto her glass-and-silver metal coffee table. "I've done a good job with this town. I've implemented improvements and I've reduced the deficit."

"You've done a good job under difficult conditions."

She jerked her head toward the discarded paper. "Then why are people challenging me?"

"You're missing the point. You're not obligated to run for a second term. Step down next January. Then you can move to wherever you want to live. Start the life you've always wanted."

"Where?" Ramona spread her arms. "Ean's not going back to New York, and you don't want me moving to Philadelphia with you."

Quincy crossed his arms over his chest, a surprisingly broad chest for such a stuffy college professor. "Stop using Trinity Falls as a crutch."

Ramona stumbled back. His words slapped her with the sharp sting of truth. "That's not what I'm doing."

"You're an intelligent, capable, independent woman. You'd do fine on your own."

"As well as I did as mayor?" Ramona blinked, battling back tears. "As well as the last time I moved to New York?"

Quincy studied her in silence for several long seconds. "What happened in New York, Ramona?"

She pressed her thumb and third finger against her eyes. "I failed. Just as I failed at being mayor." Ramona grabbed the newspaper, crushing it with her fist. "Show yourself out."

Ramona turned and hurried down the hallway, back to her bedroom. She slammed the door closed. Where would she go if she couldn't go to New York or Philadelphia? Who would she be if she couldn't be mayor of Trinity Falls? What was scarier than starting over? Starting over without a clear idea of who you were or where you fit in your community.

* * *

"Doreen's announcement that she's running for mayor made the front page." Grady Weatherington, owner of Fine Accessories, shoved his copy of *The Trinity Falls Monitor* across the table. As usual, the town center group had pushed two of the square tables together to accommodate their members for the meeting.

"It's a good article." Ean looked up from the newspaper and smiled at his mother. He caught Megan's approving regard from across the table. It was a nice change from the cool looks she'd been giving him since Friday evening. Was she ready to forgive him?

Grady ignored Ean. "What good is her campaign going to do? The election is a year away. Ramona could sell the center before then—or worse, raise our rents again."

Ean studied the newspaper photo of his mother. She looked great. Happy. Confident. He'd vote for her. "Ramona won't raise our rent before the election."

"How do you know?" Grady sounded like a petulant child.

Ean passed the newspaper to his mother. "I doubt she'll sell the center, either."

"How do you know?" Grady's voice held a bite of impatience.

Megan answered him. "With Doreen challenging her campaign, Ramona will be more aware of the impact her decisions will have on her chances for reelection."

"But you don't *know.*" Grady sighed, running his hands through his thinning hair. "Why didn't you come up with something to help us now?"

"Like what?" Megan turned the question to Grady.

"I don't know." Grady threw up his arms.

"If you don't know, how are we supposed to?" Tilda Maddox, the card store owner, rolled her gray eyes.

Grady turned toward Doreen. "No offense, Doreen, but I don't know how introducing you as our candidate is going to help me pay my rent."

"No offense taken, Grady." Doreen inclined her head. "But my campaign is about much more than your rent relief."

Ean smiled at his mother's saucy response. He didn't remember her having so much spunk. "My mother's running to help the entire town."

Grady grunted. "She can't beat Ramona. No one can. Ramona's got this town twisted to her will. No one wants to go against her."

"Maybe you don't, but Doreen does." Belinda Curby, the beauty salon owner, tapped the tip of her magenta-painted fingernail against the Formica tabletop. "You must not have read the article."

Grady scowled at her. "Is that supposed to be funny?"

"You see any of us laughing?" Tilda's voice was as dry as dust.

Grady gestured toward Doreen. "What makes you qualified?"

Ean had had enough. "My mother stepped forward to help Trinity Falls, which is something she's been doing since before I was born. No offense, Grady, but when have you ever done that? For as long as I can remember, you've looked to other people to find solutions to your problems."

Doreen squeezed Ean's upper arm. "That's enough, Ean."

"No, Doreen." Grady folded his hands on the table. "Maybe he's right. Maybe I was expecting Megan to solve my problems. But I've run out of time and no one can help me." He stood. "I'm going to have to close Fine Accessories when this rental agreement is done."

Belinda gasped. "Grady, are you sure?"

Grady nodded. "I just can't afford the rent anymore. It's draining my savings."

Tilda fisted her hands on the table. "Grady, you coward."

Grady frowned at her. "I'm not a coward."

Tilda continued as though he hadn't contradicted her. "You can't give up now. We have to stick together."

Grady turned toward Megan. "You were smart to diversify the bookstore. I should have done something similar with Fine Accessories. It's too late now."

Megan shook her head. "Grady, it may not be too late for you to revamp your company. Let me help you."

Grady shook his head. "You can't. I've run out of time and money. That's what I told Ramona when I mentioned we were gonna run someone against her."

Megan's brows arched. "You told her?"

Grady's cheeks flushed. "It came up in conversation."

Ean listened to the other association members trying to rally the accessory store's owner. Megan even offered to help him diversify his store. Still, Grady wasn't willing to even try. "You give up too easily."

Grady rewarded Ean with a glare. "My family has owned Fine Accessories for generations."

Ean arched a brow. "Isn't that even more of a reason to hold on to it?"

"I've done all that I can." Grady's gaze circled the other faces around the tables. "Good luck with Ramona. You're going to need it."

Ean considered the other business owners as they watched Grady walk away. Was he the first to go or the last?

Most of these entrepreneurs presided over businesses that spanned back generations. What would happen to Trinity Falls if its residents continued to lose the enterprises that represented their history and heritage?

He looked toward his mother. Doreen's intelligent, dark gaze focused on each member of their group. She was attentive to what they had to say. She was engaged in the town and its people, interested in their needs. How could he have ever considered giving her less than his wholehearted support?

Instead of questioning her decision, he should have been asking himself what he could do to help the town. Well, he'd ask that question now.

CHAPTER 30

"I'm proud of you, Mom." Ean broke the comfortable silence as he walked with his mother to her home after the association's meeting Wednesday night.

"Thank you, Ean." Doreen sounded startled.

The farther they traveled from the center of town, the fewer pedestrians they passed, and the darker the night became. They'd first accompanied Megan home, stopping to make sure she entered safely before continuing to Doreen's house.

"I'm nervous." His mother chuckled. "But I'm excited, too."

"I'd be worried about you if you weren't nervous." Ean tossed her a grin. "You're going to be the best mayor this town has ever seen, and I'm going to do everything I can to help you get elected."

Doreen linked her arm with his. "That means a lot to me."

"I'm sorry that I wasn't supportive of your decision right away."

"Megan reminded me that you're adjusting to a lot of changes." Doreen glanced at him. "I know I'm not the mother you remember."

Ean smiled. "That's an understatement." He sobered and held his mother's gaze. "But I like this assertive, independent businesswoman. I always thought I'd inherited my stubborn ambition from Dad. Now I wonder whether I got it from you."

Doreen's dark eyes twinkled with mischief. "You got your stubbornness from your father and your ambition from me."

Ean chuckled. "My change of mind is purely self-ish, you know. Now that I've moved back to Trinity Falls, I have to make sure that my taxes are spent re-sponsibly and that I'm getting the services I need."

Doreen placed her free hand on her heart. "I promise that if I'm elected, the roads will be main-tained. The mail will arrive on time and the water will be properly treated."

Ean nodded, satisfied. "You'll have my vote."

Doreen sighed. "I wonder if I'll have Leo's."

"Coach is pretty old-fashioned, but he cares about you, Mom." Ean patted his mother's gloved hand. "He'll come around when he sees that this is what you want to do."

"I wish I had your confidence."

They were quiet for a time. The neighbors' porch lights eased the creeping dark. Several of them had banners or flags announcing the town's upcoming 150th birthday. Ean breathed in the fresh, cool scents of Trinity Falls at night.

"After your father died, I was so lost." Doreen's

voice was low. Ean had to strain to hear her. "It's unfair that your father got sick one year after he retired. He'd worked hard all of his life. His retirement was supposed to be our second honeymoon. Instead, he suffered with cancer for a year, then died."

Ean's stomach muscles knotted with the thought of the pain his father had endured. "I wish I'd known."

"He didn't want you to see him like that. He said there wasn't anything you could do, anyway."

"I know. But I still don't understand."

"Your father had his reasons." Doreen sniffed several times before continuing. "After Paul died, I felt as though, at the age of sixty, I had to rebuild my life from scratch."

"I'd have come home sooner if you'd called me." Ean's response was just as quiet.

"It's my life, Ean." She cleared her throat. "I had to rebuild it on my own."

But she hadn't been on her own. Megan had been there, presenting her with a career opportunity. Leonard had offered her a new love life. Ean had been on the outside, unaware of what his mother had been going through. Could he ever forgive himself for allowing his career in New York to keep him so disconnected from his family and friends? Only if he never let it happen again.

"Do you think that you've rebuilt your life now?" His mother's house was paces ahead of them. Ean glanced across the street. Lights shone in Ms. Helen's house.

"Not yet. But at least I have a direction." Doreen released her hold on Ean's arm to dig her house keys from her handbag. "What about you?"

"I'm on my way." Ean followed his mother up the walkway to the front steps. "I should be able to open my practice soon."

"Congratulations." His mother's grin made him feel even prouder than when he'd earned his college scholarship.

"But I wish my relationship with Megan was as easy to figure out as my law practice."

Doreen held the door open for Ean. "Uh-oh. Is there trouble in paradise?"

Ean unzipped his coat as he crossed the threshold. "Sometimes she seems a little distant, as though she's not quite sure whether things between us will last. I think she's waiting for me to leave Trinity Falls again."

"That doesn't make sense. Why would you open a law practice here if you were planning to leave?"

"I wouldn't. That's what I told her."

"I know she cares about you." Doreen shrugged out of her coat and hung it in the closet. "Give her time, Ean. Actions speak louder than words. When she realizes you've settled in, she'll stop pulling away."

"I hope so."

But how much time would Megan need? He was growing tired of being under suspicion. What more would he have to do to earn her trust?

* * *

Ramona knocked three times on Quincy's office door Thursday morning. "Am I interrupting?"

The suddenly sexy university professor rose to his feet. His penetrating stare remained on her face as he gestured toward the guest chair in front of his desk. "No. Have a seat."

His unexpected welcome made her eyes sting. Why was she so weepy? It must be fatigue. She'd barely slept last night. She drew in a deep breath, filling her lungs with the stench of stale coffee. How much of that stuff did he drink?

"Thank you." Ramona settled onto the uncomfortable oak chair. A nervous giggle popped from her lips.

"What's wrong?" Quincy sat down again.

"The last time I was here, you didn't ask me to sit. You didn't stand, either."

"The last time you were here, you were buried under makeup and hair spray." His eyes smiled at her. "The new look suits you."

Ramona touched her face. A blush crawled up her neck. "Thank you."

Quincy's eyes sobered. "What's on your mind?"

Ramona made several false starts before the words came. "You asked why I'd left New York. I left because I wasn't good enough for Ean's world."

Quincy's coal black eyes ignited with anger. Was it at her or for her? "Who said that? Ean?"

Ramona's eyes stretched so wide, they hurt. "No! Oh no! No, of course not."

"Then from where did you get that idea?"

Ramona stood to pace the office. What little

space he had was crammed with bookcases and file cabinets. She had to move carefully. The two-toned blue carpet was faded, thin and worn. It should be replaced. She was pretty sure the eggshell walls had once been white. The room needed a fresh coat of paint. The garbage can was in the wrong place. She picked it up and moved it to the other side of his desk.

Quincy gave her a dubious look. "What are you doing?"

"That should improve your feng shui."

He arched a brow. "Stop stalling."

Ramona turned to wander the room, carefully. "Ean was my ticket to the big city. But he did his job too well."

"What do you mean?" Quincy gently prompted.

She flexed her shoulders and drew in another breath of stale coffee. "When it was my turn to step into the bright lights, I got stage fright. The female lawyers and the partners' wives were so fashionable and polished. And they were smart and well-read. They made me feel like some hick who'd just bounced off a hay wagon in the middle of Madison Avenue."

"You're polished, fashionable and smart. You were keeping up with those other women . . . until you came to the well-read quality."

Ramona gave him a wounded look. "This isn't funny, Quincy. I've never felt so out of place or alone."

Quincy was desperate. Ramona seemed broken

and lost. What should he say to make her feel better?

With her face bare of makeup and her hair pulled into a simple ponytail, she reminded him of the young woman who'd gone to New York full of confidence, then returned to Trinity Falls in defeat. How could he help rebuild her self-esteem?

He crossed to her. He cupped his hands around her slender upper arms and resisted the urge to draw her into his embrace. "Did you tell Ean how you felt?"

"Of course not."

"Why not?"

She lowered her gaze. "I was too proud."

Quincy sighed. "He may have been able to help you."

"I didn't think so at the time. So I came home. I'd only meant to stay a little while, just until I got my courage back. But then my grandfather died and I couldn't leave Megan alone." Ramona's shrug was restless. "Or maybe *I* didn't want to be alone. Then the mayor's term was up, and no one else wanted the job."

Quincy released her before he hugged her. "Why did you run for office? You'd never been political before."

"Did you see the state the town was in?" She shook her head in disbelief. "The roads were falling apart. The mayor had been in office two terms too long. Doreen was doing a great job rallying the town to raise money for the schools and clinic, but we needed infrastructure help."

Quincy's lips curved into a smile. "So you stayed because you thought your cousin needed you. Then you stayed longer because you thought your town needed you."

Ramona turned away, dragging the scrunchy from her hair. "Before I knew it, six years had gone by."

"You once asked me why I'm in love with you." Quincy deliberately paraphrased Ramona's earlier words. "It's because you have a big heart."

Ramona blinked—a slow, sexy reflex that squeezed his heart. "You're the only one in Trinity Falls who thinks so."

He paced to within an arm's length of her. "They don't see the real you."

"But you do?" She didn't sound like she believed him.

"I always have." Quincy relaxed, allowing his eyes to show the love he'd hidden in his heart for fourteen years.

Ramona looked away. "You're scaring me."

Her words chilled him. "How?"

"I don't know who I am." She blurted out the words.

"Who do you think you are?"

"All my life, I thought I was a displaced New Yorker. When I finally got my chance in New York, I failed. I thought I was the mayor of Trinity Falls, but the town's trying to replace me. I've failed again."

"It's not personal, Ramona."

"It sure feels that way. Now you're telling me you

know who I am, and you always have. How is that possible? How can you see the real me when I don't even know who that is?"

The tears in her voice tore him apart. "Don't allow New York or Trinity Falls to define you. Don't even allow me to tell you who you are. Only you can decide who you are."

Ramona's ebony eyes were watery. "How do I do that?"

Quincy approached her. He drew the tip of his index finger down her soft, café au lait cheek. "Step one, you've already removed your mask."

"And step two?"

He lowered his arm. "Stop hiding from yourself and everyone else. Start following your heart. Then you'll figure it out."

For the first time, Quincy allowed himself to hope that her plans could include him.

CHAPTER 31

"I come bearing gifts." Ean entered Megan's Books & Bakery office. He offered her a mug of coffee before closing her door.

"Thank you." Megan accepted the coffee with a smile as warm as if he'd given her a bouquet of roses.

Ean wished he had brought her flowers, red ones to match her bulky red sweater and the blush in her cheeks.

She looked well rested. In contrast, he'd barely slept in the week since Leonard George had interrupted their evening with the news that his mother was going to run for office.

Ean made himself comfortable in her visitor's chair and fortified himself with coffee. "Am I forgiven for my initial reaction to my mother's decision to run for mayor?"

"Yes." Her blush deepened. "All is forgiven."

"Good." Ean set his right ankle on his left knee and drank more coffee. "I don't think you were as upset over my reaction as you claimed to be."

"I was upset, but I'm not anymore." Megan cradled the mug in her small palms, avoiding eye contact.

Ean didn't acknowledge her response. "I think you're looking for excuses to put distance between us."

"That's not true." But she still wouldn't meet his eyes.

"Then why do you act as though every other day, you expect me to pack my bags and return to New York?"

Megan was silent for several moments. Ean waited, drinking his coffee and enjoying the view of her wide chocolate eyes, honeyed skin, full red lips and delicate features.

Finally she sighed. "All right. You have a point."

"So you believe that I'm back for good?"

"I do. I do believe you're going to stay in Trinity Falls." Megan gave him a reluctant smile. It started in her eyes and made him want to kiss her.

Ean rose, setting his coffee mug on the corner of Megan's painfully organized desk. He leaned across its mahogany surface, intending to place a quick kiss on her mouth. But as her lips softened beneath his, their kiss lengthened and deepened. Ean lost track of time and place. Megan tasted of coffee and felt like home. She moaned low in her throat, bringing Ean back to his surroundings.

He exhaled, running an unsteady thumb over her soft, damp lips. "We'll explore that further, under more comfortable circumstances."

"I'll hold you to that." Megan's promise was a soft whisper.

Ean tightened his grip on his coffee cup and sank back into the visitor's chair. He wasn't entirely comfortable and her words weren't helping. "Let's change the subject."

"More talking?" Megan pouted.

Ean tried to ignore Megan's hungry gaze as it dropped from his mouth to his lap. "I think my mom will make a great mayor for Trinity Falls. But as much as it pains me to admit this, Grady had a point last night."

Megan raised her eyes to his. "About what?"

"He said we need to do something to save the center businesses now. We can't risk waiting until next year's election."

Megan straightened in her dark blue executive chair. She looked even more confident in her role as business leader today than she had when he'd returned to town almost two months ago. "I agree with him, too. But what can we do?"

"The association has to buy the center."

"You and I already talked about that." Megan drew her fingers through her thick, dark hair. "The sale price is out of our range."

"Even if everyone pools their resources?"

"Unfortunately, yes." Her eyes were dark with concern. "Grady's not the only one whose finances are balanced on that fine edge between surviving and succumbing. It's not only the economy but the increased rent, too."

Ean stilled in his seat. "How are Books and Bakery's finances?"

"The bookstore's doing fine." She smiled. "Ramona and I won't make the *Forbes* list of the top ten thousand richest women in America, but we aren't struggling, either."

"You can try to make the list next year." Ean braced his elbows on the chair's arms and leaned forward. "Each association member wouldn't have to give an equal amount. Some of us—you and I, for example—could contribute a little more."

Megan picked up her pen and rocked it between her index and middle fingers. "The group discussed that, too. At that time, Vernon, Belinda and I were willing and able to give a bit more."

"What happened?"

Megan dropped the pen. "Even if the other members had been willing to go along with that plan, we were still too far away from the asking price to make it work."

"What's the asking price?"

Megan opened her bottom desk drawer and recovered a manila folder. She flipped through the stack of papers in the folder, until she came to the page she wanted. Reading from the document, Megan named a figure that almost made Ean drop his coffee mug.

"Is there any flexibility with that price?"

Megan closed the folder. "That's their negotiated number."

Ean sighed. "You're right. That figure is steep."

"We'd need deeper pockets than the ones we

have at the town center." Megan returned the folder to her desk drawer. "Any ideas?"

"No." Ean set his empty mug on the corner of her desk. "How about you?"

"I've been wracking my brain over this since Ramona announced her intent of selling the center to a real estate investor."

Ean dragged his left hand over his hair. He had to find a way to make this work. The election was too far away to be effective for the town center. "Maybe we could take out a loan."

"Vernon and I were willing to consider it, but the other members don't want to take on more debt." Megan shrugged. "I'm not dismissing your suggestions. It's just that we've considered these proposals before and couldn't come to a consensus to support any of them."

"Would they rather lose the town center because of their pride?"

"Would it be so easy for you to depend on someone else to save your business?"

Megan's gentle question made him face an ugly truth. No, it wouldn't be easy for him to ask someone else for help. It never had been.

Without responding to her question, Ean rose from his chair and wandered her office. Business files and ledgers shared shelf space with knickknacks and family photos. Ean paused again over the photo of Megan and Ramona as little girls with their grandparents and the author.

He slipped his hands into his front pants pockets. "I wish I could buy the center myself."

"I think we all wish we could." Her voice sounded fatigued behind him. "The amount the Realtor is asking for is fair. It's just not within our reach."

"I wonder whether it is fair. This is Trinity Falls, Ohio, not New York City." Ean turned away from her bookcase. He wandered past her printer and paused behind the visitor's chair. "Perhaps they could negotiate it down further. The only way we can secure the future of the center is to own it. Otherwise, we'll always be in danger of having a new owner try to force us out and bring new businesses in, whether Trinity Falls wants those shops or not."

"You're right. We'll keep working toward a solution."

Ean nodded. From Megan's expression, he realized they were both wondering the same thing. How much time did they have to find that solution?

CHAPTER 32

After his visit with Megan, Ean walked back to his office. His steps were brisk in the crisp, cold air as he covered the sidewalk circling the center. But he slowed when he saw the woman standing outside his office. "May I help you?"

Ramona turned to face him. "Good morning, Ean."

Ean stopped and stared at his ex-girlfriend. He'd never seen her this way before. She was bundled in her familiar fake-fur coat. But her long, luxurious black hair had been scraped back from her face and stuffed under a woolen hat. She wore flats instead of her usual stilettos. Her face was devoid of any makeup, even lipstick.

"Ramona?" Ean searched her face for some idea of what was wrong. "Are you OK?"

"Of course." With her black-leather–gloved hands, Ramona pulled her cashmere hat lower on her ears. "Why do you ask?"

"This is a very different look for you." Ean

crossed to his office door. He glanced at her again from over his shoulder.

"I thought it was time for a change. Do you have a few minutes? I'd like to talk with you."

"Sure." Ean pushed open the door, allowing her to precede him into the suite.

He led Ramona into his office and helped her with her coat. She tugged off her black leather gloves and hat, pulling strands of hair free of her uncharacteristic ponytail. Had he ever seen her with her hair pulled back?

Ean stowed her belongings on the coatrack. He waited for Ramona to settle into one of his two guest chairs before taking his seat behind his desk.

"This shouldn't take long." Ramona crossed her legs and leaned back in the armchair.

"Take your time. I don't have any appointments today." What was the motivation behind her new look? Could it have anything to do with Quincy?

"Ean, what are your intentions toward my cousin?"

That was unexpected.

Ean struggled to pull his thoughts back together. "Why are you asking?"

"If you break my cousin's heart, I'll make every waking moment of your life a living hell." There was ice in her words.

He returned her steely regard. "In all the years we were together, I think you'll agree that I treated you well."

"But Megan is my younger cousin. She's not used to standing up for herself."

Ean arched a brow. "She doesn't have any trouble standing up to me."

"She does seem to have found her spine recently." Ramona tilted her head. "Have you had anything to do with that?"

The suggestion was flattering. "I doubt it."

Ramona didn't look convinced. "As long as we understand each other, Ean. If you hurt my cousin, I'll make you sorry you were ever born."

"I won't hurt her. I promise." Ean sat back in his chair, considering this new version of Ramona McCloud. "You and Megan never seemed close."

Ramona had a tendency to bully Megan, but there was no doubt she meant what she said about the consequences of his mistreating her.

She shrugged. "We've had our differences, but she's the only family I have. And I've realized that she's worth fighting for."

"Yes, she is."

"Did you know Megan had a crush on you when she was fourteen?"

"She mentioned that to me." Ean struggled to hold her gaze.

"I don't make idle threats, Ean." Ramona seemed to be channeling her inner Mafia godmother. "Anyone in town can tell you that. With a simple word from me, no one will patronize your practice."

"I'm sure that's true." Or at least she thought it was. "But it won't be necessary."

"I hope not." Ramona held his gaze. "So what are your intentions toward my cousin?"

"I'm in love with her."

Ramona seemed taken aback by his admission. And then she smiled. "That's wonderful. When can we expect a marriage proposal?"

It was Ean's turn to be surprised. "I wasn't expecting this reaction from you. You seem . . . happy."

Ramona smiled, blinking rapidly. "In the eight years we were together, you never told me you loved me."

Ean's eyes widened. "Ramona, I—"

Ramona waved her hands to interrupt him. "This is wonderful. I know you're sincere about your feelings. You wouldn't say you love her, if you didn't mean it."

"I do."

"Great! When will you propose?"

"It's not that easy." Ean was frustrated. "I don't think she trusts me."

Ramona's jaw dropped. "Why not? What have you done?"

"Nothing, but I don't think Megan believes I'm staying in Trinity Falls."

Ramona frowned. "That doesn't make sense. You've signed a one-year rental agreement with your town house, and you've started your own practice. Why would she think you're not staying?"

"It doesn't make sense to me, either."

"Well, you're just going to have to prove it to her." Ramona stood and crossed to the coatrack.

"What more can I do?"

"You'll figure it out. But it's going to have to be big, since the town house and practice didn't work."

She slipped into her coat and put the hat back on her head. "Good luck. I'm rooting for both of you."

Ean watched Ramona walk out of his office. Their conversation had been surreal. She suggested that he prove his love to Megan. But how?

Doreen opened her front door to a tired-looking Leonard Thursday night. According to her silver-and-pearl Movado wristwatch, it was almost eight o'clock.

"Practice run late?" Doreen crossed her arms and leaned against the doorjamb. Hopefully, her body language conveyed, *You'll have to work for this.*

"It was a tough practice. I don't know if the team's ready for tomorrow night's game."

More than cold air and a front step separated them. Doreen hadn't seen or heard from Leonard in a week, since the night he'd mistakenly thought he had the right to tell her not to run for mayor. No phone call, no e-mail, not even a sighting at Books & Bakery. Had her grown lover been pouting like a spoiled child? Oh, yeah. He'd have to work for this.

"That doesn't have anything to do with me." Doreen straightened from the doorjamb and started to close the door.

"Dorie, wait." Leonard sighed. "We need to talk."

Doreen raised her eyebrows in a silent question. "About what?"

"Us."

Now, after a week of having me cool my heels, he wants to talk?

Doreen hesitated before stepping back and pulling the door wider. "Fine."

Leonard crossed her threshold and took off his winter coat. Doreen closed and locked her door as she watched him hang his coat in her front closet. She pulled her fluffy brown sweater closer around her and led him into her great room.

Doreen settled onto her thick rose-colored armchair and crossed her arms and legs. "I'm listening."

Leonard dropped onto the matching sofa. "Are you sure?"

"Don't get cute with me, Leo. You're on thin ice."

"OK." Leonard rested his forearms on his thighs. "I reacted badly when you told me you were running for mayor."

"Is that supposed to be an apology?"

"No—"

"You owe me an apology. And it had better be good."

"I'm trying to explain." Leonard stood and wandered to the other side of the room. His movements were stiff and uncertain.

Doreen squashed a sense of concern and held on to her mad. "Explain what? Your temporary insanity? Go ahead. I'm all ears."

Leonard spoke with his back to her. "You and I have been dating for five months now. But we've known each other for forever. We've been there for each other through joys and sorrows."

It was getting harder to stay angry. "We've been friends for years. I think that's why it was so easy for us to slip into a relationship."

Leonard turned. "But this is more than just a simple relationship to me. Dorie, I'm in love with you."

Doreen froze. His words scattered her thoughts and temporarily stole her voice. She worked her throat, trying to unglue the muscles.

Leonard spread his arms. "Dorie. Please. Say something."

Doreen worked her throat some more. "Leo. I . . . I don't know what to say."

Leonard dropped his arms. "Tell me how you feel."

Doreen stood. She circled the armchair, putting it between them. "You're a good friend, Leo. I care about you very much."

"But you don't love me."

"Paul hasn't even been gone a year yet." Her words were breathy. Her pulse was racing. "There's a part of me that's still in love with him."

Leonard nodded. "I understand. You and Paul were together for a very long time, even longer than Claudia and I."

"I haven't completely let go." Doreen dug her fingernails into the top of the armchair. "I don't know whether I'll ever be able to."

"I wondered if you'd be able to love me after loving Paul so much." Leonard rubbed his hands over his eyes. "When he died, you closed yourself off from everyone."

Doreen locked her shaking knees. "If it weren't for you, I would've been lost. You're a good friend."

"But I want to be more than friends." Leonard

pushed his fists into his front pants pockets. "I want to be your husband."

Doreen's grip on the sturdy armchair was the only thing keeping her standing. "I have no intention of getting married ever again."

"You can't say that. You could change your mind." A hint of desperation edged his words.

Doreen maneuvered her way to the front of the chair and sank onto its cushion. "Leo, I'm glad you're in my life. I enjoy our relationship—both in and out of bed. But that's all I'm looking for right now."

"Why?"

Doreen threw up her hands in a nervous gesture. "I'm still looking for myself. I want to know who I am, who I'm becoming now that my life has taken such a devastating turn."

"Do you think you're going to find that in the mayor's office?"

She gave him a sharp look. But his tone and expression was more confused than condemning this time. "I'd like to try."

Leonard pulled his hands free of his pockets and rubbed the back of his neck. "It's hard to hear that the woman you're in love with would rather be mayor of a town than your wife."

Doreen stood and crossed to him. "I'm honored that you think of me that way."

"I was hoping for a different reaction."

She took hold of Leonard's hands and gently squeezed them. "Before I can be a couple with anyone, I need to know who I am by myself. Can you understand that?"

Leonard heaved a sigh. "I can try."

"And I would really like for things to stay the way they are between us."

He squeezed her hands in return. "If that's all you can give me for now, I'll take it."

"And for the election, I could really use your vote."

Leonard chuckled. "You'll have to work for that one."

"Fair enough." Doreen laughed with relief. Her friend, and lover, was back.

"Have you heard from Penn about your faculty position?" Ean asked the question of Quincy in a voice loud enough to be heard in the crowded sports bar.

He, Quincy and Darius were watching the National Football League's Cleveland Browns and Chicago Bears face each other in a Sunday-afternoon competition. He washed down the bite of spicy buffalo wing with a swig of weak beer.

"They've asked me back for an interview." Quincy didn't seem enthusiastic.

"When were you going to tell us?" Darius froze as he plunged a celery stalk into Quincy's blue cheese dressing.

Quincy shrugged. "I'm telling you now."

Ean read Quincy's conflict beneath his studied nonchalance. "What's bothering you?"

Quincy exhaled an irritated breath. "Why do you think something's bothering me?"

Ean gestured with a hot wing. "First, I can hear it in your voice. Second, you're letting Darius eat your celery and blue cheese."

Quincy's jaw tightened. He moved the blue cheese away from Darius. "Would it kill you to buy your own food?"

Darius dropped the remains of a buffalo wing in an empty bowl and reached for a leg this time. "Ean's right. You seem even weirder tonight. Talk."

"Nothing's bothering me." Quincy grabbed a potato chip, avoiding their eyes. "You two are like nagging old women."

"It's Ramona, isn't it?" Ean watched closely for Quincy's reaction.

The professor tensed. "What's Ramona?"

"It must be Ramona." Darius stretched across the table to scoop a celery stalk once more into Quincy's dressing.

Ean drank some of his watered-down house beer. "Are you thinking about staying in Trinity Falls now?"

"I don't know." Quincy's smile was bittersweet. "It figures I'd get this opportunity when one of my best friends returns and the woman I care about realizes I exist."

Ean's lingering concern over their strained relationship disappeared when Quincy referred to him as one of his best friends. "You don't have to take Penn's offer, if you think you'd be making a mistake."

Darius gestured with his mug of beer. "No one would think any worse of you than they do now."

Quincy cut the reporter a look before addressing Ean. "It's a smart move for my career. No one's heard of Trinity Falls University, but everyone knows the University of Pennsylvania. More prestige, more money, better location—"

Darius interrupted. "Since when did you want to move to the big city?"

"Since I realized you were staying here." Quincy's response was long-suffering. He moved his celery and blue cheese farther from Darius's reach. "I love Trinity Falls. But there's a lot of history in Philadelphia, a lot of visiting exhibitions. I'd have better access to those things if I were at Penn."

The fact that he'd come home just as his childhood friend was leaving bothered Ean as well. "It's a tough decision. I don't envy you. But luckily, it doesn't have to be a permanent one."

Darius nodded. "Ean's right. You can always change your mind."

"Just don't wait as long as I did." Ean thought back to New York. "It took seven years to realize I may have made a good career decision, but it was at the cost of things and people who were a lot more important than my career."

The three friends were silent as they watched the Browns run several plays against the Bears. The Browns struggled against the Bears' defense, though, and had to punt. Ean was only partially aware of the on-screen action. His mind still processed his regrets—the lost time with his parents, the near loss of a lifelong friendship. How different would his life be today if he'd put those relationships above his ambition and stayed in Trinity Falls?

Darius clamped a hand on Ean's shoulder. "Who would've thought all those years ago when you were planning to become a hot-shot corporate lawyer in the Big Apple, you'd return to hang a shingle in the Trinity Falls Town Center?" Darius's jovial smile didn't mask the concern in his eyes.

Ean slapped the reporter's back. "Here I have my friends and family, as well as my career."

Darius gestured for their server to bring another round of beer. "How long do you think your shingle will remain up?"

That was a sore subject with Ean. "I don't know. It depends on what happens with the center."

Quincy selected a buffalo wing from his basket. "The election isn't for another year. And even if your mother wins, she won't take office for another two months. That's a long time."

Darius grunted. "In the meantime, Ramona could sell the center out from under the business owners, and some other evil overlord could jack up the rent again."

Quincy frowned across the booth at Darius. "Ramona's not an evil overlord."

Darius gave the professor a wide-eyed look. "Did I say, 'Ramona is the evil overlord'? You're too sensitive."

Ean ignored his friends' exchange. "I think the best solution is for the business owners to buy the center ourselves."

Darius's brows knitted. "I thought they'd already considered and rejected that plan."

"They wanted everyone to put in an equal share, and not everyone could afford to." Ean rubbed the back of his neck.

"And that bothers you." Quincy made it a statement.

Actually, he thought the business owners' objections were ridiculous. "What does it matter if someone puts in twice as much money as I do and gets a bigger vote? We all have the goal of preserving the center."

"The bottom line is you need a buyer." Darius waved a buffalo wing. "But the association doesn't trust the new owners to have their interests in mind."

"I can't blame them." Quincy received another beer from their young server.

"Neither can I." Ean thanked the server as he accepted his mug.

Darius winked at the young woman as he exchanged his empty mug for the full one. "The solution is obvious."

Quincy sighed. "Do you want to share it with the rest of us, Obi-Wan?"

Darius chuckled at Quincy's *Star Wars* reference. "Ean should get some of his fat-cat friends to invest in the center with him."

Ean was intrigued. "The other business owners wouldn't want outsiders to own the center." He was thinking specifically of Megan.

"You're not an outsider." Darius dropped the remnants of another wing into the bowl. "As long as you're at least an equal partner, the association would trust you to look after their interests."

Quincy sat back in his booth seat. "I hate to say it—I really do—but his idea makes sense."

"It does." Ean's pulse kicked up. He slapped Darius's back again. "Let's hope I can pull it off."

He knew just the men to whom he should present his proposal. It would feel good to use his former law firm's resources to help the little guys for once.

CHAPTER 33

"Megan, move in with me." Ean's husky invitation came out of the dark.

Megan's heart somersaulted into her throat and stuck there. In the aftermath of their lovemaking, she had curled against him in his bed. Now she shifted away. Cool air slipped between them. She hugged the thick comforter closer, shielding her from the cold and his invitation.

It was Sunday night and the room was dark, but Megan could make out the clean, sharp lines of his face. "Don't you think it's a little soon for that? We've only been seeing each other for two months."

"But we've known each other practically all of our lives." Ean rolled onto his side, facing her.

"For seven of those years, you were in New York." His time in New York might be a sore subject between them, but it was the truth.

So why did he want to set up house with her? Was he thinking about the future and planting roots in

Trinity Falls? Or did he just want to live together for as long as he was here?

Ean's fingertips feathered across her cheek. "Time is relative, Megan."

His touch was very persuasive. Still . . . "I'd rather wait a while longer before moving in together."

"How much longer?"

"I don't know, but two months seems too soon."

Megan returned Ean's silent regard. She felt the seconds ticking by. It was difficult to tell what he was thinking and hard to concentrate with her pulse thundering in her ears.

"What's the real reason you don't want to live with me, Megan?" His quiet question made her palms sweat.

"I've told you the real reason."

"I think you're holding something back."

"In whose house would we live?" She was grasping at straws. She knew it, and she was pretty certain Ean did, too.

"Wherever you'd like. I can move into your grandparents' home with you."

"But you've signed a one-year contract for this town house."

"Then move in here with me. Either way, I don't care. I'll be fine as long as we're together."

Who wouldn't want to hear that? "I don't want to sell my grandparents' house."

"Then don't. Does that put your mind at ease?"

The silence grew. Ean continued to play with her hair, massaging her scalp, twirling strands around his fingers. Her body was so comfortable, balanced between being soothed and being aroused. But the pressure of their conversation kept her from feeling settled.

"It's too soon, Ean." Although part of her wanted to rush home and pack. She would love to move in with Ean—wake up together, go to bed together, share closet and bathroom space—but for how long? And, after all of that sharing, how much harder would it be to say good-bye?

"Try again." Ean's voice was easy.

Megan exhaled a heavy sigh. "I don't know what you want me to say."

"Do you want to know what I think?"

"Yes, I would really like to know."

"All right. I think we have a dearth of trust in our relationship."

Megan frowned. "What does that mean?"

"I think the reason you don't want to move in with me is that you still believe that I'm going to leave Trinity Falls."

She didn't want to hurt him, but she couldn't believe he was staying. She'd grown accustomed to people she cared about leaving. Even Quincy was preparing to move to Philadelphia.

Megan swallowed. "I do trust you, Ean."

"I don't think you do. I've told you I'm staying. I've shown you I'm staying. If you don't believe what I've said or what I've done, what else can I do?"

Megan blinked to ease the stinging in her eyes. "Why are you so anxious to move in together?"

Ean rose on an elbow, holding his body above hers. "Because I love falling asleep with you beside me. I love waking up with you in my arms. I want to spend every moment that I can with you. And I don't want to waste time traveling between our two homes."

His intensity threatened to sweep her along. But she needed to protect her heart, didn't she? "I'm just asking for a little more time."

Ean rolled onto his back. His sigh was deep and long. "All right."

Megan rested a tentative hand on his shoulder. "Thank you."

Ean grunted. He slipped an arm beneath her and tucked her closer to his side. "Could we at least exchange keys?"

"I'd like that." Megan laid her hand over his heart and rested her cheek on his shoulder.

He wasn't the only one disappointed. But wasn't it easier to bear disappointment now than to suffer even greater heartache later?

A week later, Megan locked her front door after letting Ramona into her home Monday afternoon.

"Another new outfit?" Ramona tossed the amused question over her shoulder as she hung her coat on the coat tree in the foyer. "The brighter colors really do suit you."

Megan glanced from her lemon yellow jersey and rust canvas pants to Ramona's scarlet sweater and skinny black jeans. "I didn't know you owned jeans."

"More than one, and in more than one color." Ramona faced Megan.

This new Ramona would take some getting used to. Her elegant café au lait features had the barest sketch of makeup: lip gloss, powder and eyeliner. She'd styled her glossy raven tresses in a simple flip.

"Did you run out of hair spray?" Megan followed Ramona through the archway into the living room.

"If we're going to critique each other's appearance, could we at least sit down? This could take a while." Ramona settled into the red velvet armchair and crossed her legs.

"You're as beautiful as always." Megan made herself comfortable on the sofa. "Shrink-wrapped minidress or skinny jeans, makeup or no makeup, teased hair or not—it doesn't matter."

Ramona's expression sobered from her usual condescending derision. "And so are you."

Megan's eyes stretched wide at the unusual compliment. "Thank you."

"But I hope you're doing it for you, and not for Ean." Ramona waved her hand to take in Megan's appearance. "Your brighter wardrobe, styled hair and makeup are very flattering and definitely overdue. But you should make the effort for yourself, and not for some man."

Megan lost the struggle against her smile. "And who were your fashion choices for, before you decided to reduce the effort?"

"They were for me." Ramona dropped her gaze to a spot on the Berber carpet. "But I wasn't using them to boost my confidence. I was hiding behind them."

Had she heard Ramona correctly? "Why?"

"Because I didn't think I was good enough."

Ramona's sigh was self-castigating. "That's why I hid behind heavy makeup and provocative clothes. And before you ask why, I'll just tell you right now that I don't know."

Megan studied Ramona. Her minimal makeup made her look more approachable. "What made you realize that's what you were doing?"

"Not *what, who.*" Ramona hesitated several seconds before answering. "Quincy."

"Oh?" Megan thought she masked her surprise very well. "What did he say?"

"When I asked him why he was attracted to me, he didn't say my face, my figure or my hair. He talked about things I'd done." The faint blush that highlighted her cheekbones was more appealing because it was natural.

"Quincy really cares about you, Ramona. How do you feel about him?"

"I like the way he sees me." Ramona's ebony eyes were troubled. "But suppose that novelty wears off and he realizes I'm just a shallow bitch—the way everyone else in Trinity Falls sees me."

Megan's lips tightened. "A shallow bitch wouldn't have run for mayor when no one else in town would."

Ramona arched a brow. "That's what Quincy said."

"'Great minds think alike.' Quincy's had feelings for you for years. He sees what's inside you. He always has."

Megan understood Ramona's uncertainty. She also liked the way Ean saw her. His characterization of her was very different from the way she saw herself. But in a good way—a way that made her stronger and more confident.

Ramona sighed. "It's been years since we've talked like this."

"I like it." They were sharing confidences like . . . family.

"So do I." Ramona checked her gold Movado wristwatch. "Are you free for lunch?"

"Yes." Megan stood. "Where do you want to go?"

"How about Trinity Falls Cuisine? I'll drive." Ramona slipped back into her coat.

A burst of surprised laughter escaped Megan. "Just don't interrogate the server again." She zipped her winter coat, then held the front door open for Ramona to precede her.

"I won't." Ramona's cheeks flushed again. "What's Ean doing?"

"He has a business meeting." Megan locked the front door behind them, then followed Ramona down her walkway to her car. If it wasn't thirty degrees with snow on the ground, they could have walked to the restaurant.

"With a client?"

Megan shrugged, ill at ease. Had he been evasive that morning, or had that been her imagination? "He said it has to do with his practice."

"Sounds mysterious."

Megan thought so as well. She settled into the passenger seat of Ramona's silver Honda Accord. "I'm sure I'll get more details at dinner tonight."

Ramona started her engine. "Ean cares about you. A lot."

"I know." Megan buckled her seat belt. "I care about him, too."

Enough to move in with him? Yes, definitely. She imagined Ean's reaction when she told him tonight. Her decision made, Megan felt warm despite the cold.

A few minutes later, Megan trailed Ramona to the restaurant's hostess station. She blinked a bit in the darkened interior before glancing at the nearby booths and tables.

"Good afternoon, ladies. Welcome to Trinity Falls Cuisine. Table for two?" The young hostess looked uncomfortable in her skinny black pants, starched white shirt and narrow black tie.

At Ramona's nod, she led them to a booth in the same area of the restaurant in which she, Ramona, Quincy and Ean had unexpectedly had dinner together weeks before.

Megan froze.

Near the same booth sat Ean with three older men. Their Park Avenue suits branded them as outsiders.

Ramona had noticed them, too. "Those are Ean's former law partners." She left their booth and made a beeline for Ean.

"Ramona, wait." Megan found herself hissing to thin air. She gritted her teeth before following in her cousin's wake.

"Hello, Ean." Ramona turned to face his companions. "Gentlemen, what a surprise to see you here in Trinity Falls. Welcome."

CHAPTER 34

Ean and the three outsiders stood, stepping away from their table. They wore their wealth, privilege and power like cologne. Megan swallowed hard. What were Ean's former law firm's partners doing here?

"Ramona, I thought you'd never eat here again." Ean's easy smile faded when he noticed Megan.

Megan ignored the chill seeping into her bones. "I was surprised she picked this restaurant as well." She sealed her lips to trap any further comments inside her mouth.

Why are you having lunch with your former firm's partners?

When were you going to tell me about your meeting with them?

Ean's expression was guarded, as though he'd heard the questions. He gestured toward the tall, imposing silver-haired man beside him. "Let me introduce you. Megan McCloud, this is Hugh Bolden, my former boss."

Hugh extended his hand. His laser blue eyes seemed to take her measure. "Pleasure."

Ean continued down the line. "August Craven."

Megan released Hugh's hand to accept August's greeting. The older gentleman's smile deepened the creases on his cocoa skin. "Nice to meet you."

Ean moved on to the final introduction. "Jorge Arnez."

Megan stepped forward to greet the youngest and tallest of the group. The thick waves of his inky black hair hinted at threads of gray. His large hand enveloped hers. "It is a pleasure."

Megan released Jorge's hand. "It's good to meet you as well."

"How long are you gentlemen staying?" Ramona made the question sound natural.

Jorge responded for the group. "This is just a day trip."

"A day?" Ramona sounded surprised. "Trinity Falls may be small, but you won't get to see much in one day."

Megan felt Ean's eyes on her. She turned to him. *Tell me they're not here to ask you to return to New York.*

Ean smiled and cupped her cheek. "I'll see you later."

Megan's breath caught in her throat. She'd gotten a brush-off when she'd needed reassurance.

"Enjoy your lunch." She led Ramona back to their table.

Their server, a young man in need of a haircut, appeared. He traded a basket of fresh rolls for their drink orders. They both asked for iced tea with lemon, then he left.

Ramona opened her menu. "Breathe."

"What?" Megan's thoughts were spinning so fast. She would either pass out or throw up.

"You're turning blue." Ramona lowered her menu. "What's wrong?"

Breathe in. Breathe out.

The restaurant was full. A quick look around confirmed Megan's suspicions. Most of the diners were looking from Ean, to his visitors, to her and back again. Their attention skittered away when they saw her watching them.

"What's wrong?" Megan struggled for composure. "Do you really think Ean's former bosses flew in from New York just to visit Trinity Falls, Ohio?"

"No-o-o." Ramona gave the simple word a few extra syllables. "But why do *you* think they're here?"

"It's obvious. They want Ean to return to New York."

Ramona frowned. "How is that obvious?"

Beneath the table, Megan clenched her fists to stop their trembling. "Why else are they wearing Lord and Taylor suits? This isn't a visit. It's a business meeting."

Ramona slid a look across the aisle toward the table of very well-dressed men. "They do look fine."

"Focus." Megan's hands itched to shake her cousin.

"What?" Ramona gave Megan her full, wide-eyed attention. "Just because his former bosses are here doesn't mean they're trying to get him back."

"Then why are they here?"

Ramona continued. "And even if they were trying to talk him into returning to the firm, that doesn't mean he would. He's in love with you."

Shock punched her in the gut. Megan sucked in a breath. "How do you know?"

Ramona rolled her ebony eyes. "I'm not blind."

Megan had hoped for a stronger endorsement, perhaps something like, *I can see it on his face. I could hear it in his voice; He told me.*

Their server returned with their drinks and took their meal requests. Ramona asked for the grilled salmon and Caesar salad. Megan picked the chicken noodle soup and sandwich at random.

Megan sweetened her iced tea. "I know Ean cares about me, but does he care enough to stay in Trinity Falls?"

"Why wouldn't he stay here?" Ramona stirred the lemon slice into her drink.

Megan lifted her gaze toward Ean's table. "I—"

"Stop staring." Ramona interrupted her.

Megan lowered her eyes. She sipped her iced tea. It was a struggle to keep her gaze from returning to Ean and his group. She squeezed her drink's lemon garnish into her beverage. "You've said yourself, repeatedly, that Trinity Falls is slow, boring and backward."

"It is." Ramona sipped her drink.

"Ean spent seven years in New York. How can he be satisfied with Trinity Falls after that?"

"Where have you been for the past two months?" Ramona set her glass on the table. "No one twisted

Ean's arm to get him to return to Trinity Falls. He came back on his own."

"I know that." Her glass was cold and wet between her palms. "He'd had enough of the rat race and came home to spend more time with his family and friends."

"So you *were* listening." Ramona pulled apart a wheat roll and slathered it with butter. "His father was dying, and he didn't even know. Do you really think the firm's partners would be able to persuade him to go back to working for them after something like that?"

They sat in pensive silence for several minutes. Ramona finished a buttered roll. Megan toyed with her drink. Finally their server returned with lunch. Once Megan and Ramona assured him they didn't need anything more, the young man disappeared.

Megan stared at her soup and sandwich. "Maybe they wouldn't be able to change his mind this time, but suppose they try again?"

Ramona's sigh was short and irritated. "Now you're borrowing trouble."

"Maybe because I'm scared." Megan stirred her chicken soup as she watched Ramona slice her salmon salad into more manageable pieces.

Her cousin stabbed a forkful of the salad and chewed. She seemed deep in thought. "Let's say, for argument's sake, Ean does decide to return to New York. Why couldn't you go with him?"

The question caught Megan by surprise. "He hasn't asked me."

Ramona rolled her eyes again. She spoke with

exaggerated patience. "For argument's sake, let's say he did. What's keeping you in Trinity Falls?"

Megan spread her arms. "Our bookstore, our grandparents' house. This town is my home."

"Home is where your heart is. Is a store and a house more important than your relationship with Ean?"

The server appeared to check on their meals and refill their iced tea. He then crossed to Ean's booth. Megan's gaze followed the young man as he returned Ean's credit card and left the receipt for the bill before going back to his station.

Megan looked away. A week ago, Ean had asked her to move in with him. Today he was having lunch with the principals of his former law firm. A meeting he'd never mentioned to her. What did Ean really want? Did he want to settle down to a small-town life with her? Or was he considering returning to his cosmopolitan life in the Big Apple?

Megan sighed. "I don't know if I could live in New York."

Ramona forked up more of her salad. "It does take some getting used to. But perhaps a better question would be, could you live without Ean?"

Megan stared at her half-eaten sandwich and cooling chicken noodle soup. "I don't know if I can do that, either."

She looked up as Ean and his companions stood to leave the restaurant. His eyes found hers as he drew closer. Ean offered a smile Megan couldn't return.

Ramona's voice cut through the fog in her mind. "You'd better figure it out."

Megan knew her cousin was right. She also knew she was running out of time.

CHAPTER 35

Megan opened her front door to Ean later that afternoon. He wore the sexy grin that usually made bubbles pop in her stomach. Today the bubbles sat like bricks. She stepped back, pulling the door wider.

Ean shrugged out of his coat. "You're probably wondering why I didn't tell you I was having lunch with my ex-bosses."

Megan locked her front door, then turned to watch Ean hook his winter jacket onto her coat tree. "I know what you were doing."

His smile wavered. "You do?"

"Your firm wants you back." Megan stepped away from the door. She crossed her foyer, past her cheery if overdecorated Christmas tree, into her living room.

"What makes you think that?" His voice seemed cooler.

"Their suits." Megan faced him. More than the width of the living room separated them. "If they were here to visit with you, they would have worn casual clothes. Since they wore business suits, it was obviously a business meeting."

Ean had changed his clothing since she'd seen him at lunch earlier today. At the restaurant, he'd worn a gunmetal gray suit. His cool green shirt and dark green tie had complemented his olive green eyes. Now, in addition to his dark blue jeans, he wore a bronze sweater that spanned his broad pectorals and hugged his washboard abs.

His smile disappeared. "And that business was offering me my old job back." Ean paused in the archway between the two rooms, ironically beneath the mistletoe.

"What other business could they have with you?" Megan narrowed her eyes. *What does he have to be angry about? I'm the one being misled.*

"They couldn't have any other reason for meeting with me. And, of course, I'd accept their offer, even though I've signed a yearlong contract on my town house and a three-year lease on office space." Ean shoved his hands into the front pockets of his jeans. "You're very insightful to deduce all of that from our business suits."

Megan frowned. "Why are you angry?"

"What makes you think I'm angry? Is it because I'm wearing a bronze sweater?"

Megan crossed her arms over her chest. "Are you mocking me?"

"Yes."

"Why?" She hadn't expected Ean to be happy to

have her confront him, but she hadn't expected mockery, either.

"Because your suit theory is the dumbest thing I've ever heard." He dragged both hands over his hair.

"What?" Megan dropped her arms and clenched her fist.

"I've told you that I'm staying. I've shown you. I've even asked you to live with me. What more do I have to do to convince you that I'm not leaving?"

"How can you go from always wanting a successful career in New York and leaving that career to return to Trinity Falls, Ohio?"

"I'm fourteen years older." Ean stood with his legs braced and his hands planted on his hips. "You're the one who told me people don't stay the same. Why won't you believe that I've changed?"

"Everyone leaves, Ean."

"Not me. And, obviously, not you."

Megan spread her arms. "What was I supposed to think when I saw you having lunch with your former bosses?"

"That I'd tell you later why I met with them. That I'd have a damn good reason not to tell you in advance about the meeting." Ean tugged his jacket from her coat tree. "I never thought you'd consider me a liar."

Megan gritted her teeth. "All right. Tell me now. Why were you meeting with them?"

Ean regarded her in silence as he zipped himself into his coat. "I asked you to move in with me. Did you tell me you wouldn't because you didn't have faith that I'd stay in Trinity Falls?"

"You're changing the subject." Megan's cheeks burned.

"Am I?" There was pain in Ean's eyes. "All this time we've been together, I thought we were in a relationship."

"We were. . . . We are." What was he saying?

"But you never trusted me."

"I . . ." All her anger drained away. Is that how it seemed?

"If we don't have trust, we don't have a relationship. All we have is sex. The sex is great, but I was hoping for something more." Ean turned for the door.

Megan hurried after him. Her words rushed over each other. "Ean, you caught me by surprise. I wasn't expecting to see your firm's partners. I didn't know what to think." She laid her hand on his shoulder, hoping he'd face her.

Ean turned to her. "You should have asked me."

"I'm asking you now. Please." Her eyes stung with tears. Her voice trembled with fear. "Tell me, why were you meeting with them?"

"No, I don't think I will." Ean's face was expressionless. "You chose to believe the worst of me, instead of asking for an explanation. That's what matters now."

Megan watched Ean leave, unable to stop him. She'd allowed fear to dictate her relationship with him. She'd actually believed she could fall in love and still protect her heart. The pain in her chest let her know just how stupid she'd been.

Christmas Eve, Books & Bakery reflected Megan's love of this time of year. Decorative snowflakes and stars swung from the store's ceiling. Bookshelves were trimmed with tinsel, ribbons or bows. A real seven-foot evergreen dominated the center of the store. Every inch of it was as overdecorated as the Christmas tree in her home.

The store was merry and bright with the holiday, but Megan felt like Scrooge. She'd wanted to cancel this emergency Tuesday-night association meeting so she could go home and sulk behind the closed door of her darkened bedroom. But Ramona had asked her specifically for the opportunity to address the group. She couldn't say no, but she wished she had.

"Good evening, everyone." Megan waited for their attention. They all looked at her, looked at Ean, then looked away. Was their breakup that obvious?

"I want to thank everyone for coming tonight." Megan started again. "It's Christmas Eve. I'm sure you all had other plans. But Mayor McCloud asked to address our group, so I'll turn the meeting over to her. Mayor?"

Megan sat as Ramona stood to address the six-member business association.

From the corner of her eye, Megan slid a glance at Ean. She hadn't seen him since Monday evening.

But tonight he sat on the other side of Doreen, close enough to touch. He looked as though he'd slept like a baby last night. She hadn't. If she looked the way she felt, she was probably frightening small children and animals.

Ramona cleared her throat. "Good evening, everyone."

Murmured responses circled the two tables the group had pushed together prior to the meeting.

Ramona continued. "I won't keep you long. As you know, last spring, the original town center owners defaulted on their loan. Ever since that time, the town has been looking for new ownership for the center."

Tilda Maddox shifted in her seat. "We don't need the history lesson, Mayor. Just tell us if you're going to raise our rent again."

Perhaps Megan should have been used to Tilda's rudeness by now, but she wasn't. "Tilda, be patient. The mayor is putting her announcement in context."

Ramona inclined her head toward Megan in silent thanks before continuing. "As I was saying, the town declared the default and hired a rental agency to collect the rents and a real estate agent to find a new owner." Ramona paused to look around the tables at the members. "I'm pleased to announce that we have a new owner for the Trinity Falls Town Center, the limited partnership of Fever, Craven, Bolden and Arnez."

Megan's jaw dropped. Her pulse was drumming in her ears. A look around the table revealed she wasn't the only one in shock.

"What did you say?" She wasn't even aware of asking the question.

Ramona's eyes were bright with laughter. "Ean and his friends, the partners of the law firm of Craven, Bolden and Arnez, are the new owners of the Trinity Falls Town Center." Ramona gestured toward Ean. "Ean is the majority owner. The town council members and I are confident that Ean and the other owners have the best interests of the town and the center's businesses in mind."

Megan managed to close her mouth. She turned to Ean. "Was this the reason for your business meeting Monday?"

"Yes." Ean's olive eyes were blank.

Megan wanted to curl into the fetal position, pull a blanket over her head, hide under the table. "Thank you."

"You're welcome." Ean's tone was cool as he stood. "Thank you, Mayor McCloud."

"Thank you, Ean." Ramona sent Megan an empathetic look as she reclaimed her seat.

Ean looked around the table, but avoided Megan's eyes. He feared he'd get lost in her gaze and not find his way back. "I realize this announcement comes as a surprise."

"You've got that right," Tilda barked. "Why didn't you tell us you were planning this stunt?"

Ean pinned her with a look. "I wasn't obligated to discuss my decision with you."

Tilda's eyes widened. "Sounds just like a damn lawyer." Her response was a low grumble.

Grady's frown was more perplexed than antagonistic. "We let you become a part of this group. It would have been common courtesy to let us know what you were planning, so this wouldn't come as a surprise."

Megan leaned forward, setting her elbows on the table. "We didn't *let* Ean join the association, Grady. Every business in the center is invited to join the group, although each business has the right to decline our invitation."

Doreen nodded. "For months, we've been trying to figure out an answer to this ownership problem. Instead of jumping down Ean's throat, we should be thanking him for coming up with a solution."

The glow of pride in his mother's eyes eased his temper.

"Hold on, Doreen." Belinda's voice claimed Ean's attention. "So, does this mean you're not running for mayor?"

"Oh no. I'm still running for mayor." Doreen turned to Ramona. "Nothing personal."

Ramona returned Doreen's smile. "Same here."

"Ean." Megan raised her voice above the cacophony of private conversations. "What plans do you and your partners have for the center?"

The store experienced sudden and complete silence. Ean met Megan's gaze. Her eyes held an important question. It showed she understood the significance of this business venture. It also meant she was willing to treat him as a professional regardless of what was happening in their personal relationship.

He missed her so badly. And it had only been one night. Does this get any easier?

Ean cleared his throat. "My partners and I have discussed the business center and our roles in it at length. We recognize that most of these businesses are family-owned companies that have served this town for generations. We want to preserve that."

Belinda shrugged. "So what does that mean to me?"

Ean looked at each association member in turn, settling his gaze on Megan again. "It means we're rolling back rents to what they were prior to the town taking over the center."

A startled silence descended on the table as though all of the air had been sucked from the store. Then a collective gasp rose, followed by a round of applause.

Through it all, Ean kept his attention on Megan. Her expression swept from puzzlement, to shock, to amazement and finally joy. She sprang from her chair. She took a step forward as though to embrace him. He knew the moment she remembered they'd broken up. The pain in her eyes matched the ache in his chest. Ean looked away.

Grady swept him into a surprise bear hug, which lifted him from his feet and realigned his spine. "Ean, my man, you are A-OK in my book. A number-one OK in my book! This is the best news I've gotten all year! The greatest Christmas gift I could ever get *ever*!"

That quickly Ean morphed from an interloper, who'd overstepped his boundaries, to the accessory store owner's best friend. The older man released him. Ean gasped for air. He saw Megan grinning and wiping tears from her eyes. Tears of happiness, as well as laughter?

The image was bittersweet. In his mind, Ean had pictured himself making this announcement, then sweeping Megan into his arms. Instead, Grady had squeezed the life from him.

Damn it! He'd never done anything to cause her to mistrust him. He missed her so damn badly. But, apparently, their relationship had existed only in his imagination.

About an hour later, Ean was asking himself for the fourth time, *Why am I putting myself through this?*

He glanced at Megan seated beside him in his silver Lexus coupe. Her seat belt was secured across her slender body. After the meeting, they'd accompanied Doreen to her front door. They wished her a hasty "good night" before rushing back through the biting cold to his car. He checked his mirrors before pulling away from the curb in front of his mother's house.

He would drive Megan home before continuing to his town house. Ean had taken Megan home from the bookstore so many times in the two months since he'd returned to Trinity Falls. He'd enjoyed her company in the past. Tonight it was torture. In the quiet, warming confines of his car, with the darkness surrounding them, Ean sensed her beside him. He tugged his gaze from her elegant profile. He smelled her soft powder fragrance. He tasted her skin with his mind.

Torture.

But it was only three blocks. Ean tightened his grip on the steering wheel. He could handle this, as long as they remained quiet.

"I owe you an apology." Megan's voice broke the merciful silence. "I should have realized that you weren't meeting with your former bosses for yourself. You were meeting with them for the center."

"Apology accepted." Ean halted his car beside the Stop sign. With the roads empty, he continued through the intersection.

"I'm serious, Ean. I'm very sorry."

Ean's throat muscles flexed. "So am I, Megan. I'm sorry you didn't trust me."

"It's not that I didn't trust you." There was a muted rustle as Megan shifted in her passenger seat.

"So what was it?" *Don't look at her. Don't reach out to her. Keep your eyes on the road and your hands on the steering wheel.*

"I was afraid the partners would make you an offer you couldn't refuse."

"Just as I said." Ean's lips curved in bitter amusement. "You didn't trust me to keep my word."

"Ean, I was—"

"But I didn't just give you my word. I gave you a rental contract, a lease agreement and membership in the local business association." Ean clenched his teeth to stop his words. What good would they do? They'd gone over this before.

The car was silent for several minutes. Ean

braked at another Stop sign, then breathed in relief as he steered his Lexus toward Megan's block.

"You're right to be angry." Megan's words wobbled with emotion. "I should have believed you. I shouldn't have allowed my fear to confuse me."

Ean tried to harden his heart against Megan's sorrow. He couldn't. But he couldn't dig his way out of his own hurt and disappointment, either. Ean parked his car in her driveway.

He wrenched the emergency brake into place before turning to face her. "I thought we were more than bed partners."

"We were!"

"I told you I was thinking of a future with you. Did you think I was lying?"

"I was confused." Her voice cracked. Her tears broke free.

Ean turned away before he started crying, too. He shoved his driver's-side door open and stepped out of the Lexus. He barely noticed the burst of cold air that wrapped around him as he circled his car.

He pulled open the passenger door and extended his free hand. "Come on."

The feel of Megan's small, gloved hand in his made him want to hold on forever. Ean released her and stepped back as soon as she was steady on her feet. He fisted his hands to keep from tracing the tears rolling slowly down her cheeks.

Megan swiped away her tears, then looked at him. "Please. Give me another chance, Ean."

The entreaty in her wet chocolate eyes pierced his heart like an ice pick, over and over and over again.

Ean swallowed twice before attempting to speak. He opened his mouth, then swallowed again. "I can't keep proving myself to you."

"You won't need to."

How he wanted to believe her. "You're ready to trust me this time?"

"Yes." Megan wiped more tears from her cheeks.

Ean ignored the cold and returned Megan's regard for a long, silent moment. It would be so easy to pull her into his arms and cover her mouth with his own. His body wanted to touch her, to taste her again. But his heart hadn't healed from the wound of her distrust.

He stuffed his gloved hands into his jacket pockets. "You've said that before."

Megan blinked, long and slowly, then squared her shoulders. "I understand. It's my turn to prove myself to you. And I will."

She walked past him to her front door. Ean watched her enter her home. She'd left the light on in her foyer as usual. He stared blindly at her house before getting back into his car.

Damn it! He'd taken her at her word when she'd said she believed he was home for good. She'd lied. Now she was claiming she could prove she trusted him. What could she possibly do to convince him that their relationship was more than just sex? Really, really great sex.

CHAPTER 36

"Good. You're here." Ramona's pronouncement broke Megan's concentration.

Megan glanced up from her year-end accounting report to find her cousin striding into her office at Books & Bakery. It was Saturday morning, four days before New Year's Eve. She laid her pencil on her desk. "It's good to see you, too." And she meant it. Girl talk was a powerful thing. It had healed a decaying family bond. It could probably forge a bridge to world peace.

Ramona settled into one of the dark blue visitor's chairs in front of her desk. "I've already spoken with Doreen, but I wanted to talk with you about this myself."

A sliver of unease grew in her gut. "About what?"

Ramona crossed her legs, smoothing her purple velvet maxiskirt over her thigh. "I've decided to withdraw from the mayoral race."

Megan's expression felt frozen. "What changed your mind about running?"

"I've thought about this a lot since Doreen announced her campaign." Ramona wrapped her hands around the overstuffed arms of the guest chair. "I don't really enjoy being mayor. I never have. But Doreen has a passion for that kind of responsibility. So I've decided to withdraw my candidacy and endorse her campaign."

Megan's eyebrows rose. "I'm sure she's thrilled to have your support."

Ramona waved a dismissive hand. "She deserves it. I told her I wished her every happiness and great success. And I meant it."

Remarkable. Megan examined her cousin's features and listened hard to her voice. She didn't detect even an ounce of regret in Ramona's expression or her tone.

"What are you going to do with all your spare time?" *Do I really want to know the answer?*

Ramona's shoulders rose and fell in a movement that was almost theatrical. "Well, now that someone who actually wants to be mayor is running, I'm going to follow my own dream."

"You're moving to New York." Megan answered her own question.

"I haven't decided yet. I'd like to try a cosmopolitan city, but New York isn't the only big city out there." Her cousin's eyes were bright with excitement.

Megan wished she could feel the same. "I've heard Philadelphia is nice."

A faint blush filled Ramona's cheeks. "I've heard that, too."

Megan coughed, trying to dislodge the lump building in her throat. "I've known this day was coming. Now that it's here, I don't feel prepared."

"It's not as though I'm leaving next week or even next month." Ramona offered her a smile that wasn't quite steady around the edges. "It'll take me a while to figure out where I'm going and what I'm going to do once I get there."

"Why are you leaving?" Megan's voice faded at the end of her question.

"I need a bigger playground, Megan." Ramona's response lacked conviction. "I need more excitement. I wasn't up for the challenge before, but my experiences over the past six years have given me more confidence. You've become more confident, too."

Megan nodded, buying herself time to clear the burning mass from her throat. She looked away, blinking rapidly. She wouldn't cry. That would be too ridiculous. "I just feel as though, now that we're growing closer, you're moving away."

"Something tells me you'll be too preoccupied to even miss me." Ramona's voice was thick with amusement—and a hint of sorrow.

Megan couldn't hold back the tears. She swiped them angrily away. "I don't know about that. Ean and I haven't seen or even talked to each other since the night you announced the center's sale."

"That was five days ago."

"I know."

"You didn't even speak on Christmas Day?" It was Ramona's turn to gape at Megan. "Why are you giving each other the silent treatment over such a small misunderstanding?"

"It's not that small. He doesn't think I trust him." Megan pulled a tissue from the box on her desk and wiped her nose.

"Because you wanted to know why he was meeting with his former bosses?"

"And because I didn't want to move in with him."

"Oh, Megan." Ramona sighed. "Does this have anything to do with your fear that he's not going to stay in Trinity Falls?"

Megan nodded. "But now I really do believe that he's going to stay."

"Then tell him."

"I did. He didn't believe me." Megan rubbed her forehead. "I have to figure out a way to show him that I believe him. But I don't know what to do."

"It's going to have to be something pretty big. I mean, the man did just buy the town center for you."

Megan blinked. "He didn't buy it for me. He bought it for the town."

Ramona chuckled. "I'm pretty sure your involvement went a long way toward swaying his decision."

Megan dropped her head into her hands. "If that's true, now I feel worse."

"You'd better find a way to make it up to him soon. There's nothing worse than living with regret."

"Trust me. I don't want to live with this feeling any longer than I have to."

* * *

Megan slowed to an easy jog along the sidewalk three blocks from her home. She'd pushed herself during her New Year's Eve jog this Tuesday morning, adding an extra mile to her workout. The air was cool against her heated cheeks. Sweat dripped incongruously from her brow. She'd hoped the exercise would clear her thoughts and help her come up with a plan to win back Ean. But her mind had remained painfully blank.

Her gaze slid toward Doreen's house. Was Ean inside? Maybe she should cross the street and check. Doreen was probably awake. She wouldn't have to ring the bell. She could just knock. . . .

"Megan McCloud, get out of the cold!" Ms. Helen's admonishment shot like a bullet from her porch.

Megan jumped a foot above the sidewalk. She pressed her hand to her chest and stumbled to a stop in front of the older woman's home. "Ms. Helen, you scared ten years off my life."

"Good." The older woman stood shivering in her doorway. "I hope I scared some sense into you, too. Now come inside before you freeze to death."

Her muscles were still recovering from the surprise attack. Nevertheless, Megan hurried to obey Ms. Helen's order. She wasn't far from home, nor was she cold—thanks to her run. But the older woman was in maximum-fuss mode. Experience had taught Megan that Ms. Helen would continue to target her until Megan surrendered. She toed off her shoes before entering her neighbor's home.

"Good Lord, child. What would your grandparents

think to see you out running in the cold?" Ms. Helen continued the chastisement as she let Megan into her foyer.

The room was warm and cheerful with the holiday spirit. Christmas greeting cards were suspended from a cord Ms. Helen had tied across the top of her windows. The air was fragrant with the scents of pine from the thick, natural Christmas tree and apples from a nearby candle.

"Ms. Helen, you worry like this every time you see me jogging in the winter." She would have taken an alternate route home, but Megan had secretly hoped to run into Ean.

Ms. Helen grunted. "And you never listen. Come on back. I'll fix you some tea to warm you up."

Megan pulled off her ear warmers and tugged off her gloves. She followed her neighbor through her living and dining rooms, and into her kitchen. The older woman looked comfortable in a red velour lounge suit that picked up the healthy blush of her cheeks. Her oversized, fuzzy purple slippers were silent on her hardwood flooring.

Ms. Helen had enhanced the kitchen's white-and-yellow color scheme with hand towels, pot holders and Christmas curtains that added the season's green-and-red accents.

Megan settled into a chair at the table and watched her hostess prepare their tea. "Happy New Year, Ms. Helen."

"Happy New Year to you, too, baby." Ms. Helen

spoke with her back to Megan as she pulled mugs, tea bags and sugar from her cupboards.

With a smile, Megan shook her head at the familiar exchange. "Did you have a good Christmas?"

"Oh yes. This year, all of the cousins returned to Trinity Falls with their children. They left yesterday. It was a good visit."

Megan nodded. Ms. Helen's relatives were scattered across the country and took turns hosting the family's Christmas reunions. "Will they come back for the Founders Day celebration this summer?"

"They'd better." Ms. Helen's tone was stern. "This one's the sesquicentennial. It's too important to miss."

"I hope Jack Sansbury feels the same way."

The kettle boiled. Ms. Helen turned off the burner and poured the hot water into two mugs. "He's the last member of the town's founding family. He'll come around by then."

Megan accepted the tea from her hostess. "Thank you."

"I haven't seen Ean running with you for a few days now." Ms. Helen settled into the chair across the table. "When are you two going to settle this foolishness and make up?"

Megan dropped her gaze. "I wish I knew, Ms. Helen."

Ms. Helen grunted. "I was young and stupid once. But I didn't know it at the time. Well, I knew I was young. Didn't know I was stupid."

Megan smiled. "How did you come to find out you were stupid?"

"I fell in love." Ms. Helen laughed at Megan's expression. "You'd never imagined that I'd had a torrid love affair, did you? Actually, I've had more than one."

"Why didn't you ever marry?" Megan looked with new eyes at her elderly neighbor.

Ms. Helen blew into her mug of hot tea. "I came close to marriage during my first love affair. I met him while I was teaching at the college. Well, it was a college then. It's a university now."

"Was he a professor, too?" Megan recalled Ms. Helen had taught physics at what was then Trinity Falls College. She'd been Dr. Helen Gaston in those days, decades before the town's children began calling her "Ms. Helen."

Ms. Helen nodded. "He taught political science."

"What happened?" Megan prompted. Ms. Helen wasn't telling the story fast enough.

Ms. Helen's gaze became distant as though she was reviewing the events from her past. "He was a fine man. Tall, lean, broad shoulders. He had a great butt. Far too sexy to teach political science. And I told him so."

Remarkable. Megan had known Ms. Helen her entire life but had never heard the story of her lost love. Had anyone?

"What happened?" She prompted again.

Ms. Helen's gaze came back into focus. "He wasn't from Trinity Falls and didn't want to stay. But I didn't want to leave. I was born here. I grew up here. I'd attended universities in big cities, but Trinity Falls was my home." She arched an eyebrow. "Sound familiar?"

Megan nodded. Ms. Helen's story was her own. "So he left."

"He left. He became a campaign advisor to a political candidate in Chicago." Ms. Helen sipped her tea. "I was devastated for a long time. A very long time."

"I'm so sorry." Megan could only imagine the older woman's heartache. She was experiencing a smaller version of it now.

Ms. Helen seemed to shake off the memories. "I heard he married a stunning young woman with excellent political connections."

"Oh no."

"A few years later, he went to prison."

Megan blinked. "What?"

"He was caught embezzling from that Chicago politician's reelection campaign fund." Ms. Helen propped her chin on her fist and lowered her voice. "I'd always wondered if he stole the money to please his wife. She looked to be used to the finer things."

"Oh." What else could she say?

"'Oh,' indeed." Ms. Helen lowered her arm to the table. "Do you know the difference between my lover and yours?"

"Besides the fact that Ean would never embezzle money?"

Ms. Helen chuckled. "Yes, besides that."

"What is it?" *Am I really having this conversation with Ms. Helen?*

"My lover left Trinity Falls. Yours came back. Your fear of losing him became a self-fulfilling prophesy. He didn't leave Trinity Falls, but he did leave you."

The words were hard to hear. "I shouldn't have given in to my fear."

"No, you shouldn't have."

Megan felt worse. "Do you have any advice for me?"

"Yes, I do."

Megan's heart jumped. "What is it?"

"Don't wait too long to make things right."

"This isn't much of a New Year's celebration." Quincy's voice rumbled into Ramona's town hall office Tuesday afternoon.

Ramona's heart lurched. She spun her chair away from her computer monitor and pointed it toward her doorway. Even after several blinks, the suddenly sexy university professor didn't disappear like an apparition conjured by her secret fantasies.

"It's New Year's Eve." Her response was faint. She cleared her throat and tried again. "I thought you were in Florida."

"I got back this morning." Quincy paced forward.

His long legs were clad in dark blue jeans. His broad-shouldered torso was gift wrapped in a sage green crewneck. Ramona's heart thudded in her chest. They were the only two souls in the building.

Everyone else had the week between Christmas Eve and New Year's Day off. She swallowed hard.

"You usually stay until after the New Year." She couldn't pull her gaze from him as he drew closer.

Quincy settled into the visitor's chair in front of her desk. "I hadn't realized you'd noticed."

Neither had she, until this moment. Ramona's gaze dropped to her desk. It was sturdy . . . sturdy enough to bear the weight of two people.

She raised her eyes to Quincy. "What made you come back early this year?"

Quincy cocked his clean-shaven head. "What made you drop out of the mayoral race?"

His coal black eyes locked with hers. Was he trying to read her thoughts? Funny, today she wouldn't mind that.

Ramona crossed her arms. He wasn't to know she was giving in to him so easily. "Did Darius tell you that?"

"I read it in the *Monitor*'s online edition."

"Oh." She regarded him stubbornly.

Quincy's rugged features softened into a smile. His dark eyes brightened with humor. "Are you going to tell me?"

Ramona dropped her arms and looked away. "You were right."

"What did you say?"

"You were right."

"Excuse me?"

Ramona smothered a smile. "Shut up."

Quincy's chuckle strummed the muscles in her lower abdomen. "This is a historic event. As a professor of history, I have to make sure it's properly chronicled."

Ramona rolled her eyes. "I'll give you some injuries to chronicle, if you don't stop making fun of me."

Quincy flashed a grin. "What was I right about?"

"You said I was using Trinity Falls as a crutch. I am." She dug deep for the fortitude to hold the history professor's gaze. "It's safe here. I have followers, even if I don't have friends. So when I do screw up—like I did as mayor—most people won't tell me."

"You put the town on the right track, so stop saying you screwed up." His dark eyes glowed with irritation. "Because of you, Trinity Falls is becoming more economically stable, and long-awaited repairs have finally been completed."

Ramona blinked. "Then I guess it was all that success that made the good people of Trinity Falls want to make me a one-term mayor."

"Honey, people only spoke out against you when you started to take a wrong turn. But you were smart enough to hand the wheel over to someone else."

"Thanks for that." Ramona nodded, although she hadn't heard a single word he'd said after "honey."

"Now that you're not running again, what are you going to do?"

Ramona shrugged. "Move."

"Where?"

"I haven't decided yet." She frowned. The look

in Quincy's eyes and the tone of his voice were guarded. What had he wanted her to say?

Quincy tightened his grip on the arms of Ramona's cushioned guest chair. He didn't want her to know he was growing desperate at the thought of her leaving Trinity Falls, and the possibility he'd never see her again.

His shrug felt unnatural. "There's no rush, is there?"

"Of course not. I don't have a timetable. Besides, I don't want to move in the middle of winter."

"Good." The word emerged with more force than Quincy had intended.

A glimmer of a smile twinkled in Ramona's ebony eyes. "I'm glad you approve."

Act cool. "Since you don't have a timetable or a particular city in mind, maybe you'll consider Philadelphia in the spring."

She gave him another one of her long, slow blinks that mesmerized him. "Philadelphia? With you? Has Penn offered you the job?"

"No." Quincy struggled to put the brakes on his accelerating anxiety. "But the telephone interview went well. I'm hopeful they'll invite me for an on-campus interview in the spring."

"I thought you didn't want me to follow you to Philadelphia."

"I didn't say—"

"I can paraphrase what you said." She crossed her arms again. "You *said*—and I'm practically *quoting* now—that I was an independent, capable, intelligent woman, who would do fine on her own."

"Yes, that's what I said."

"So have you changed your mind? Am I no longer a capable, independent, intelligent woman? Do I need you now?"

Quincy rubbed his hands over his face. He felt her rising tension. Why was it so hard for him to communicate with her? *Because I'm afraid.*

He tried harder. "I didn't want you to move to Philadelphia with me if you were only interested in Philadelphia, not me."

Ramona tilted her head, causing her loose raven tresses to slide to her right shoulder. "Are you asking me to move to Philadelphia with you so that we could live together? Before we've even dated?"

"We've been on a date." His palms were starting to sweat. "I brought you food from Trinity Falls Cuisine; salmon, your favorite."

She laughed at him. "Eating takeout in my dining room is not a date."

Quincy briefly considered texting Darius for advice. He was certain the reporter would know how to handle this volatile situation. "What would you consider a date, then?"

Irritation was edging out amusement in her eyes. "Quincy, you're thirty-two years old. I'm sure you've been on at least one first date in your life. And I'm sure it didn't involve eating salmon out of a Styrofoam container."

His cheeks were growing warm. "No, it didn't."

"I'm talking roses, music, a meal with silverware and plates. A kiss."

"A kiss"? Quincy stood and strode around her

desk as Ramona continued her list. She was up to tablecloths and fancy clothes. But she came to an abrupt stop when he spun her seat to face him and gripped the arms on either side of her chair. Her eyes widened as he lowered his mouth to hers.

He'd wanted to kiss her silent for years. Hell, he'd wanted to kiss her for forever. He'd gone out of his mind wondering what she'd taste like. Now he knew. Her taste was a mix of contradictions, like the woman herself. Sweet and spicy. Sharp and tender. Hot and cool.

Quincy reluctantly drew back. His gaze lifted from her moist, plump lips to her dark, dreamy eyes. "Ramona McCloud, will you go out with me?"

Her lips parted with a smile. "Oh yes. I'll go out with you, Quincy Spates. But I'll plan the evening."

"Fair enough." Quincy stepped back, drawing Ramona up and into his embrace. Her eyes drifted closed as he lowered his head to hers. "As long as we start right now."

CHAPTER 37

"This was the worst Christmas I've ever had." Ean fixed his gaze on Darius's flat-screen television. He was more interested in avoiding his friend's eye contact than in this New Year's Eve college football bowl game.

"It was your first Christmas without your father. How's your mother?" Darius reached forward to bathe his tortilla chip in the salsa bowl sitting on his coffee table.

"She's better today." Ean glanced at Darius. "It was nice of you and Leo to stop by."

The words seemed inadequate. Ean grew quiet as he remembered the dozens of people, including Darius and Leonard, who'd dropped in on him and his mother. Even Ms. Helen had paid a visit. Life in a small town; everyone knew everyone's business, and rallied around their neighbors in need. Their friends truly seemed interested in helping them through their first Christmas without Paul Fever.

Darius washed down his chips and salsa with a swig of soda. "Your mother makes the best pies."

That was Darius's way of saying, "You're welcome."

Darius grunted. "Quincy had the right idea. Convince your parents to retire to Florida, then spend the holidays with them, surrounded by beaches and palm trees."

"Which makes coming back to the snow even harder." Ean's tone was dry. The joke helped lift his mood, at least temporarily.

Darius's tidy two-bedroom apartment bordered on barren. In fact, if it hadn't been for the calendar in the kitchen, one wouldn't have any idea it was the holiday season. Ean couldn't remember the last time Darius had gotten into the Christmas spirit.

"How was your Christmas?" Ean turned to his childhood friend in time to see his features stiffen.

"I survived it." Darius munched on another chip as he stared at the television. "I always look forward to sharing dessert with your family."

"We enjoy your company." Ean's gaze was once again drawn to his surroundings.

Darius's bookcase served as the only window to his personality. It was crammed with nonfiction books, most on current events. The pictures on his fireplace mantel chronicled Darius's years with Ean and Quincy. There were no family photos. You wouldn't guess his parents lived two blocks away.

"How are things with you and Megan?" Darius's

question distracted Ean from his concern for his friend.

"We exchanged Merry Christmas voice mail messages Christmas morning." Ean barely registered the wide receiver's touchdown reception in the end zone.

Darius grunted again. "That's lame."

"I know." Ean's face heated. Perhaps he and Megan were both cowards, too afraid to face each other. "What exactly is the problem?" Darius seemed to have shaken off his maudlin mood in preference to interrogating Ean on the subject of his love life—or lack thereof.

"I told you. She doesn't trust me."

"And you're basing this charge on her misunderstanding the reason your ex-bosses came to town." Darius leaned forward and grabbed another fistful of tortilla chips from the bowl on his coffee table.

"That's right." Ean heard the righteous indignation in his voice.

"What would you have thought if the situation had been reversed?"

"If I'd been the one who saw Megan having lunch with her former boss?"

"Right." Darius gestured with a chip. "But she hadn't told you that her boss was coming to Trinity Falls, or that she was meeting her boss for lunch."

"I wouldn't have thought anything. I would've waited for her to explain the situation to me."

"Really?" Darius arched a brow.

"Really." Ean added a firm nod for emphasis.

"That's interesting." Darius's eyes said he didn't believe Ean. "I'd thought lawyers were more suspicious."

"You were wrong."

"Frankly, dude, I'd have been suspicious of you, too."

Ean frowned. What was Darius's point? "Why would I even consider an offer from my former bosses? It was my decision to leave the firm and move back to Trinity Falls. No one forced me."

"Then why didn't you tell Megan you were meeting with them?"

"You know why." Ean sighed. "I didn't want to get her hopes up in case the partnership to buy the center didn't work."

"But in her mind, you were keeping secrets." Darius gestured with the chip again. "How can there truly be trust in a relationship if the people involved in it are keeping secrets?"

Ean refused to acknowledge that Darius was making sense. "And in my mind, she should have asked a question, instead of coming at me like some overzealous government prosecutor."

Darius laughed. "Maybe she came at you kind of strong, but you're expecting too much of her, man."

"It's too much to expect trust from the woman with whom I'm in a relationship?" Ean's eyes stretched wide. "The reason she refused to move in with me is that she's afraid I'm not going to stay."

Darius settled back into the corner of the sofa

and balanced his left ankle on his right knee. "Have you ever put yourself in Megan's shoes?"

"What's that supposed to mean?"

"Megan is a classic 'fear of abandonment' case, and she has good reason. Every significant person in her life has left her. Her parents died when she was young. Her grandmother died when she was in high school. Her grandfather died before she graduated from college. And her cousin's always threatening to leave Trinity Falls."

"I never thought of that." Ean remembered Megan's words *"Everyone leaves, Ean."* He wanted to smack himself.

"It's no wonder she's waiting for you to leave, dude, especially since you've left before."

Ean searched his friend's face. "How did you know all this? Did she tell you?"

Darius shook his head. "She didn't have to. I'm a journalist. I've got mad observation skills."

Ean chuckled without humor. "In other words, I'm a self-centered asshole."

Darius threw back his head and laughed. It was the first genuine amusement he'd heard from his friend all day. "Don't put words in my mouth, man. You've only been back two and a half months. That's not enough time, even for someone with my observation skills. It's also not enough time for Megan to fully believe you aren't going to leave her."

Ean drained his can of root beer as he mulled over Darius's words. His friend's theory made sense. Why hadn't he realized it on his own? He'd been blind, self-centered and—yes—stupid. Ean clenched his teeth. Maybe he hadn't been back long enough to recognize the reasons behind Megan's hesitation, but he'd known Megan practically their entire lives. He should have realized her personal experiences would make her cautious about his commitment.

"What should I do?" Ean looked up as Darius handed him another can of soda. He hadn't noticed his friend had left the room for drinks.

"Ah, you've recognized my wisdom." Darius sank back onto the sofa and popped open his soda. "Be patient. Stop pressuring her to trust you. Let her set the pace, and the trust will come."

Ean nodded, but his heart was still heavy. "What if it's too late? What if I've pressured her so much that I've already pushed her away?"

"Then you'll need to consult someone with much more wisdom than me."

"Who?"

Darius gulped his soda. "I'd start with your mother."

Megan let herself into Ean's townhome Tuesday evening with the key he'd given her two weeks earlier. She pressed a hand to her abdomen. The butterflies in her stomach must be hosting a rave. She dried her sweating palms against the thighs of her black jeans, then bent to haul her two stuffed suitcases—one at a time—across his threshold. She took her time shoving them into a corner beside the staircase. After locking the front door, she was out of delaying tactics. Megan took a deep breath and straightened her shoulders. It was time to plead her case.

She mounted the stairs, letting the sound of the shower lead her to the master bedroom. The water stopped as she crossed the threshold.

Ean had set a change of clothes on the bed, stone gray slacks and the burgundy sweater she liked. A chill trailed down her spine. Where was he going? It was New Year's Eve. With whom was he celebrating?

Megan sank onto the foot of the bed and lifted his sweater. Was she too late? Had he given up on her?

Ean emerged from the bathroom, wrapped in a cloud of steam and nothing else. The scent of soap and shampoo trailed after him. He took her breath away. He appeared like a mythological hero—larger than life, brave, bold. She yearned to trace the sculpted muscles under his dark, damp skin, but this was too important. She couldn't afford distractions.

Ean stopped when he saw her. Surprise and confusion swept through his olive gaze. She was used to a warmer welcome.

"Megan?" He sounded uncertain.

Megan released his sweater and stood on shaky legs. She braced her calves against the mattress for support. "I'm sorry to barge in on you. I hadn't realized you were on your way out." She gestured with a trembling hand toward his neatly laid-out clothing.

Ean's attention dropped briefly to his bed before returning to her. He was silent for several long seconds. Was he trying to think of a way to ask her to leave?

"How did you get in?" He crossed to the bed and began to dress.

Megan's eyes ate up his long legs and tight hips. She dragged her gaze up his muscled torso to his face. "You gave me a key to your townhome, remember?"

"Oh yeah." He pulled his slacks on over his underwear. "I thought you were a mirage."

What's that supposed to mean? It was time to stop stalling. Megan wrapped her arms around her waist. "I've contacted a Realtor."

Ean seemed startled. "Why?"

The sound of the zipper closing over his fly drained the moisture from her mouth. Megan remembered his question. "I'm putting my grandparents' home on the market. I want to move in with you. I was afraid to, before. But I shouldn't have let fear control my feelings for you. You were right."

"I was wrong." Ean's flat statement interrupted Megan's halting admissions.

"What?" *Oh, God, did I wait too long?* Did Ean not want her to move in with him anymore?

"I was an ass."

"What?" Now she was thoroughly confused.

"*You* were right. I was on my way to tell you that. I had no right to pressure you into moving in with me, making that kind of commitment in only two months." Ean pushed his hands into the front pockets of his gray slacks. "We'll go at your pace."

At her pace? Was he willing to give her another chance? Did he believe her now?

Megan spread her arms. "But I'm ready to make that commitment to you. I do believe that you've come home to stay. But even if you haven't . . . If you want to return to New York, or move to Philadelphia or Timbuktu—I'll go with you."

Ean's body froze. When he'd walked into his bedroom and found Megan sitting on his bed, he'd thought he was hallucinating. He'd thought all the nights of wanting her had caused his mind to snap. Now he thought he might be dreaming. "You'd leave Trinity Falls for me?"

Megan brushed her hands over her eyes. "A house and a store are not more important to me than you."

Ean didn't remember moving. But suddenly Megan was in his arms. He was holding her so tight and kissing her so deep. Her body against his, her heat seeping into his skin was healing the aches he'd borne over the past week. He tasted joy, relief, hunger—hers and his.

He plunged his tongue into her mouth, seeking her response. She pulled him even closer, digging her fingertips into his shoulders. Ean lowered his left hand to her firm buttocks and squeezed. Megan pressed her hips tighter against his burgeoning erection. She was with him. She responded with him and to him. His blood rushed through his veins. He wanted her now; he needed her always. Ean cupped her hips to raise her against him. He started for the bed. Megan wrapped her legs around his waist.

"You believe me now?" Megan's breathy question confused him.

"Believe what?" He laid her on the mattress and covered her body with his own.

"That I know you're staying in Trinity Falls. That I trust you. That our relationship is more than sex."

Ean raised himself on his forearms and looked into her hot chocolate eyes. "I believe you. But I want you to take your grandparents' home off the market."

She gave him her long, slow blink, which always melted his heart. "But I want to move in with you."

He pressed a quick, hard kiss against her soft lips. "I want to live with you, too. But your grandparents left you that house. I'd rather we lived there, if that's all right with you."

"I'd like that." Megan's smile started in her eyes. She cupped the side of his face. "Happy New Year, Ean. Welcome home."

Ean pressed a kiss into the palm of her hand. "My home is in your arms, and that's where I want to spend the rest of my life."

He lowered his head to seal his promise with a kiss. Tonight they'd celebrate their new beginning, the New Year and Trinity Falls.

Trinity Falls Fudge Walnut Brownies

Ingredients

1½ cups of margarine
1 cup cocoa
1 teaspoon of nutmeg
2½ cups of sugar
2 teaspoons of vanilla
4 eggs
1½ cups of wheat flour
2 cups of walnuts

Preparation

Preheat oven to 350 degrees.

In one bowl, mix margarine, cocoa and nutmeg. In a separate bowl, mix sugar, vanilla and eggs, one at a time. Combine the contents of the first two bowls, then stir in flour and walnuts. Mix well.

Spray a baking pan with nonstick cooking spray. Pour brownie mix into pan and bake for 30 minutes in a 350 degree oven. Cool for 30 minutes before cutting into squares.

Don't miss the next novel in the Finding Home series,

Harmony Cabins

On sale in February 2014

CHAPTER 1

Audra Lane strode with manufactured confidence to the vacation cabin rental's main desk and faced the man she thought was the registration clerk. She curled her bare toes against the warm polished wood flooring and took a deep breath.

"You're probably wondering why I'm wearing this trash bag."

"Yes."

That was it. That single syllable delivered without inflection or emotion in a soft, bluesy baritone.

Audra's swagger stalled.

Maybe that was his way. His manner wasn't unwelcoming; it was just spare. He'd been the same when she'd checked into the cabin rentals in Where-the-Heck-Am-I, Ohio, less than an hour earlier.

In fact, the entire registration area was just as Spartan as the clerk. Despite the large picture windows, the room seemed dark and cheerless in the middle of this bright summer morning. There weren't chairs inviting guests to relax or corner tables with engaging information about the nearby town. It didn't even offer a coffee station. Nothing about the room said, "Welcome! We're glad you're here." There were only bare oak walls, bare oak floors and a tight-lipped clerk.

What kind of vacation spot is this?

Audra pushed her questions about the room's lack of ambience to the back of her mind and addressed her primary concern.

She wiped her sweaty palms on her black plastic makeshift minidress. "I'd left some of my toiletries in my rental car. I thought I could just step into the attached garage to get them, but the door shut behind me. Luckily, I found a box of trash bags on a shelf."

She stopped. Her face flamed. If he hadn't suspected before, he now knew beyond a doubt that she was butt naked under this bag.

Oh. My. God.

She'd ripped a large hole on the bottom and smaller ones on either side of the bag for a crude little black dress, which on her five-foot-seven-inch frame was *very* little.

Audra gave him a hard look, but his almond-shaped onyx eyes remained steady on hers. He didn't offer even a flicker of reaction. His eyes were really quite striking, and the only part of his face she could make out. When he'd checked her into the rental, she'd been too tired from her flight from California to notice his deep sienna features were half hidden by a thick, unkempt beard. His dark brown hair was twisted into tattered, uneven braids. They hung above broad shoulders clothed in a short-sleeved dark blue T-shirt. But his eyes . . . they were so dark, so direct and so wounded. A poet's eyes.

How could the cabins' owner allow his staff to come to work looking so disheveled, especially an employee who worked the front desk? Did the clerk think he looked intimidating? Well, she had been born and raised in Los Angeles; he'd have to try harder.

Without a word, the clerk turned and unlocked the cabinet on the wall behind him. He chose a key from a multitude of options and pulled a document from the credenza.

"Sign this." He handed the paper to her.

The form stated she acknowledged receipt of her cabin's spare key and would return it promptly. Audra signed it with relief. "Thank you."

"You're welcome." He gave her the key.

A smile spread across her mouth and chased away her discomfort. Audra closed her hand around the key and raised her gaze to his. "I don't know your name."

"Jack."

"Hi, Jack. I'm Au . . . Penny. Penny Lane." She continued when he didn't respond. "Thanks again for the spare key. I'll bring it right back."

"No rush."

"Thank you." Audra turned on her bare heels and hurried from the main cabin. That had been easy—relatively speaking. At times, she'd even forgotten she was wearing a garbage bag . . . and nothing else. It helped that Jack hadn't looked at her with mockery or scorn. He'd been very professional. Bless him!

Jackson Sansbury waited until his guest disappeared behind the closed front door. Only then did he release the grin he'd been struggling against. It had taken every ounce of control not to burst into laughter as she'd marched toward him, the trash-bag dress rustling with her every step.

He shook his head. She'd been wearing a garbage bag! Oh, to have seen the look on her face when the breezeway door had shut behind her—while she'd been naked in the garage. Jackson gripped the registration desk and surrendered to a few rusty chuckles.

It had been so long since he'd found anything funny.

He wiped his eyes with his fingers, then lifted the replacement key form. A few extra chuckles escaped. She'd signed this form, as well as the registration form, "Penny Lane." Jackson shook his head again. Did she really expect him to believe her parents had named her after a Beatles song?

Jackson lifted his gaze to the front door. She'd given a Los Angeles address when she'd registered. Who was she? And why would someone from Los Angeles spend a month at a cabin in Trinity Falls, Ohio, by herself and under a fake name?

* * *

"Benita, when you told me you'd made a reservation for me at a vacation cabin rental, I thought you meant one with other *people*." Audra grumbled into her cellular phone to her business manager, Benita Hawkins.

Although still tired from the red-eye flight from California to Ohio, she felt much more human after she'd showered and dressed.

"There aren't any people there?" Benita sounded vaguely intrigued.

"The only things here are trees, a lake and a taciturn registration clerk." Audra's lips tightened. Her manager wasn't taking her irritation seriously.

"Hmmm. Even better."

Audra glared at her phone before returning it to her ear. She could picture the other woman seated behind her cluttered desk, reviewing e-mails and mail while humoring her. "What do you mean, 'even better'?"

"I told you that you needed a change to get over your writer's block. You're having trouble coming up with new songs because you're in a rut. You see the same people. Go to the same places. There's nothing new or exciting in your life."

That's harsh.

Audra stared out the window at the tree line. She'd noticed right away that none of the windows had curtains. The lack of privacy increased the rentals' creepiness factor.

A modest lawn lay like an amnesty zone between

her and a lush spread of evergreen and poplar trees that circled the cabin like a military strike force. In the distance, she could see sunlight dancing off the lake like diamonds on the water. But the area was isolated. Audra didn't do isolated. She'd texted her parents after she'd checked into the resort to let them know she'd arrived safely. Maybe she should have waited.

"This place is like Mayberry's version of the Bates Motel." She turned from the window. "How is this supposed to cure my insomnia?"

"Writing will cure your insomnia."

"Have you been to these cabins?"

"No. When I was growing up in Trinity Falls, Harmony Cabins went into bankruptcy and was abandoned. They've only recently been renovated."

"I'm coming home." But first, she'd take a nap. The red-eye flight was catching up with her.

The cabin itself was lovely. The great room's walls, floors and ceiling were made of gleaming honey wood. The granite stone fireplace dominated the room. But a large flat-screen, cable-ready television reassured her she'd have something to do at night. The comfortable furnishings that were missing from the main cabin were scattered around this room: an overstuffed sofa and fat fabric chairs. The décor was decidedly masculine, though; it was black leather and dark plaids. That would explain the lack of curtains at the windows.

"You promised me you'd give it thirty days, Audra." The clicking of Benita's computer keyboard sounded just under her words. "I sent the rental a nonrefundable check for the full amount of your stay in advance."

Audra frowned. Benita's check had allowed her to register as Penny Lane. "It was your check, but my money. If I want to cancel this anti-vacation vacation, I will."

They both recognized the empty threat. The cost of a monthlong stay at a cabin rental was too much to waste.

Benita's exasperated sigh traveled almost twenty-five hundred miles and three time zones through the cell phone. "You owe the record producer three hit songs by the end of the month. How are they coming?"

Audra ground her teeth. Benita knew very well she hadn't made any progress on the project. "How can you believe this place is the solution? You've never even been here."

"Do you really think I'd send you someplace that wasn't safe? I have family in Trinity Falls. If there were serial killers there, I'd know it."

Audra tugged on her right earlobe. She was angry because she was scared, and scared because she was outside her comfort zone. "I don't want to be here. It's not what I'm used to."

"That's why you *need* to be there. And this is the best time. Trinity Falls is celebrating its sesquicentennial. The town's hosting a Founders Day celebration at the beginning of August. I'll be there."

"One hundred and fifty years. Big deal."

Benita chuckled. "I'll see you in a month."

Audra stared at her cell phone. Benita had ended

their call. "I guess that means I'm staying." She shoved her cell phone into the front pocket of her jeans shorts and turned back to the window. "In that case, I'll need curtains."

The chimes above the main cabin's front door sang. With three keystrokes, Jackson locked his laptop and pushed away from his desk. The cabins had had more activity today than they'd ever had.

Jackson paused in his office doorway. It wasn't a surprise to see that the chair of the Trinity Falls Sesquicentennial Steering Committee had returned to his front desk. Doreen Fever was a determined woman.

"Afternoon, Doreen." He knew why she was there. She wanted every citizen to be involved in the festivities surrounding the town's 150th birthday. The problem was, Jackson wasn't a joiner.

"I'm still amazed by how much you've accomplished with the rentals in so little time." Doreen gazed around the reception area.

"Thank you."

Doreen was the town's sole mayoral candidate. She also was the artist behind the bakery operation of Books & Bakery and the mother of a former schoolmate—though Doreen looked too young to have an only child who was just two years younger than Jackson. Her cinnamon brown skin was smooth and radiant. Her short, curly hair was dark brown. And her warm brown eyes were full of empathy.

Jackson didn't want anyone's empathy. Not even someone as genuine and caring as Doreen.

"I hear you have a lodger," Doreen folded her hands on the counter between them.

"Not by choice." How did the residents of Trinity Falls learn everyone else's business so fast? His guest hadn't even been here a full day.

Confusion flickered across Doreen's features before she masked it with a polite nod. "A young woman."

"I noticed."

"I'm glad to see the cabins' renovations are going well and that you're taking in customers."

"Thank you."

Doreen gave him a knowing smile. "The elementary school was grateful for your generous donation. I take it that was the check from your guest? Are you sure you don't need that money to reinvest in the repairs?"

"The school needs the money more. I appreciate your stopping by, Doreen." He turned to leave.

"Jack. You know why I'm here." Doreen sounded exasperated.

Good. He could handle exasperation. Pity pissed him off.

He faced her again. "You know my answer."

"The town will be one hundred and fifty years old in August. That'll be a momentous occasion, and everyone wants you to be a part of it."

Jackson shook his head. "You don't need me."

"Yes, we do." Doreen's tone was dogged determination. "This sesquicentennial is a chance for

Trinity Falls to raise its profile in the county and across the state. You, of all people, must have a role in the Founders Day celebration."

"That's not necessary."

"Yes, it is." Doreen leaned into the desk. "This event, if done well, will bring in extra revenue."

"I know about the town's budget concerns. I have an online subscription to *The Trinity Falls Monitor.*" Reading the paper online saved Jackson from having to go into town or deal with a newspaper delivery person.

Doreen continued as though Jackson hadn't spoken. "If we host a large celebration with high-profile guests, we'll attract more people. These tourists will stay in our hotels, eat in our restaurants and buy our souvenirs."

"Great. Good luck with that." He checked his watch for emphasis. It was almost two o'clock in the afternoon. "Anything else?"

She softened her voice. "I know that you're still grieving Zoe's death."

"Don't." The air drained from the room.

"I can't imagine how devastated you must feel at the loss of your daughter."

"Doreen." He choked out her name.

"We understand you need time to grieve. But, Jack, it's not healthy to close yourself off from human contact. People care about you. We can help you."

"Can you bring her back?" The words were harsh, rough and raw.

Doreen looked stricken. "I can no more bring

back your daughter than I can resurrect my late husband."

Paul Fever had died from cancer more than a year ago. He'd been sixty-seven. In contrast, leukemia had cut Jackson's daughter's life tragically short.

Jackson struggled to reel in his emotions. "People grieve in different ways."

Pity reappeared in Doreen's warm brown eyes. "I went through the same feelings. But, Jack, at some point, you have to rejoin society."

"Not today." Some days, he feared he'd never be ready.

The persistent ringing shattered Audra's dream. She blinked her eyes open. Had she fallen asleep?

Her gaze dropped to the song stanzas scribbled across the notebook on her lap. Had it been the red-eye flight or her lyrics that lulled her to sleep?

She stretched forward to grab her cell phone. "Hello?"

"Did we wake you?" Her mother asked after a pause.

Audra heard the surprise in the question. "It was a long trip." She refused to believe her writing had put her to sleep. "Is everything OK?"

Ellen Prince Lane sighed. "That's what we're calling to find out. We thought you were going to call us when you arrived at the resort."

"I sent you a text when I landed." Audra scrubbed a hand across her eyes, wiping away the last remnants of fatigue.

"A text is not a phone call." Ellen spoke with exaggerated patience. "How do we know that someone didn't kidnap you and send that text to delay our reporting you missing?"

Audra rolled her eyes. Her mother read too many true-crime novels. Her father wouldn't have suspected foul play was behind a text from her.

"I'm sorry, Mom. I didn't mean to worry you."

"This whole idea worries me." Her mother made fretting noises. "Why couldn't you have stayed in Brentwood to write your songs? Why did you have to go to some resort in Ohio?"

Audra wanted to laugh. No one would mistake Harmony Cabins for a resort. But this probably wasn't a good time to tell that to her mother.

"We discussed this, Mom. Benita thought a change of scenery would cure my writer's block." And even though she had her doubts, Audra didn't want to add to her parents' worries.

Ellen tsked. "How long will you be gone?"

They'd discussed that, too. "About a month."

"You've never been away from home that long."

"I know, Mom."

"You don't even know anything about that resort."

"Benita's friend owns the cabins. I'm sure I'll be comfortable here."

"How will you eat?"

"There's a town nearby. I'll pick up some groceries in the morning."

"What do they eat there?"

Audra closed her eyes and prayed for patience.

"I'm in Ohio, Mom. It's not a foreign country. I'm sure I'll find something familiar in the town's grocery store."

Ellen sniffed. "There's no need to take that tone."

"I'm sorry."

"Your father's very worried about you, Audra."

Yet her mother was the one on the phone. "Tell Dad I'll be fine. The cabin is clean and safe. There are locks on all the doors and windows. I'll be home before you know it." She hoped.

Audra looked toward the windows beside the front door. She needed curtains. She didn't like the idea of the windows being uncovered, especially at night. She'd feel too exposed. She checked her wristwatch. It wasn't quite three in the afternoon. It wouldn't be dark until closer to nine P.M. She had a few hours to figure something out for tonight.

Her mother's lengthy sigh interrupted her planning. "Your father wants to talk with you. Maybe he can get you to see reason."

Audra rubbed her eyes with her thumb and two fingers. This experiment was hard enough without her mother's overprotectiveness.

"My Grammy Award–winning daughter!" Randall Lane boomed his greeting into the telephone. He'd been calling her that since February when she'd been presented with the award for Song of the Year. Before that, she'd been his Grammy Award–*nominated* daughter.

Audra settled back into the overstuffed leather sofa. "Hi, Daddy."

"Will you be home in time for my birthday?"

She frowned. Her father's birthday was in October. It was only July. "Of course."

"That's all that matters."

"Randall! Give me back that phone!" Ellen's screech crossed state lines.

"Your mother wants to speak to you again. Have a nice time in Ohio, baby."

Her mother was as breathless as though she'd chased her father across the room. "Aren't there coyotes and bears in Ohio? And mountain lions?"

Audra's heart stopped with her mother's questions. She was a West Coast city woman in the wilds of the Midwest. Talk about being a fish out of water.

She swallowed to loosen the wad of fear lodged in her throat. "They don't come near the cabins."

"How do you know?"

"I just do," she lied. "I'll be fine."

"I think you should come home, Audra. What does Benita know about writer's block? She's your business manager, not a writer. I'm your mother. I know what you need. You need rest."

Her mother had a point. Audra hadn't had a full night's sleep since she'd taken the Grammy home.

She stood and paced past the front windows. "Benita may be right. Maybe I need to get completely out of my comfort zone to jump-start my songwriting."

Ellen sniffed again. "Well, I disagree. And so does Wallace."

Audra stilled at the mention of her treacherous ex-boyfriend. They'd broken up more than a month ago. Her mother knew that. "Why are you talking with him? What does he have to do with anything?"

"He wants to apologize to you. He wants your forgiveness."

That made up her mind. She was definitely staying at the Harmony Cabins for at least a month. "Please don't tell Wallace where I am. Even if I forgive him, we're never getting back together."

"You should give him another chance, Audra. He knows he's made a mistake."

"Wallace used me. I'm not giving him or anyone else the chance to do that again."